THE SECRETS OF TREE TAYLOR

DANDI DALEY MACKALL

ALFRED A. KNOPF 〜 NEW YORK

THIS IS A BORZOI BOOK PUBLISHED BY ALFRED A. KNOPF

Visit us on the Web! randomhouse.com/teens

Educators and librarians, for a variety of teaching tools, visit us at RHTeachersLibrarians.com

Library of Congress Cataloging-in-Publication Data
Mackall, Dandi Daley.
The secrets of Tree Taylor / Dandi Daley Mackall.—1st ed.
p. cm.
Summary: In small-town Missouri in tumultuous 1963, Tree Taylor, thirteen, wants to write an important story to secure a spot on the high school newspaper staff, but when a neighbor is shot, she investigates and learns that some secrets should be kept.
ISBN 978-0-375-86897-9 (trade) — ISBN 978-0-375-96897-6 (lib. bdg.) — ISBN 978-0-375-89982-9 (ebook)
[1. Secrets—Fiction. 2. Reporters and reporting—Fiction. 3. Community life—Missouri—Fiction. 4. Family life—Missouri—Fiction. 5. Nineteen sixties—Fiction. 6. Missouri—History—20th century—Fiction.] I. Title.
PZ7.M1905Sf 2014
[Fic]—dc23
2013001577

The text of this book is set in 11-point Bembo.

Printed in the United States of America

May 2014

10 9 8 7 6 5 4 3 2 1

First Edition

To Maureen Daley Pento,
the world's best big sister then . . . and now

1

Soul

The morning the gun went off, I was thinking about Tolstoy and the Beatles, and maybe, if I'm being honest here, a little about Ray Miller and how his eyes were perfect little pieces of sky.

The Beatles I thought about all the time, especially Paul. My friend Sarah could have Ringo. Just give me Paul McCartney.

I wouldn't have been thinking about Tolstoy if he hadn't popped up in my writing notebook as my first quote of the summer. All year I had collected quotations from famous writers and had copied one quote onto each page of my otherwise empty social studies notebook. Our school library had biographies of writers, but the public library had whole books of quotations. My primary goal for the summer was to become a great writer—at least, great enough to earn me a spot on the school newspaper my freshman year.

My first quote happened to be from Tolstoy:

A writer is dear and necessary for us only in the measure of which he reveals to us the inner workings of his very soul. —Count Leo Tolstoy

How on earth was I supposed to reveal the inner workings of my very soul?

To be fair, I had tried to write something dear and necessary—well, worthy—the day before the shooting. I figured I'd need a worthy article to convince Mrs. Woolsey to give me the only freshman reporting spot at Hamilton High next year. Two seniors would run the paper, but each class got one reporter. I wanted ours to be me.

As for "necessary," well, that's what this position was to me. Being on the *Blue and Gold* staff would be my first step toward becoming a real writer. An investigative journalist. Or maybe a female version of Walter Cronkite, interrupting regularly scheduled television programming with breaking news for the nation.

Randy Ridings had been editor of the *Blue and Gold,* and now he ran the town's only newspaper, the *Hamiltonian.* And Becky Smith, also an ex-staffer, got a job in the mailroom of the *Kansas City Star* last year.

I sure needed that *Blue and Gold* job a heap more than Wanda Hopkins did. Wanda hadn't written anything important last year when she was our junior high reporter. Since the junior high occupied the same building as the high school, seventh and eighth graders got one reporter for the *Blue and Gold.* But Wanda didn't report. She'd been too caught up reigning as queen over her many friends.

And too busy entertaining Ben, then Dennis, then Eric . . . then Ray.

Ray, with the eyes like two pieces of sky.

I tried writing about the Cold War and the Russian premier Nikita Khrushchev banging his boot on a podium and declaring, "We will bury you!" I tried writing about President Kennedy's promise in front of God and everybody to put a man on the moon by 1970 . . . and how embarrassing it would be if we didn't get there before the Russians.

But I ended up ripping the pages from my notebook and pitching them into the wastebasket.

What did world events have to do with me, Tree Taylor, age thirteen, living in Hamilton, Missouri, population 1,701? (And that census had been taken before the shoe factory closing that forced dozens of families, including our census taker, to leave town.) We hadn't even been all that worried about the Cuban missiles aimed at the U.S. What would the Communists want with us farmers anyway?

Nope. Everything dear and necessary happened far away. And certainly not in my soul, thank you, Count Tolstoy.

My second day of writing went much better, even before Mr. Kinney got shot right up the road from my house. Ben Franklin had a lot to do with it. (Not with shooting Mr. Kinney. With getting me off to a better writing day.) The quote for the day was:

Either write something worth reading, or do
something worth writing. —Benjamin Franklin

So even before the whole Kinney shooting business gave me something worth writing about, I'd penned two worthy goals for the summer of '63:

1. *Write such a fantastic investigative report that even Mrs. Woolsey can't turn me down for the freshman spot on the Blue and Gold staff.*
2. *Experience my first real kiss. A kiss delivered by a boy. A boy who is not related to me. A kiss worth writing about.*

Jack, my lifelong buddy, and Sarah, my best-friend-who-was-a-girl, already knew how much I wanted to write for the school paper. But I wouldn't talk to anybody about my kissing goal. I would keep *that* a secret.

Barefoot and still in my fuzzy pj's, I tiptoed out of the house at dawn. I eased the screen door shut behind me and skipped over the dewy wet front step, where I usually sat. Instead, armed with nothing but a Bic pen and my writing notebook, I plopped cross-legged, Navajo-style, right onto the warm sidewalk.

I'd barely finished writing the day's date on my journal page when I heard gravel crunch in the distance. A car going way too fast bounced up over the hill in a cloud of dust. From the backyard, Midge barked.

"It's just Jack!" I hollered to our family mutt, a terrier mix that looked kind of like a hairless lamb.

Jack Adams came flying up our road in Fred, his '53 Chevy. Brakes screeched, and the car came to a stop. "Hey, Tree!" he called out the driver's window.

Jack claimed credit for getting everybody to call me Tree instead of Teresa. Tree is all I ever remember answering to, so I couldn't say about that.

"Hey, Jack!" I called back.

His parents and mine had been friends longer than Jack and I had been alive. He was four years older than me, but it had never mattered. We'd always been close. We talked to each other about everything in a way I never could with my sister, even though Eileen was only three years older than me.

Music blared from Jack's radio—"The Loco-Motion" by Little Eva. Jack's non-steering-wheel hand hung out the window and drummed against the car door in perfect rhythm. Made me want to jump up and dance, but I resisted.

"You working this afternoon?" he shouted above Little Eva's invitation to "Come on, come on, do the loco-motion with me."

I sighed. "All afternoon. Tonight too. What a drag." It had seemed pretty neat when I'd gotten the job of basketgirl at the town's swimming pool. It only paid a quarter an hour, but there weren't any other jobs for a thirteen-year-old girl. Plus, I'd have the edge on the lifeguard job when I turned sixteen. "You working today, Jack?"

He smiled, flashing the biggest, whitest teeth in all of Caldwell County. People said I had big brown eyes, but Jack's eyes made mine look like pennies. He had a classic face, with bones, instead of flesh, shaping his chin and jawline. "Me? Nah, man. I'm up and grooving early for no reason. You know me."

I did know Jack. If he was up this early, it had to be work. Jack's summer job was the pits. Donna, his mother, had pulled strings to get him on at the IGA, Hamilton's only grocery

5

store. He worked in the meat department, cutting and wrapping gross, raw meat in slick white paper. Jack hated the job. But what he hated even more was his mother's prying. Donna, who had never met a piece of gossip she didn't like, called him a couple of times a day at work, always with the same question: "What's new at work today, Jack, honey?"

"So, writing anything great?" Jack asked.

"I wish."

"Wishing is great." He revved his engine as the Beatles launched into "Please Please Me." "Guess I'll see you later. I might stop by the pool if I get off in time and haven't slit my throat from boredom."

"Thanks for the warning." I waved my pen at him.

He honked goodbye. Then he and Fred the Car disappeared into another cloud of dust as they rounded the curve at the end of our road.

I couldn't stand the thought of Jack not being around next year. He'd be off to Northwest Missouri State, where, no doubt, he'd have a dozen dates on weekends and never come home. In the yearbook, his class had voted him "Most Likely to . . . Everything." To succeed. To get rich. To find fame. To marry a movie star.

Every time I thought about school without Jack, I got a pain in my stomach, as if my guts were being twisted like a wet towel.

I breathed in the scent of two horses and a dozen cows from across the road. Our house was the last house in town—not that there was much difference between Hamilton's town and country.

A block away, the McPherson dogs kept barking like squirrels were teasing them. I would have turned those poor hounds loose myself if I hadn't been afraid they'd kill chickens and meet a fate worse than being tied up all day and night.

Our Midge liked chickens a little too much for us to let her run free like our other dogs always had. But Midge still had a great life—big backyard, the shade of our tamarack tree, lots of food and water, toys and love. She hardly ever barked except to say hey.

Dad and I kept watch over all the dogs in the neighborhood. Not everybody in Hamilton believed they owed it to their pets to take good care of them. Some of the very same folks who got so upset about the Russians sending dogs and monkeys into space kept their own dogs chained and hungry half the time.

Maybe I could write a hard-hitting investigative report on "The Hamilton Hounds." Or "The Hounds of Hamilton." I'd work in alliteration, like "horror" and "hunger."

But as I sat under a cloudless blue sky, with the cry of a mourning dove underscoring the sweet music of song sparrows, I didn't feel up to writing about horrible, hungry hound dogs.

I wanted Jack to come back so I could hear John Lennon and Paul McCartney singing "Please Please Me." I wanted Tolstoy to drop in and explain what he meant about the inner workings of my soul. I wanted Ray Miller, with his sky eyes. . . .

And that's exactly what I was thinking when the gun went off.

2

A Bad Scene

I knew a rifle when I heard it.

Only this one was too loud. Louder than all the McPherson hounds put together. The shot had come from my right, no more than a block away.

The door to our house flew open. The screen slapped back. Out flew my dad in his plaid robe and leather slippers. He struggled to knot the robe's long belt around his waist. His eyes were wide, but he didn't even glance my way.

As he stumbled past me, one of his slippers slipped off. He stepped back and slid his foot in again. His thick, wavy hair stuck out all over like a black Brillo pad.

I scrambled to my feet. "Dad, what—"

He swung around, and the look on his face shut me up fast. He raised his arm, pointed straight at me, and, in a voice he'd never used on me before, said, "Stay put, Tree!"

Then he wheeled around and took off up our road toward the rifle blast.

I stood right where I was, frozen as much by my dad's gruff voice as by the gunshot. I watched him shuffle to the end of our block, past the crossroad, up to the first house on the left.

When he reached the rundown one-story house, he slowed.

I think I knew from the start where he was headed: the Kinney place.

There was something about that house that always creeped me out. The first time I heard the nursery rhyme about a crooked house, I thought they were talking about the Kinneys: "There was a crooked man, who walked a crooked mile. He had a crooked house and he had a crooked smile." Or something like that.

My stomach did the twisty thing. The problem wasn't just the crooked house. It was the crooked man. Old Man Kinney.

I always went out of my way to avoid Mr. Kinney and his house. Every time I passed him sitting in that rocker on his front porch, his glare gave me the willies. The guy looked permanently ticked off, like he just knew I would rob him blind if he ever left home. And he was always home.

I edged to the end of our yard so I could see better. The door to the Kinney house cracked open, and a shadowy figure stepped into the light of the doorway. I was pretty sure the woman was Mrs. Kinney. In all the years we'd lived on this same street, I'd only seen her a few times and never exchanged so much as a word. Jack told me once that Mrs. Kinney was the same age as both our moms, but I didn't believe him. She looked old enough to be our mothers' mother.

Dad stood at the foot of the Kinneys' decrepit porch. Its peeling gray planks reminded me of an old fishing dock. He was looking up and saying something to Mrs. Kinney, but I couldn't imagine what.

I watched him as if he were a stranger on television—John Wayne, or Ben Cartwright from *Bonanza*. Whatever my dad said worked, because the woman stepped all the way out and crossed the porch toward him.

That's when I saw it. In her arms, tucked against her hip and across her breast like a much-loved baby, lay a rifle.

Before I realized what I was doing, I was running toward them.

Gravel dug into the soles of my bare feet. I kept going.

At the crossroad, I had to hobble to the side and lean against a walnut tree to catch my breath. I brushed the gravel from my callused heels. Then I watched the scene unfolding on the Kinneys' front porch.

Dad moved closer to the steps. Mrs. Kinney, still clutching her rifle, loomed over him, only a couple of feet away now.

I wanted to charge the porch, to knock that gun out of her arms.

But I didn't. I kept watching, not sure if I was more afraid of startling her and making her shoot . . . or of having my dad see that I wasn't staying put.

I had to get closer. I tiptoed toward them. It wasn't that hard to stay out of sight, ducking between the maples, oaks, and elms that lined every piece of the road. I aimed for the fattest tree on the Kinneys' property, a cottonwood that would have taken four grown men to circle it, hand to hand. From there, I'd at least be able to see what was going on.

The last stretch to the big tree opened wide in front of me. I darted across the grass.

My dad's gaze stayed fixed on Mrs. Kinney's face. It wasn't much of a face—wrinkled in a way I wondered if you could blame on age. Her cheeks and forehead were the color of lemon-lime Squirt, with patches of yellow and splotches of blue and purple. Her nose bent to the side, hinting at the letter L.

But it was her eyes that set her apart from every other human. I could not stop staring at her tiny eyes, colorless and flat, as if all the seeing had drained out of them. I had never seen that kind of empty.

I squatted behind the twisted tree trunk and waited.

Without a word, my dad set his foot onto the bottom porch step. He didn't look down but stayed locked into Mrs. Kinney as he took the next step. In slow motion, he turned and lowered himself onto the top step, sitting with his back to that woman with the rifle.

I felt like I had to keep my eye on her for the both of us. I stared at her until my eyes watered with the pain of not blinking.

Just when I was afraid she'd never move again, she did. She let out a sigh that I swore shook the leaves of the cottonwood, raining down puffs of white on my head. Then she shuffled the rest of the way to Dad and sat down next to him. The gun came to rest on her lap, its nose stretching to my dad's knee.

"Doc," she said, like they were in the middle of a conversation. She said something else, but her head was turned. I couldn't hear her.

Dad squinted, like he was straining to listen. He stared straight ahead, same as her. It was like they were both watching a picture show. Then he got to his feet and crossed the porch to her front door. He opened the screen and walked inside.

Mrs. Kinney didn't so much as shift her eyes to watch him go. I caught a glimpse of her faded cotton apron and her gray shoes, which my mom would call "sensible" but would never wear herself.

I have no idea how long my dad stayed inside. So long my knees grew stiff from squatting.

I slipped around the tree, but I couldn't see inside the house. I wanted to look in the window. I wanted to make sure Dad was okay in there. I wanted to see for myself whatever there was to see.

But before I could make my move, the front screen opened and Dad came out. His face said nothing about what he'd seen. He walked over and sat back down beside Mrs. Kinney and looked straight ahead again, as if he'd only stepped out for the intermission and was back in time for the rest of the show.

Then without saying a word, he slid that rifle off Mrs. Kinney's lap and out of her hands.

I heard a car coming from the direction of town. When it got closer, I could see it was the sheriff's car. Both the car and the sheriff were old. I didn't know much about cars, but this one was black and roundish, like police cars in old crime movies. There was no siren. Maybe the old patrol car didn't have one. Sheriff Robinson, a one-man police force, had been sheriff when my granddad, instead of my dad, was the only doctor in the county.

The car eased to a stop in front of the Kinney house as if it had all the time in the world. The motor kicked off with a sputter that shook the cruiser. Sheriff Robinson climbed out like he'd been stuck in the seat. He took a minute to square himself on his scuffed cowboy boots. He tipped his hat back, then glanced at the sky before taking off the hat and tossing it onto the front seat. What hair the sheriff had left was thin and gray. He wasn't fat or skinny, tall or short, not somebody to stand out in a crowd. With his hand shielding his eyes in a sun salute, he crossed the lawn and stood in front of my dad, the rifle, and Mrs. Kinney.

I should have felt relieved that the law had arrived, but I didn't.

"Neighbor called, Mrs. Kinney," Sheriff Robinson said, glancing from her to Dad and back. "Said you'd had some trouble."

Mrs. Kinney shifted her gaze to squint up at the sheriff, but she didn't answer him.

My dad spoke up. "Alfred's been shot, Sheriff."

Sheriff Robinson scratched his head. "That right? You've seen to him, have you, Doc?"

"He's bandaged. Grazed his shoulder. I used their phone to give Carl a call and get the ambulance out here. Alfred ought to spend a couple of nights in the hospital, to be on the safe side."

Sheriff Robinson looked down at Mrs. Kinney, who was staring at her hands in her lap. "Guess I'd best have a chat with

Alfred." He stepped between Dad and Mrs. Kinney and walked on into the house. The screen slapped behind him, and I jumped a little.

Yelling came from the house, and it wasn't coming from Sheriff Robinson. The cusswords were loud and clear, but the rest sounded garbled, like radio stations during a storm.

When the sheriff strode out onto the porch again, his face was red as raspberries. "Need to decide what we're going to do about this, Doc," he said, like they were talking about a flooded basement or a burnt cake. Not about whatever must have gone on inside that house.

Dad met the sheriff's gaze. "Not much we can do about it, Leo," he said. "Accidents happen."

3
Accidents Happen, Man

Accidents happen.

I tried to replay everything I'd seen and heard, starting with the gunshot and ending with my dad's words to the sheriff. But it was like trying to tune in the television when the vertical control was out of whack. The pieces were there, but they didn't line up.

I sure hadn't been thinking *accident.* I thought . . . well, I guess I couldn't have said what I thought. Not really. Maybe without my knowing it, my brain had been making up a sensational story I could write about.

Only . . .

Mrs. Kinney had the rifle.

Dad had more information than I did. He'd been inside the Kinney place and I hadn't. Plus, Doc Frank Taylor, M.D., was the smartest person in Hamilton. Probably in Missouri. Maybe in the whole United States of America. And maybe Mr. Kinney came out and told him it was an accident.

Sheriff Robinson scratched his head. "Well, Doc, Mr. Kinney has some peculiar notions about the shooting."

Dad's gaze stayed fixed on the sheriff. "Pain can make a man say peculiar things, Sheriff."

"You got a point there," Sheriff Robinson said, not sounding all that sure. "I can't say I know the man very well. Not like you do, Doc."

Like nearly everybody else in town, the Kinneys doctored with my dad. When Mrs. Kinney fell and broke her arm last Christmas Eve, Dad set it for her while we waited for him at church.

Dad never talked about his patients, but I heard things at school. Or from Jack. Or from Sarah. Sarah's dad farmed, but he worked as a handyman on the side. He'd been fixing plumbing at the Kinneys' once when Mrs. Kinney was laid up on crutches. She told him she'd toppled off a ladder.

Accidents happen. They sure did in that house.

Even an accident was worth writing about in Hamilton, though. People were always blowing off fingers or getting third-degree burns from Fourth of July fireworks, Dad's most hated day of the year. Farmers got tangled in hay balers, or crushed in tractor rollovers, or kicked by horses. We got our share of hunting accidents, of course. And all of those things ended up on the front page of the *Hamiltonian*.

I had a feeling there was a big story in this shooting. And I wanted to be the one to get it.

Whatever did happen inside the Kinneys' house, it was going to be my ticket to the *Blue and Gold* staff. This would be my first investigative report, and I'd prove to Mrs. Woolsey that she should choose me. Not Wanda.

I might even end up with a better story than the *Hamiltonian*. Our weekly paper under old Mr. Ridings didn't believe in publishing "negative news," anything that might get people riled. On the other hand, Mr. Ridings had supposedly turned the newspaper over to his son. Jack knew Randy Ridings better than I did, and he said Randy wanted to make the paper more interesting, more modern.

All at once, the whole town descended on us. A siren wailed on and off, like it couldn't make up its mind. An ambulance swooped in from the west, probably on loan from Cameron, a bigger town up Highway 36. Behind the dented white ambulance, a parade trailed up our dusty road. Gawkers pulled their cars to the side, shy of ditches, smashing lavender and clover.

I felt sorry for the Quiet House, only two houses down from the Kinneys'. Eight-year-old Gary Lynch lived in the tiny greenish house with his mother. Gary had leukemia and couldn't get out of bed. The shades never went up in the Quiet House, and nobody visited. Dad said we couldn't get sick by visiting Gary but he could get sicker if we gave him our germs. I wondered if Mrs. Lynch would venture out to see what the fuss was about.

From all sides, car doors slammed and out climbed a motley crew of Hamiltonians, some in sweatpants, some in shorts, a few in robes and pj's . . . like Dad.

Like me!

I had to get out of there. Fast.

I didn't really care if anybody saw me in pj's. But I still had to make my getaway. If I didn't, sooner or later I'd be spotted. Then word would get back to Dad.

Keeping my head down, I sneaked home, zigzagging from tree to tree. I didn't stop until I made it to my house. I scooped up my writing notebook from the sidewalk, where I must have dropped it. And I hustled inside.

There was no sign of my sister. Eileen had slept through the whole thing.

From the kitchen I heard Mom's telephone voice and figured she was talking to Donna, Jack's mom.

"She *what?*" Mom asked.

I peeked into the kitchen and saw Mom seated on the phone stool. She had on a sleeveless flowered dress that made her waist look tiny under the wide belt. But she still had her curlers in. She lifted her hand in a half wave, half plea to wait until she got off the phone.

"No. He isn't back yet," she said into the phone. "He bolted out of bed like we'd been bombed. First thing I thought was: another missile crisis."

Mom went wordless for a couple of minutes, which confirmed my guess that Donna occupied the other end of the line.

I slid into the breakfast booth. Mr. Rose had built it for us in exchange for Dad taking care of Mrs. Rose, who'd died last year of tuberculosis. We ate most meals with Mom and Dad facing Eileen and me across our speckled Formica table. The booth seats, two long cushioned benches, opened to store newspapers and magazines underneath—Mom's idea, and a pretty neat one, if you asked me.

Mom laughed at something Donna said. She took a swig of her black coffee and kept listening.

From habit, I glanced toward the window. I'd grown up watching birds nest in the elms just outside. But last summer Dad stuck a giant air-conditioning unit into the window. Now I couldn't see anything except a tan box with knobs and vents.

I tuned in to Mom's one-syllable end of the conversation and tried to figure out Donna's stream of consciousness on the other end. Sooner or later, Donna Adams would know things. She would have made a great investigative reporter.

"So you think this has something to do with *that*?" The way Mom said this, I knew she was watching her words because of me.

Fine. Let them guess what was happening at the Kinney place. I knew more than either of them.

I shoved aside my empty cereal bowl and silverware and opened my notebook. *I'm going to tell it like it is. Tree Taylor the Writer is going to write.*

4
Tell It Like It Is

I sat at our kitchen table with my notebook in front of me. But I had no clue where to begin my Kinney story. I'd written a lot—stories, school reports, journal stuff. I just hadn't ever written a real article. And I'd never investigated.

I flipped through my journal until I found the quote I was looking for:

> I keep six honest serving-men (they taught me all I knew); their names are What and Why and When and How and Where and Who. — Rudyard Kipling

It was a little dippy, but Kipling's advice was exactly what I needed. I'd had to memorize the same journalism questions in Miss Jones's seventh-grade language arts class. We learned them in a different order, but I decided to go with Kipling's order instead of Miss Jones's.

What: An accident. More than likely. Probably.

Why: Good question. Was the gun loaded, and nobody
  knew it? Was Mr. Kinney cleaning his rifle? At
  that hour? Why did Mrs. Kinney have it when Dad
  and I got there?

When: About 6:55 a.m., May 25, 1963. But what
  happened at 6:54? And at 6:56?

How: A rifle. But how do you shoot yourself in the
  shoulder? Did he drop the rifle? Did she?

Where: The Kinneys' house, East Samuel Street,
  Hamilton, Missouri. Bedroom? Living room?

Who: Mr. Kinney. But who is he, really? And what
  about his wife?

I stopped writing because my five questions had turned
into a dozen. And I had zilch for answers.

I wished Dad would come home. I needed to know if he
was one hundred percent positive the shooting had been an
accident.

I stopped chewing my Bic and tried again. Only this time,
I posed my questions to Mrs. Kinney. I imagined her sitting
across from me in the breakfast booth, that rifle stretched
across her lap.

Who are you, really?

I pictured thin, dry lips barely moving as she answered:
"You know who I am, Tree." She let out a sigh like the one on
her front porch. *"I reckon I'm Alfred Kinney's wife. That's all.
I'm not like your mother over there, with friends to talk to on
the telephone."*

It was weird. As I wrote, I could almost hear Mrs. Kinney's flat, twangy voice. True, I wasn't sure I'd ever heard her speak. But I knew how a lot of Hamilton women spoke. A country accent? A dialect? Ways of saying things that Mom always corrected Eileen and me on. "Warsh" instead of "wash." "Fanger" instead of "finger." "Fixin' to" instead of "going to."

I wrote it all down in my notebook and turned the page for more.

Yet in the time it took me to write my next question, my imagination fizzled on me. The skinny woman across the table began to fade ... dissolve ... disappear like a lump of sugar in a cup of hot coffee.

You go on and ask your daddy what happened, Mrs. Kinney whispered.

I looked up from my notebook. And just before the image of Mrs. Kinney disappeared, I thought I saw her grin.

"Finally! I thought Donna would never get off." Mom hung up the phone on the wall, where Dad had mounted it because I kept tripping over the cord. He'd refinished the little round table beneath the phone and caned the seat of the phone stool. Mom needed to be comfortable when she talked to Donna. Sometimes she curled her hair or did her nails during those conversations.

She walked to the sink and ran the water before filling her glass. She took a long drink, then turned to me.

No way my mother and Mrs. Kinney were the same age. Mom had blue eyes and page-boy blond hair, and strangers sometimes thought she and Eileen were sisters. Before World War II broke out, Mom worked as a nurse in a big Chicago hospital. She signed up for the army because she couldn't stand the thought of her five brothers on a battlefield with no nurse around.

Mom and Dad met in boot camp and got married in their army uniforms two months later. For the rest of the war, they were army doctor and army nurse overseas, only in different countries, like France and Germany, or maybe England. After the war, they moved to Hamilton, and Mom started working as Dad's nurse three days a week. Patients from out of town made passes at her all the time. I'd have bet money that nobody had made a pass at Mrs. Kinney in a hundred years.

Mom leaned against the sink and wiped her hands on a dish towel. "A very bad thing has happened, Tree."

I knew what she was going to say, of course. But I tried to act like I didn't.

"You might as well hear it from me." She drank the rest of her water and set her glass in the sink. "Our neighbor Mr. Kinney had an accident this morning."

I looked down so she couldn't see my face. Jack was always telling me, "It's written all over your face, Tree."

"He . . . is . . . well, he's on his way to the hospital."

"Ah," I said, nodding like the Kit-Cat clock in Eileen's room.

Mom's eyes narrowed. "He suffered a gunshot wound, honey."

I was lousy with secrets. And I wasn't even sure why I'd been turning this into one. "I know, Mom."

The wrinkles disappeared from her forehead. Maybe she'd

been afraid I'd burst into tears or scream in terror. Maybe I should have.

Then the wrinkles came back. "Wait—did you hear the gunshot, Tree?"

I nodded.

"Were you scared, honey?"

"I'm okay."

"Did you see your father?"

"He ran down to their house. I was sitting outside, writing, when the gun went off."

"Why didn't you say anything?"

"You were on the phone."

Mom began ripping the pink spongy curlers out of her hair. "Did you talk to Dad? Is he all right?"

"He's okay. The sheriff is there." *I* should have been there too, where the action was. Randy Ridings was probably there by now, collecting facts, interviewing neighbors. And what if Wanda had the same idea I did about getting a story for the school paper?

Mom set the fistful of curlers onto the counter and ran her long red fingernails through her hair. She and Eileen had the same hair. I got Dad's wild and wavy black hair. "Tell me your father didn't go down there in that raggedy robe and those awful slippers."

My mom would never have left the house in a robe and slippers, not even if the house were on fire.

I shrugged. "Mom, do you know the Kinneys very well?"

"Not really. Lois—she was Lois Dodge then—went to

school with your dad, I think. Maybe she was a year behind him. Your dad skipped two grades."

Jack was right as usual. Mrs. Kinney must have been about the same age as our moms. "But she looks so old."

Mom came over and sat on the edge of the booth bench opposite me. Her feet stuck out, and I saw that her pink slip-ons matched the big flowers on the full skirt of her dress. "Lois Kinney has had a hard life."

Mom was looking right at me, talking to me like I was one of her friends instead of one of her girls, the younger one. I felt like I was on the verge of uncovering something, part of a truth I'd need if I really planned to write about this. "How has her life been hard?"

"What's going on?" Eileen, still in her powder-blue baby-doll pajamas, shuffled into the kitchen. She and Mom had bought matching pj's on their last shopping spree to Kansas City. I got the latest issue of *Mad* magazine, which was exactly what I asked for.

Eileen yawned. "Why are people crawling all over our street?"

Mom jumped up from the table. "I'll tell you about it later, honey . . . after you've had a chance to wake up." She glanced over at me and shook her head. Mum's the word. Mustn't sully Eileen's morning with upsetting news. "Break-fast?"

"I'm off." All hope of getting real answers out of my mother left the room the minute Eileen stepped in. Honesty went down the tubes as my sister slid into the breakfast booth and downed her OJ. Eileen never wanted to hear anything ugly or disturbing. She refused to watch *The Twilight Zone* or *Alfred Hitchcock* with Dad and me. As far as my big sister knew, everyone died in his or her sleep after a long and happy life. And "dead" wasn't a word you said out loud.

I needed to talk to Dad. He shot straight with me. When my grandmother was dying, he told me right out that he didn't think she had long to live. I appreciated that. Grandmother Taylor and I had never gotten along too well. Knowing that my visit with her would probably be the last time I'd see her helped me be extra nice. Otherwise, I might have snapped back at her when she told me to stop my yelling, when all I was doing was talking normal.

I had to get Dad off by himself if I wanted the truth. Besides, there was no way I could spend another minute in the house—not while everything was happening right down the street. Mom wouldn't approve, and Dad wouldn't be happy to see me at the Kinneys'. But that was just too bad. I flipped toward the back of my notebook, where I knew I'd written a tough writer's quote:

Writing is hard work and bad for the health.
—E. B. White

"Guess I'll go get dressed," I announced as casually as I could. "I'm working this afternoon." I slipped back to my bedroom and changed into my swimsuit, white shorts, and a sleeveless tie-top.

Crooked house, here I come!

5
Town Gossip

It wasn't easy sneaking out of my house. The tamarack tree that shaded our back door used to barely brush the screen when you opened it all the way. But since last summer, the delicate branches had grown so that we had to duck and turn sideways to get out.

Then Midge pounced on me, barking her head off.

"Shush, girl." I scratched her floppy ears.

She dashed off and trotted back with her chewed-up rubber ball. Her tail wagged so hard, her whole body swayed. Three years ago, somebody had dumped her by the side of the road. Dad spotted her on his way home from a house call and doctored her back to health.

"Sorry, buddy. No fetch. I've got work to do."

Midge whined as I made my escape.

About a dozen people were milling around the Kinneys' front lawn. Mr. Kinney would have had a fit. Down at the Quiet House, a shade looked half hoisted. Even Mrs. Lynch must have gotten caught up in the ruckus.

"Hello, Tree." An older woman I recognized nodded at me. She belonged to a big group of Hamiltonians who knew Eileen and me because of our parents but whose names had never stuck in my brain.

"Hello." I nodded back.

"Dreadful business." She clutched her collar at her throat. Her black blouse and straight black skirt would have looked at home in a funeral parlor. "I'm surprised your daddy let you be here."

I shrugged and kept walking. Strolling around to the side yard, I couldn't see Dad or Sheriff Robinson. No ambulance, either.

Six or seven people huddled on the sidewalk. I sidled over there, close but not too close.

Olan Stemple and his wife seemed to be talking at the same time. They farmed eighty acres east of town. Their seven grandkids ranged from kindergarten to high school. "We went to school with Alfred," Mrs. Stemple began.

"In a one-room schoolhouse in Mirable," her husband continued. "Course, that school's been tore down nigh onto forty years or better."

"Post office is still there," Mrs. Stemple chimed in.

I wanted them to stick to the subject. It would really help my article if I knew what Mr. Kinney was like when he was young.

Thankfully, John Rounds asked my question for me: "What was the old man like back then?" Mr. Rounds ran the hardware store. His right hand clutched one suspender like he couldn't quite trust it to hold up his baggy gray trousers.

Both of the Stemples opened their mouths to speak, but Mrs. got words out first. "Young Alfred was the school bully."

"Even when there was other fellas bigger than him," Mr. added.

"My, yes." Mrs. Stemple glanced at the Kinneys' house as if Mr. Kinney were still in there and she wanted to make sure he couldn't hear her. "He used to terrorize us at lunch."

"Just take whatever he dang well pleased from lunch pails. Money too, if a body had some."

"And fights," his wife added. "Not just schoolyard scuffles, neither."

"All-out fights that *he* always started."

Mr. Rounds snapped his suspender. Everybody in the huddle jumped, including me. "So he was always a mean son-of-a-gun, eh? Shame, really. Wife seems okay. Good deal younger than Alfred."

"Don't know how she puts up with him," said a long-faced woman.

"Alfred Kinney tried to kill himself once," Mrs. Stemple whispered.

"Years back, afore he took a wife," her husband added. "Ran his car straight into the stone barn out yonder past our place."

Irma Jones, a woman in Mom's bridge club, said, "That's not how I'd commit suicide—not that I ever would, of course. I wouldn't shoot myself, either."

Mr. Arndt, another farmer, took off his faded John Deere cap and wiped his bald head with a handkerchief. "You sure he didn't just fall asleep at the wheel? That's how I remember it."

The Stemples exchanged a look, but I couldn't tell what it meant.

"Doc ruled it an accident," Mrs. Stemple said.

"Old Doc Taylor, Senior," Mr. Stemple added. "And that was that."

Mrs. Stemple got in the last word: "Course, Doc Junior reckons this here one's an accident too."

I edged away from the group, which had begun breaking apart anyway. I pictured Mr. Kinney sitting on the porch, scowling like he hated the world and everybody in it. What did he do all day? I couldn't ever remember hearing music coming from that house. Shoot—without music, *I* might kill myself.

Maybe there was a way to tell when somebody had shot himself on purpose or by accident, or if somebody else did the shooting and if that was an accident or not. I needed to ask Dad.

My dad never "talked doctor" or used fancy words I couldn't understand. He paid attention to words. He hated language that colored over the truth of things. Like calling all that fighting in Korea a "conflict," even though Dad said it must have felt like war to the soldiers there. The newspapers, when they wrote about Vietnam, called it "the Vietnam conflict." But Dad said it was getting mighty close to a war, no matter what they called it.

I couldn't wait to talk to Dad. Only he was nowhere in sight. He'd probably ridden along in the ambulance.

Mom would kill Dad when she found out he was riding all over the state of Missouri in his robe and slippers.

6
Basket Cases

The day had turned into what Dad called "a real mugger," and it wasn't even June yet. School let out in early May, thanks to all the farmers who would have pulled their sons out anyway to get the planting done on time. It felt like sweat dangled in the air, an invisible curtain of yuck. The sun shone from straight up in the sky, which meant it could already be noon.

I had to get to work. D. J. Bretz, the pool manager, said he hired me because I was never late to anything. I ran home, changed into flip-flops, and biked to the pool.

When I got there, the stack of metal baskets reached from the floor to the counter. My job as basketgirl was to set out baskets for the swimmers to put their clothes in. Each basket had a number and a big safety pin with a matching number so I'd know which basket to get when swimmers wanted their clothes back.

Sarah hadn't shown up yet, so I got started on my own. I straightened out the pins and placed the empty baskets in order on the shelves. Easy as pie, which might have explained the quarter-an-hour pay.

Every few minutes, I peered out to the road, hoping to see Sarah. I'd talked D.J. into hiring her. Sarah and I had been best friends since birth. Our moms started it, letting us play at one house or the other. I loved Sarah's farm. I thought pumping water and using the outhouse were cool—they didn't get indoor plumbing until we hit fourth grade.

Sarah liked coming over to my house and playing in town. She loved my dad too. They had a funny routine going on for as long as I could remember. Dad used to teach our Sunday School class, and one Sunday he told us about the Bible verse that says nothing is impossible with God. So every Sunday after that, Sarah arrived with a new impossibility for Dad: "What if a guy got his head chopped off? It would be impossible for him to stay alive." Then Dad would come up with some way it could be possible, like sewing ligaments or freezing the guy. Dad hadn't taught our class for years, but Sarah still tried to stump him every time she saw him.

Sarah finally showed almost a half hour late. "Before you say a word about me being late, I want you to know I've been ready for hours. I got up at dawn, thinking Dad would have to work the back forty acres today and I'd have to help. Turns out, he's not planting the back forty this year. So that gave me *and* my big brother all kinds of time. But when I told Mack I wanted to get to the pool early for once, he couldn't be bothered to get himself in gear. So, yes, I'm late as usual."

"No sweat." I'd already figured Mack was to blame. He never wanted to drive Sarah anywhere.

Sarah helped me clear the counter of loaded baskets. "So, what's the skinny, Tree?" she asked.

"You mean with the Kinneys?" I reached for the last metal basket waiting to be shelved. It had boy clothes in it, some of them pretty gross.

"No. With the Russians and all those atomic bombs," she said sarcastically. "*Yeah,* with the Kinneys. What's your dad say about the old kook shooting himself?"

"Haven't seen Dad. I think he must have ridden in the ambulance to the hospital."

"This is your big chance, Tree." She stopped long enough to face me. Her wrinkled green blouse clashed with her red plaid shorts.

I faced her back. "Sarah, Mr. Kinney could have died, you know."

"That's what I'm saying! Mrs. Woolsey has *got* to let you on the *Blue and Gold* staff if you nail this story. Besides, I heard the bullet barely grazed his arm."

Two little boys slid their basket onto the counter. Sarah didn't move to get it, so I did. "Wait!" I hollered after them. "You forgot your pin."

Swimmers were supposed to take the numbered safety pin from their basket so they wouldn't forget the number. If everybody did it right, this job was a piece of cake. If they didn't, it was the crumbs.

The bigger of the two kids hustled back and grabbed the pin from my hand. Then he ran to catch up with his brother.

Like it would have killed him to say thank you?

The whistle blew. "No running!" Lifeguard Laura Brown,

my least favorite guard, lived to rule with her pool power. She and my sister, Eileen, liked the same guy, Butch, who had no problem dating both of them. Jack said Butch was a hound dog and he went out with Laura to get what he couldn't get from Eileen. When Jack said that, I acted like I knew what he meant. But I wasn't totally sure—at least, not until the following week, when Mom, Dad, Eileen, and I were all watching an episode of *The Saint,* a spy thriller series on TV. Mom made Dad change channels. But I caught enough of the Saint in action with a beautiful woman thief to know that the Saint was no saint. And things clicked into place so that I fully understood that Butch was no saint, either. And neither was Laura.

"Hello? I'm talking to you, Tree." Sarah stuck a green Life Saver in her mouth and gave me a red, my favorite. "You won't get another break like this one. Not in Hamilton." She was shorter than me, kind of stocky, with a really pretty face. Her hay-colored hair fell below her ears, thick and coarse. When we'd walked the midway at the carnival that stopped in Hamilton last summer, we tried to ignore the guys yelling at us to throw darts at balloons or baseballs at milk cans. Then one of them hollered after Sarah, "Hey, kid! Did your dad run over your hair with a lawn mower?" Sarah's mom had cut her hair too short, and kind of uneven.

When the guy made that crack about Sarah's hair, I felt awful for her. But Sarah burst out laughing. She turned around and actually, sincerely laughed at what the guy said. Then he laughed too. A nice laugh—*with* Sarah, not *at* her. Plus, he gave her three free games.

"Please tell me you're going to write about this Kinney thing." Sarah shoved a basket onto the shelf—the wrong shelf. "Of course, you could always write an exciting article on Hamilton's first-ever Steam and Gas Engine Show instead."

Funny. I'd considered doing that. A lot of people in Hamilton were already fired up about having old steam engines and ancient farm machines come from all over the state on the Fourth of July. Dad hoped the tractor pulls and wheat-threshing competitions might cut down on the fireworks. My parents' friends had been digging through attics for antiques to show. Mom had started sewing prairie dresses for Eileen and me. But apparently Sarah didn't share their enthusiasm.

I moved the misplaced basket to the right spot. "I'm investigating. I'm way ahead of you," I insisted, hoping it was true.

"Hey! Basketgirls!" Wanda Hopkins plopped her basket onto the counter and stuck out her chest—what there was to stick out.

I did a double take. I'd seen two-piece suits at the pool. But never one this skimpy. Wanda had straight brown hair, glasses, and a bony figure. But she had everyone convinced she was the sexiest girl in our class. I didn't get it. It made me wonder if "sexy" was something I would never understand. And never be.

"My feet are burning on the pavement, you guys," Wanda whined. "Do I have to stand here all day?"

"I'll take this one," Sarah whispered. She trudged over to the counter and frowned at Wanda. "Didn't you read the sign in the ladies' room?"

Wanda wrinkled her nose. "What sign?"

"The one that explains that you're supposed to wear your swimsuit and leave your bra and panties in the basket—not the other way around."

It took Wanda a moment to get it. "Guess you haven't heard of bikinis down on the farm." She studied Sarah from head to toe, her gaze resting too long on Sarah's middle. "Just as well."

With that, she spun around and changed her voice from mean to syrupy sweet. "Ray! Wait up!"

Ray Miller came strolling out of the locker room. Deeply tanned, he looked even better shirtless than he had in the T-shirts he wore to class. His was an honest tan, showing the lines left by his work shirt. A farmer's tan. He was no sun worshipper. Not like Butch or Michael the Lifeguard, who babied their tans worse than girls. Ray's denim swim trunks looked awesome on him. They could have passed for shorts and probably did.

Wanda waved at Ray. She fumbled with the basket pin. Finding nothing on her bikini to pin the number to, she clutched it in her hand and trotted over to Ray. She ran like a girl.

No punishing whistle warned Wanda the Wonderful to stop running. Where was Laura the Lifeguard when I needed her?

I joined Sarah at the basket counter and watched Wanda and Ray lay their towels side by side. If this turned into a beach party movie and they rubbed suntan lotion on each other, I'd barf.

"I don't even think Wanda can swim," I grumbled, staring at her basket. The rat-tailed comb she used to tease her bouffant back into shape was there, plus her frilly white blouse and the form-fitting red pedal pushers nobody could pedal in without splitting a seam.

"If she ever did try to swim, I shudder to think what would happen to that suit. *I* don't want to be around to see it." Sarah glanced back at me. "Can Ray swim?"

"Of course." I'd never seen him swim. But he could play football. And baseball. And basketball. He could do anything. He was *Ray Miller.*

Ray.

With the sky-blue eyes.

So, if he really could do anything, why couldn't he fulfill my second summer goal? For there was no doubt in my mind or soul that if I could choose any boy in my class to give me that kiss worth writing about, it would be Ray.

7
Rumors

As the day wore on, I felt as if somebody had split me into two Trees. One Tree couldn't stop thinking about Alfred Kinney. In the snippets of conversations I'd been hearing over the baskets (basketgirls were invisible, so we heard all kinds of gossip), the only thing everyone agreed on was that Mr. Kinney was a not-so-nice old man. People used other words to describe him, but I wasn't allowed to say those.

The other Tree couldn't help watching the Wanda-and-Ray Show. She giggled. He grinned. She rolled over to face him, then stuck a wad of gum into her mouth. Purple. I knew this because she chewed the pale purple lump with her mouth open.

"Why do people think it's okay to do that?" I muttered to Sarah.

"Do what?"

"Chew gum with their mouths open!"

Wanda chewed like a largemouth bass. Did guys think

that was cute? As she talked, a *snap* and a *pop* came from behind the teeth of her half smile. She used *pop*s as exclamation points. Some writer! "Oh, Raayy . . . *pop!*"

Sometimes I felt like the youngest person in our class, which I was. And sometimes I felt like the oldest person in the world.

A hand waved in front of my face. "Calling all Trees!" Sarah squinted into my eyes. "You okay?" She alone knew about my longtime crush on Ray, although neither of us would have reduced my feelings to a "crush."

"I'm fine," I lied. "I just wish we could get off early. I want to talk to my dad." I glanced up at the fluffy clouds drifting across the sky. The whole Kinney incident already felt like it was drifting out of my reach.

"Better do your rain dance," Sarah said.

I'd always danced, mostly when nobody was looking. But my rain dance was different.

Legend had it that it all began on a perfectly clear day in fourth grade. My class was headed outside for recess, but Sarah and I wanted to play dodgeball in the gym. So out of the blue, I announced that I'd do a rain dance so we could stay in. And there, in the hallway, with my whole class looking on, I launched into my first-ever rain dance. I whooped and spun and twirled. All of a sudden, thunder boomed and the skies opened. We got indoor recess.

But I had to sit it out because I'd danced in the hallway.

D.J., pool manager extraordinaire, paraded into the basket room, clipboard in hand, whistle around his neck, his big bare feet slapping the damp cement floor. Reddish blond hair curled along his forearms and legs and burst like a hairy sun across his bare chest. His permanent sunburn made him the color of cherry Kool-Aid. As always, a dab of zinc oxide accented his nose, bright white under his dark shades.

D.J. had graduated with Jack. His folks wanted him to go to the teachers college in Maryville, but he took the manager's job at the pool instead. "Did I hear someone say 'rain dance'?" he bellowed.

"My idea," Sarah said.

"And a fine idea it was, young Sarah." He turned to me. "What say ye, fair Tree?"

I spotted one promising cloud, wispy and white but low to the ground. I stuck out my finger and registered a breeze out of the southeast. "I do see a rain dance in my future."

"Right on, Tree Man!" D.J. exclaimed.

D.J. always closed the pool at the first hint of lightning, and often at the first raindrop. If the weather cleared, he'd reopen . . . unless it was close to closing time. Then we'd go home early.

I looked around the pool, hoping not to see any drop-off kids, the ones whose parents wouldn't show up until the last possible minute. But there they were—three boys, ages six to nine, huddled on towels.

"A lot of good rain will do us," I muttered. "The Cozad boys are here. Their mother won't pick them up, even if I dance up a thunderstorm."

"Somebody ought to tell her we're not babysitters," Sarah complained.

★ ★ ★

The afternoon dragged on. With school out, the pool had become the town hangout. And babysitting service.

And dating service.

I'd been trying hard not to look at Wanda and Ray. But I couldn't help myself. Their towels were touching.

"Man!" Sarah exclaimed, and I was afraid she'd caught me staring at Wanda and Ray. But I was wrong. She had just come back from her break. "Have you heard the rumors flying around? Two seventh-grade girls claim they know for a fact that the Kinney shooting was a hunting accident."

"Right. What was he hunting in that house? Cockroaches?"

"Then there's Mikey Mouse." That was her name for Michael the Lifeguard, who could be pretty Mickey Mouse when it came to pool rules.

"What's Michael know about it?"

"Nothing," Sarah said. "But he thinks he does. Mikey says he heard that Mr. Kinney died in the ambulance."

"That's crazy!"

She shrugged. "Don't shoot the messenger. At least *I'm* out there interviewing people."

She was right. I grabbed my notebook from my basket. "My turn!"

Sarah handed me a pencil and gave me a little shove. "Go! I've got the baskets covered. Investigate. Interrogate. Initiate."

I loved my best-friend-who-was-a-girl. Sarah would have been behind me if I'd told her I'd decided to fly to the moon.

I headed poolside and moved in the opposite direction

from Wanda and Ray. Two of Jack's friends let out howls of laughter as they made their way to the pool.

Only the whistle blew right then and Lifeguard Laura shouted, "Everybody out! Swimmers' break!"

The taller of Jack's friends swore.

I couldn't blame him. D.J. claimed that getting swimmers out of the pool at the top of every hour was a safety thing. I didn't buy it. Like if somebody drowned at the bottom of the pool, this would be our chance to see him? But the Cameron swimming pool guards did the same thing.

It took all of my courage to walk up to Jack's classmate, Ben, even though most of Jack's friends liked me okay.

Ben's basketball-sized head didn't fit his hockey-stick body. He had to keep hiking up his paisley trunks. He squinted down at me. "Hey, Tree. What's happening? Jack around?"

I shook my head. "But I wanted to ask you what you thought about the Kinney shooting?"

"That was pretty crazy," Ben said.

I think he was about to say more, when the not-Ben guy butted in. "Look at her!"

Lifeguard Laura stepped to the edge of the pool, first making sure all eyes were aimed her way. She raised her arms and executed a perfect surface dive, rolling over to do the backstroke the length of the empty pool. That little exhibition was, I believed, the real reason lifeguards whistled swimmers out every hour.

8

Twistin' and Turnin'

"See you, Tree. Tell Jack hey for me." Ben and his buddy took off to join Laura's admirers, who flocked around her lifeguard stand like pigeons waiting for popcorn.

I tried interviewing more people. One kid said Mr. Kinney took a bullet to the gut. Another claimed he shot himself in the foot and doctors had to cut off his leg.

Then I spotted Penny Atkinson sitting on a striped towel off in the far corner of the pool deck. I didn't know her very well, which was weird since we only had forty-nine kids in our grade. Maybe since she'd moved to Hamilton in the fifth grade, she was still the new girl. The rest of us had been born here. People moved out of Hamilton, Missouri. They almost never moved in.

"Hey, Penny!"

She jumped like I'd startled her. "Hi, Tree."

Neither of us said anything. That's what happened every time I tried to talk to Penny—nothing but awkward silence.

Penny was the kind of girl nobody noticed—here or at school. She never got into trouble. She turned in her work on time, and her work never got noticed, either. When she did talk in class, you got the feeling she was trying out speech and kind of surprised by the sound of her own words.

Small talk wouldn't cut it. Not with Penny. I whipped out my notebook. "I'm asking people what they know about Mr. and Mrs. Kinney."

Silence.

I stared down at her penny-red hair, her bangs so long they hid half her face. "Don't you have anything to say about them?" The question came out sharper than it should have. But I was tired of people not helping with my investigation.

Penny didn't look away. "Okay. I saw Mr. and Mrs. Kinney together. More than once."

I was so surprised she'd said anything that I didn't know what to ask next. I squatted so she didn't have to stare into the sun. "Now we're getting somewhere. So you saw them together. What were they doing?"

"Whatever *Mr.* Kinney wanted." Penny's lips grinned, but her eyes didn't.

Her answer threw me, but I recovered. "Yeah? Anything else?"

"Well, I guess I won't be seeing Mr. and Mrs. Kinney together for a while." She paused, and I thought she might be finished. "So I guess Mrs. Kinney can do whatever *Mrs.* Kinney wants for a change."

I wrote it down. Word for word. "Thanks, Penny."

She nodded, and I went back to being a basketgirl.

Most people's stories about the Kinneys sounded like gossip. But not Penny's. I suspected she had a whole blizzard of things she could have said and she'd only offered me a snowflake.

For my supper break, I bought a frozen Milky Way from the snack bar and took my seat on one of the picnic tables outside. Across the gravel road sat Hamilton High, an L-shaped brick building with room for 350 students, grades seven through twelve. J. C. Penney, born and raised in Hamilton, had donated the cash for our new school. I'd be headed back there in early August, the price we paid for getting out in early May.

Supper over, I trudged back to the basket room and was reaching for an empty basket when Sam Cooke broke through the radio with "Twistin' the Night Away."

Without thinking, I launched into my own version of Chubby Checker's twist. I loved twisting, but it had gotten old fast . . . until I made it my own.

"Turn it up, D.J.!" Sarah shouted.

I couldn't help myself. I twisted low, kicked off my flip-flops, and twirled, all without losing the beat.

D.J. let out a whoop. "Lay it on me, Tree!"

I grinned but kept my eyes shut. I wasn't sure why that helped, but it always did.

In every other part of life, I felt lame in front of people. I couldn't sing in the choir—Eileen had inherited Mom's singing voice. My knees shook when I had to say the least little thing in school.

But dancing was different. When I was dancing, *I* was different.

The music ended. I opened my eyes and found Sarah staring at me.

She shook her head slowly. "Tree, you need to get yourself on *American Bandstand.*"

"Was that a rain dance?" Laura the Lifeguard demanded, not smiling. I suppose you could call her pretty, but Eileen was twice as pretty. Maybe three times. And Eileen smiled. Not at me especially, but she smiled. Laura's permed hair framed hazel eyes and a tiny nose. But her face wasn't what most guys looked at. Unlike Wanda, Laura didn't have to stick out *her* chest.

She frowned at me. "Well? *Was* that a rain dance?"

"Why? You want to close early? Got a big date?" *With Butch, my sister's creep of a boyfriend?*

She sneered in a way that made me check to see if I had Milky Way smudges on my chin.

I resisted twisting to "Peppermint Twist." But when I heard the first note of Bill Haley's "Rock Around the Clock," it was all over. "Come on, Sarah!" I begged, grabbing her hands and stepping out. "I can't dance by myself."

Sarah stood like a statue while I rock-'n'-rolled out of control.

"Cutting in here."

Jack.

I hadn't heard him come in. Jack Adams was the best dancer I knew . . . although he claimed I was the best. We'd danced together so many times that we could sense each other's moves.

Jack grabbed my hands, and we started with classic steps—*right foot forward, right foot back, left foot back, left foot forward*—and moved into bridges and back-turns, sidearms and wraps. He spun me dizzy, and then we both spun until the music stopped.

"Man," Sarah said. "You guys are good."

"Far-out rockin' great!" D.J. shouted.

"I'd second that," said a thin voice from the poolside counter. A white-haired woman, whose face resembled a shriveled potato, handed in her basket. "I used to cut a rug myself in my day."

"It's the best, isn't it?" I said, still a little out of breath.

"It is indeed, dear." She smiled, then walked to the corner of the pool, where the railing was.

I watched her until she made it safely into the pool's shallow end.

Jack snatched a basket and started off toward the locker room.

I headed him off. "Jack—wait up."

"I'm all danced out, Tree."

I put my hand on the empty basket so he couldn't leave. "You heard about Mr. Kinney, right?"

"Not you too, Tree." He sighed. "It's all I heard about today. And that includes the twelve phone calls from Donna." Jack only called his mother Donna when she wasn't around.

"I'm not looking for gossip."

"Right. You just want to write about it so you can get on the school paper. Ask Donna for details. I'm sure she's got more than anybody." He started off again.

"Jack, please? I need to know what *you* know about Mr. and Mrs. Kinney."

This time he came back and gave me his full attention. "Okay. I don't know him at all. But I like Mrs. Kinney. She stops by the IGA and asks me to cut her meat *exactly* the way her husband likes it."

I could tell he had something else to say. I waited.

Jack sighed. "I don't know, but I've always gotten the feeling things wouldn't go so well for her if she brought the wrong cut of meat home."

9
Rain Dancing

"Jack Adams!" Laura the Lifeguard had apparently given up her post in favor of personally welcoming Jack to the Hamilton pool.

Jack studied my face. "You good, Tree?"

"Yeah. I'm okay."

Laura wouldn't leave Jack alone. Maybe being a leech was how she kept Butch in her clutches. That, and what went on in that bedroom scene right after *The Saint* broke for a shaving-cream commercial.

With Laura trotting after him, Jack jogged to the high diving board. Lifeguard Mike blew his whistle, but Jack waved as if the whistle were a friendly hello.

I watched Jack climb the ladder to the high dive. I'd gone off the high board only once. Nothing had prepared me for the fact that water, a liquid, could hurt like a solid.

Jack raised his arms exactly like Laura did before her exhibition dives. Then he shot into the air like he meant to dive.

Only instead of flipping over, he came down feet first. But it wasn't a jump, either. He grabbed one knee and hit the water with the force of a cannon.

It had to hurt like hades. But, man, was it worth it! Jack's cannonball shot up a spray of water that rained down on the unsuspecting Laura. She sputtered and screamed like she'd never been wet before.

Jack climbed out and jogged off. Mike tried to blow his whistle, but he was laughing too hard.

A smattering of applause accompanied Jack as he disappeared into the locker room.

Around seven, the pool emptied. Not a swimmer in sight . . . except for the Cozad boys, wrapped up in towels. I didn't know if they were protecting themselves from the evening breeze or from third-degree sunburn.

I used the lull to catch up on D.J.'s copy of last week's *Hamiltonian*. Two articles surprised me—one criticizing the school board and the other reporting on the rise in auto accidents in Caldwell County. Randy must have written both articles. Old Mr. Ridings would have thought they were too negative.

"Can you believe this?" Sarah whispered. "Mrs. Cozad's here. Maybe we can get off early after all."

"You're kidding," I whispered back. We still had ninety minutes till closing.

But no sooner had the boys left than the stragglers arrived, a handful of people who actually liked to swim. I waited poolside and tried to interview a couple of them, but they were too serious about swimming laps.

This was turning out to be the longest day in the history of history.

"Time for a rain dance," I whispered to Sarah.

I didn't need music for my rain dance. In fact, the song playing now—"Sherry" by the mellow Four Seasons—made my job harder. The only way to dance to that song was to "non-dance." That's what Jack and I called the way most kids faked slow dances at sock hops after ball games. They leaned on each other and swayed. Non-dancing.

I did the best I could.

About a half hour later, D.J. burst into the basket room. "Tree, did you do your rain dance?"

"I did," I admitted.

"Freaks me out every time. I knew I felt a raindrop!"

"No lie, D.J.?" To tell the truth, my rain dances only worked half the time. Plus, I only did them when there was a good possibility of rain . . . unless I was desperate, like tonight.

Sarah and I left the basket room to stand with D.J. and watch the pool turn into a tiny ocean of dots as raindrops plunked the surface.

The last of the swimmers hoisted themselves out of the pool.

"Let's split while the splittin's good!" Sarah shouted.

I lifted my face to the sky and let the rain splash me. We'd only be closing twenty minutes early, but it felt like a snow day.

Then, as suddenly as it had started, the rain stopped.

"Dance again, Tree!" Sarah commanded.

Before I could, D.J. muttered, "What a drag. Lifeguards! Get back here."

They'd both abandoned their lifeguard chairs. Laura was halfway to the locker room.

"Why?" Michael whined. "Who's going to come swimming with only fifteen minutes left to closing?"

For once, I had to agree with Michael.

D.J. was staring out toward the street.

I looked where he was looking. Mrs. Cozad's beater pickup cruised across the lot and up to the sidewalk. Her boys, their towels still wrapped around their shoulders, were piled into the back like bales of hay.

"Out!" she shouted to the boys. Then she marched her ducklings up to the pool ticket window and flashed her family pass.

We all followed D.J. through the basket room to the ticket counter.

D.J. placed both palms on the counter. "Can I help you?"

"My boys want to swim some more," Mrs. Cozad said.

D.J. glanced at the skinny boys staring at their feet and shivering. "Sorry, Mrs. Cozad. We're closing."

"You can't close! They got fifteen minutes of swimming left." She glanced at her watch. "And I've got to be somewheres."

"We're closing," D.J. repeated.

"It's not raining!" she snapped.

D.J. didn't lose his cool. "Threat of lightning."

"*I* didn't see any lightning."

"That's why we have trained lifeguards," D.J. said evenly.

"Shoot. I'll be back in ten minutes. You can keep them out of the pool if it makes you feel any better."

D.J. lowered his voice. "Take your kids home, Connie."

The Cozad boys sprang to life. Their little bony faces broke into grins, showing yellow teeth. The oldest boy ran barefoot to the truck and hopped in back. The others followed.

Mrs. Cozad glared at D.J. Her eyes had tiny red lines in them. Without a word, she wheeled around and stomped back to the truck, slamming the door after her. When she floored the gas, her boys had to grab the sides of the truck to keep from falling out.

10

Deep

D.J. grabbed his clipboard and keys. "Flee the scene, cats. Later."

I nodded. "See ya!" I called after Sarah.

"Not if I see you first!" she called back.

D.J. offered me a lift, but I had my bike.

Pedaling just fast enough to keep moving, I gazed up at the sky. Through the clouds, I could make out both Dippers and the North Star.

I took the side streets with the most hills. I never minded hills. I tried to keep the vision of the starry sky in my head. But the second I looked away, my mind filled with images of Mr. Kinney lying in a pool of blood shaped like Texas. True, I hadn't seen him wounded and bloody. But I'd imagined him that way so often during the day that the pictures felt real.

Then my brain shifted to Mrs. Kinney, clutching the rifle like it was hers.

I turned onto Prairie Street. I needed to bike past Mrs. Gurley's house, where the scent of her lilacs floated over the whole block like a lavender fog. I tried to let the stars and lilacs kidnap my mind so I wouldn't think about the Kinneys anymore.

But they were the ones I was going to have to write about. Stars and lilacs wouldn't get me a spot on the *Blue and Gold* staff. True, most of the articles in the *Blue and Gold* covered boring school news. But every kid from seventh grade to senior, plus their parents, read that paper. And when Jack was in junior high, he said the *Blue and Gold* broke a big story about the civics teacher getting himself fired "on moral grounds."

If I wanted to be the one to break this story, I needed to get on it. By now, Randy Ridings would be out doing his own investigation.

I felt pretty sure Dad wouldn't tell Randy squat, though. So I might still have an advantage.

When I turned onto our street, I could see Dad's car in our carport. The old station wagon, which Eileen and I had dubbed Buddy, was showing its age in scratches and dents. I wheeled my bike in front of Buddy and saw that Dad had left his window open. Again. He was always doing things like that. We got at least three calls a week from some patient telling us Doc had left his hat after a house call. Eileen said our dad was the original absent-minded professor.

I rolled up the window and reached for Dad's hat, a tan fedora. Then I changed my mind and left it there. At least when Dad started looking for it, I'd know where to find it.

"I'm home!" I hollered to an empty living room.

"Hang up your wet suit!" Mom shouted from the bathroom. The bathroom door was closed, and wisps of smoke seeped from under the door.

I had never seen a cigarette in my mother's possession—not in her lips, mouth, or fingers. Not even in her purse. But a couple of years earlier, I realized that unless our bathroom was occasionally on fire, my mother smoked now and again. We never mentioned it, even though she knew that I knew, and I knew that she knew that I knew.

I didn't think Mom and Dad talked about the cigarettes, either, except in hints. Dad cut out articles from his medical journals that claimed smoking was bad for you. As far as I knew, Mom never acknowledged these articles, which he placed on her side of the bed. But I'd caught her reading them.

Our family had other secrets like that. Nobody came right out and said that Grandmother Taylor had hated kids, but it was true, and we all knew it. Nobody ever explained why Cousin Virginia had gotten married while she was still in high school, and had a baby six months later.

I had honestly believed that Eileen's hair was Marilyn-Monroe-white-blond all on its own . . . until Jack convinced me to rummage in Eileen's wastebasket after she washed her hair. I found a bottle of Liquid Sunshine hidden under some Kleenex.

Who knew what other secrets lurked in the corners of the Taylor household? I just wished some of them could have been mine. It wasn't that I couldn't keep a secret—I could. It was just that I didn't have any secrets of my own worth keeping—except maybe Summer Goal Number Two.

I found Dad in the den, a tiny room carved out of the hallway outside his and Mom's bedroom. To enter the bedroom, you had to go through the den. Dad had squeezed a little desk and one chair into the space.

When I walked in, he stopped reading. He was holding a copy of the *New York Times,* which he usually picked up in Kansas City, from the same shop that sold my *Mad* magazines. "Do you know who Senator Mansfield is, Tree?"

I almost answered, "A senator," but I had a feeling Dad wasn't in a joking mood. "Not exactly," I admitted.

"He's the Senate majority leader. And he's a brave man who's getting sucker-punched by the media."

"How come?" There was only the one desk chair, so I could sit on the floor or stay standing. I stood.

"Mansfield, like our own Senator Symington, started out believing America needed to become involved in Vietnam. But after flying there and seeing for themselves what was going on, they changed their minds. Both oppose the war in Vietnam now. And for coming to their senses, they're being called 'wishy-washy' and a lot worse."

Months ago, I'd found an old issue of *Life* magazine in the bathroom and read an article, "Vicious Fighting in Vietnam." I'd asked Dad about it, and he told me straight out why he was against Vietnam. The next day, I asked kids at school what they thought about Vietnam. Most of them didn't know what I was talking about. But everybody said they were for America beating anybody, including Vietnam. I didn't bring it up again at school.

After I got home, I asked Mom if she was for or against Vietnam. She growled a little, like she was tired of Dad talking about Vietnam and now here I was doing the same. "America for the

Americans," she said. "That's what I've always said. And that's all I'm going to say. Now, go and wash up for supper."

I didn't bring up Vietnam with Mom again, either.

Dad swiveled his chair to face me. "Sorry. I have a feeling that's not why you're here."

I shook my head.

"How're you doing, Tree?"

"Okay."

"About this morning, I wanted to say I'm sorry for yelling at you. I didn't know what I'd find, and I wanted you safe."

"That's okay."

"Well, I don't know what you heard. . . ." He paused. Waited.

My stomach tightened. What I heard? What I *overheard*? Had he seen me behind the cottonwood? Did he know I'd been spying on him? That I'd seen Mrs. Kinney with the gun?

Dad looked down at his hands, which were clutching the arms of his desk chair. He had big fingers and knuckles, and calluses on his palms. Nobody would have guessed that he delivered babies and stitched up cuts with those hands. I knew that for a fact because when a carny at the state fair tried to guess Dad's occupation by examining his hands, the guy guessed steelworker, gardener, and carpenter.

Finally, Dad looked up again, and his face had changed from worried to not at all worried. It felt like we were playing that game where you frown, then pass your hand over your face, turning the frown into a smile. "Well, whatever you heard at the pool, just ignore it. I'm sure rumors are all over Hamilton by now."

I breathed easier. "That's all people were talking about at the pool. I heard a lot of things about the Kinneys."

"Tree, haven't I taught you not to pay attention to gossip?"

"Yeah. Only how do I know it's gossip if I don't really know what's true and what's not?" To me, I sounded very logical.

"Well, what have you heard?" The smile on his face was slipping back to frown.

"Rumors were flying all over. Mr. Kinney got shot in the gut. Or the arm. Or the foot. A couple of people said he died in the ambulance."

Dad's grip tightened on the chair arms. The chair creaked like it was in pain. "Nonsense. Foolish people like to talk about other people's troubles. It makes them feel better about their own, I suppose. Alfred—Mr. Kinney—will be fine. He's in the hospital, where they can keep an eye on him."

"How did it really happen, Dad?"

"The accident?"

I shrugged. "If it *was* an accident. Could you tell if Mr. Kinney fired the gun, or if maybe—?"

"You can stop right there, Tree." Dad's voice had a quiet control I'd seen him use on other people. "I won't have gossip repeated in my house. I get enough of it everywhere else." He got to his feet.

"But, Dad, I just—"

"I'm tired. And I'm not talking about the Kinneys—not even to you."

"Then could we talk about it tomorrow?"

"Let it go, Tree." He walked out of the tiny room, taking all the air with him.

11

Game On

Sunday night I sat at our card table with Jack and Eileen, playing Monopoly while our parents banged out a rousing rendition of "Sleepytime Gal" in the TV room.

Almost every Sunday night, our family went over to Jack's or he and his parents came to our house. The grown-ups played old music from the forties. And I don't mean they played records. They played instruments—Dad on the trumpet, Bob Adams on the trombone, Mom on the sax, and Donna on the piano, singing along.

For better or worse, we were the only kids in the world who knew every word to "Shine, Little Glow-Worm," "It Had to Be You," and "Chattanooga Choo Choo."

We'd done this for so many years that we'd progressed through playing with stuffed animals and blocks to playing War and Go Fish to competing in Monopoly and Wahoo and sometimes chess or poker. Jack said I could finance my college education through five-card draw and seven-card stud.

If we got together early enough, Jack would round up friends for baseball or Capture the Flag. Unfortunately, Sarah could never come, because nobody wanted to drive her into town and then back out to the farm at night.

A few times, Penny and her older sister, Karen, came over for baseball. But Penny acted like she was afraid of the ball, and Karen was way more interested in Jack than in sports of any kind. Their stepbrother, Chuck, showed up a couple of times. He was Jack's age, but I got the feeling Jack didn't care much for Chuck. And Jack liked everybody.

Partly out of self-defense against our parental songbirds, Jack, Eileen, and I listened to our own records. We'd inherited Grandmother Taylor's stereo when she died. It was built for Mom and Dad's LPs, but if we popped in plastic centers, we could play our 45's, and they sounded great. Eileen had a little suitcase full of records she'd bought with her babysitting money, and usually she was pretty good about sharing them. So no matter what else we did on Sunday nights, we played music.

And danced.

Except not Eileen. Jack and I had coached her to the point where she could pull off the pony and twist well enough to make it through sock hops without embarrassing herself.

But Jack and I liked to rock-'n'-roll. I firmly believed that each new song brought its own new dance step with it. Like, if I listened right, my feet and body could follow the only rhythm possible for that song.

Jack *felt* music the same way I did, which was why we loved dancing together.

Now, as we played Monopoly and listened to our parents pound out "When the Saints Go Marching In," I could almost believe nothing had changed. I hadn't heard the rifle blast. Mr. Kinney hadn't been carted away in an ambulance. And my dad hadn't shut me down when I tried to talk to him about it.

I shifted in my seat and heard a crinkle. I'd forgotten about the note. I reached into the back pocket of my holey, faded blue jeans and pulled out the typed note I'd found taped to the handlebars of my bike when I got home from church. I'd read it right then and there:

```
To observe people in conflict is
a necessary part of a child's
education. -Milton R. Sapirstein
```

I'd known the minute I saw the note that it came from Jack. I wasn't crazy about the "child" reference. But I figured he was just looking out for me, like always, in case the shooting on our street had freaked me out. I just didn't know why he'd denied leaving it when I called to thank him.

"Why won't you admit that you left me a note, Jack?"

"I'm telling you, you've got it wrong, Tree. Must be some secret admirer leaving you love notes."

I admit that I sometimes dreamed about Ray leaving me love notes, but this was not one of them. "Some love note. And some secret," I muttered. It was like Jack to do something nice but not want anybody to know he did it. A week before my twelfth birthday, Jack left flowers for me every day. I had myself convinced the flowers came from Ray, and I tried not to let on how disappointed I was when I caught Jack red-handed with a fistful of red carnations.

We'd been waiting for Eileen to pay up for landing on Boardwalk with three houses. As usual, Jack the Risk Taker owned most of the property and Eileen the Conservative had almost all the Monopoly money. As for me, I was simply hanging on, confident I'd come in second as soon as one of them lost. Jack helped by pretending not to notice when *I* landed on his properties.

Jack turned to Eileen and held out his palm. "Any-time now."

Eileen plunked a fistful of small Monopoly bills into his hand. "There." Her fingernails were painted the same color as Mom's, bright red. They matched the dress she still had on from church, a red-striped shirtwaist with a white collar. I'd changed the second we got home.

"Ouch!" Jack dumped the money and examined his palm.

"What's the matter?" I scooted my chair over for a better look.

A cut ran about two inches across his palm, curving like another lifeline. It separated when he spread his fingers.

"Cut my hand chopping beef yesterday." He shook his hand, like he could shake off the pain.

I couldn't stand to think of Jack in pain. Paper cuts are killers. I couldn't imagine what a cut from a butcher's knife might feel like.

Eileen-who-wanted-to-be-a-nurse disappeared, then re-turned with a bottle of sting. The antiseptic probably wasn't named Sting, but it should have been. With all the bedside manner of a charging rhinoceros, Eileen shoved me out of the way and dumped half a bottle of that stuff onto Jack's cut.

"Yeow!" Jack cried.

"Don't be a baby," said Eileen the Compassionate Nurse.

"Does it hurt bad?" I asked as Eileen taped up his hand.

"I don't know," he said. "I mean, what's bad to you might not be bad to me."

"That doesn't make sense," Eileen said.

She said this at the same time I shouted, "Exactly!"

I went on to explain. "Haven't you ever wondered what other people's pain really feels like?" I'd thought a lot about this. "I would love to invent a *feeling machine* that would let people trade pains—just for a minute—so we'd know what the other person was feeling. Like right now, I could press the machine into your hand"—I touched my small hand to Jack's big one, palm to palm—"and I'd know exactly how you felt. Wouldn't that be the coolest?"

"Heavy," Jack said. I could tell he was mulling it over.

"I think that would be a drag," Eileen objected. "*I* don't want to feel anybody's pain."

"And therein lies the difference between the Taylor sisters." Jack grinned over at me. "I'd buy your compassion machine in a heartbeat, Tree."

Then he grinned at my sister. "And I'd buy you a heart in a heartbeat, Eileen."

She threw her little metal game-piece shoe at him. "Sometimes I hate you, Jack Adams! I quit."

Jack smiled after her. "I love your sister, Tree. She'd be lost without me."

With Eileen gone, Jack and I decided we wanted to do something outside. He called a couple of people before phoning the Atkinsons. After he hung up, he said, "Chuck said he'd drive the girls over."

"I thought you told me Chuck joined the army," I said.

"The reserves. He'll be a weekend soldier. But he hasn't started yet."

"Capture the Flag?" I suggested, remembering how awful Penny and Karen were at baseball.

We waited outside until Chuck drove up in his old Chevy. He pulled too far onto the lawn. I just hoped he wouldn't leave tire tracks.

The night smelled like cut grass and the promise of rain. Only a handful of brave stars made it through the night clouds. I pulled back my hair into a ponytail to get ready to play.

"Hi, Jack!" Karen jumped from the car before Chuck shut off the engine. She dashed up to Jack. "Dibs on being on your side." Karen hadn't dressed for baseball or Capture the Flag. She'd dressed for Jack. Her blue polka-dot dress hugged her chubby figure, the wide white patent leather belt straining at her waist.

I met Penny and Chuck as they stepped out of the car. Chuck looked like a giant next to Penny. He might not have been taller than Jack, but he outweighed him. His hair was so long it hung below his ears, and his bangs hovered over his eyebrows. No army haircut—not yet, anyway.

"You said you were dropping us off!" Penny was saying when I walked up.

"Changed my mind. And don't be so stupid, Mouse." Chuck glanced at me, then strutted off to Jack. "Where's

65

Eileen? Man, don't tell me she's not home! I'd go AWOL for that chick."

I stood with Penny for a few seconds. A woodpecker hammered in the distance. Crows argued on the telephone wire across the road. "So, Penny, up for a little Capture the Flag?"

"Sure." She walked with me to the side yard, where Jack was setting up the flags and marking off prisons.

"Ladies against gents?" Jack shouted.

Karen groaned.

"You're on!" I shouted back.

The object of the game was to get the other team's flag and plant it next to yours. If you got tagged in enemy territory, you went to prison and could only get out if one of your teammates came and tagged you. The guys would have a big advantage when it came to capturing us. But with three of us, we could divide and conquer to get their flag.

After two games, we'd each won one.

"Stupid game," Karen muttered. She'd proved to be more worthless than ever, since she didn't want to get her dress dirty. "I quit!"

"You can't quit!" Chuck shouted. The boys had lost the last game, and Chuck had kicked the flag and sworn a blue streak. "We have to play a tiebreaker!" He turned on Penny. "Get over there, you dumbhead. You heard me!" When she didn't, he stiff-armed her, and she stumbled out of his way. "What—are you girls chicken?"

"*I'm* chicken." Jack waved his flag in surrender. "It's getting too dark to play. Besides, you girls are too tough."

Karen ran up and hugged Jack. "You're the best, Jack!"

Penny hadn't said two words during the last game. But she'd surprised all of us by running fast and grabbing the flag to give us the victory.

"No, Karen." I grinned at Penny. "*Penny* is the best. She could have beat the guys single-handed."

"Very true." Jack wrenched free from Karen's clutches and handed Penny the flag, a white handkerchief. "Congratulations."

Penny grinned and took the flag from him. "I accept."

Music still blared from our house. The quartet would be at it another hour or more. "So now what do you want to do?" I asked.

After a few seconds of silence, Chuck jumped up and dashed to the road. "I know!" He glanced down the street toward the Kinney place. "Let's go see where that guy shot himself."

12
Far-Out!

Chuck mimicked putting a gun to his head and firing. "So, Tree, what's your dad say about Old Man Kinney trying to kill himself?"

I didn't answer.

"I thought it was an accident." Somehow, Karen had ended up next to Jack again.

"Maybe . . . maybe not." Chuck walked backward up the street a couple of feet. "Let's see for ourselves!"

I didn't want to agree with Chuck, but I liked the idea of checking out the house. Maybe we'd find a clue.

"So, what's the plan, Chuck?" Jack asked. "You going to waltz up to the door and ask Mrs. Kinney if you can search her house?"

"I'm not going to ask her anything. I'll see what I can see." Chuck turned to Penny and me. "Who's in?"

Penny shook her head. "I'll stay here."

"Big surprise," Chuck muttered.

"Me too," Karen said. "We could talk about what we're doing for the steam engine show. I'm making my own costume." She batted her eyelashes at Jack. "Maybe we could dress up as a famous couple, Jack. Like Mr. and Mrs. Daniel Boone?"

Jack ignored her. His gaze hadn't left Chuck.

I wouldn't go unless Jack did. But I really hoped he'd go. "Chuck's going to do this with or without us, Jack."

"She's right. Better come keep an eye on me."

Jack shook his head, then glanced at me. "Okay. But nobody bothers that woman. Got it?"

Chuck whooped. The rest of us, except Penny, fell in. Karen had changed her mind and now wormed her way next to Jack, which left me beside Chuck.

I was glad to finally be going to the Kinney place to investigate, but I wished it was just Jack and me. Not Chuck. I wished Chuck were already in the army. Soon as I thought it, I felt guilty. What if Chuck ended up going to Vietnam, and I'd wished it on him? "Chuck, do you think the army will send you to Vietnam?"

"No way!" He elbowed me, hard. "Reserves and National Guard. That's the way to go. It's poor schmucks like D.J.— guys who aren't signing up and aren't going to college—who are going to end up getting drafted and shipped off to Vietnam. Not me. I'm not waiting around to be drafted."

"D.J.'s no schmuck!" I said.

Jack stopped his conversation with Karen and turned to Chuck. "There are no schmucks in Vietnam—at least no American schmucks. Soldiers there are fighting your fight, Chuck. You ought to show more respect."

I wanted to ask Jack what he meant, but Karen had glued herself to his side. And anyway, we'd reached the Kinneys' house.

Now that we stood facing it, our mission seemed pretty lame.

"Where did he do it?" Chuck asked. "I heard it was on the porch." He walked closer, while the rest of us stayed back, near my old hiding place, the cottonwood.

"This is a bad idea," Jack muttered. "Chuck, come back, man. You're going to scare the woman to death."

Even with Jack there, I felt scared. What if Mrs. Kinney still had that rifle stretched across her lap?

Chuck bent over, hands on his knees, to inspect the porch. "No blood here."

Clouds hid nearly all the stars. The TV from a house across the street gave the only light in flickering shadows. I glanced down the road at the pitch-dark Quiet House and imagined Gary asleep in his bed. The Kinney house couldn't have been blacker inside if the windows had been painted black.

An owl hooted.

"This is spooky," Karen whined. She clasped Jack's arm with both hands. "Let's go back."

"'Fraid of a little ghost, Karen?" Chuck didn't bother lowering his voice. "I'll bet Old Man Kinney's ghost isn't waiting for him to kick the bucket. It's probably already haunting this old shack." He walked all the way up to the front window.

"Chuck!" Jack called.

Chuck pressed his nose to the glass, his hands cupping the

sides of his head. "Looks like the lady of the house is out on the town."

I thought about what Penny said at the pool, about Mrs. Kinney being able to do whatever she wanted now that her husband was laid up.

"What's that?" Karen squealed.

Inside the house, a single flame-light swept across the room. I gasped. "I see it!"

Chuck laughed. "Yeah, right." He was staring at us instead of the window.

"Chuck!" Jack shouted. "They're not kidding, man! Something's in there."

Chuck tilted his head like he knew we were kidding. Then he turned and peered in the front window. "What—?" He jumped from the porch so fast, he landed in a bush. Then he stumbled to his feet and took off running back up the road.

Karen was crying, burying her head in Jack's side.

Jack burst out laughing. "It was just a light. A lantern maybe. Chuck probably woke Mrs. Kinney up. I hope she scared him more than he scared her."

I knew Jack was right. But as we walked home, I made sure Karen wasn't the only one next to Jack.

After the Atkinsons left, Jack and I went back inside and cleaned up our Monopoly game. Jack never divided his money pot into denominations, so we bundled ones, fives, twenties, and everything together, something that would have put my sister over the edge.

"I've been thinking," Jack said.

"About what? Karen's proposal to be Mr. and Mrs. Boone at the steam engine show?"

"Very funny. No, I was thinking about your compassion machine. That's a great idea, Tree."

"Yeah? Thanks."

We picked up Monopoly stuff while strains of "I'll Be Seeing You in All the Old Familiar Places" came floating in. My mind drifted back to the Kinney house. I felt bad for waking up Mrs. Kinney. "Jack?"

"Hmm?" He shoved the Monopoly board on top of the piles of money and forced the lid on the box.

"If we could use a compassion machine on Mrs. Kinney, what do you think she'd be feeling right now, with her husband in the hospital?"

Jack put both hands on the card table and leaned back, his chair rearing on its hind legs. I knew he was really thinking about this, which was one of the best things about Jack. He took me seriously. Always had. "Relieved," he said at last.

"What?"

"I think Mrs. Kinney's feeling relieved, at least for now."

"Don't you think she's sad? They've been married a long time."

Jack shrugged. "The Kinneys are married, but it's a bent marriage. Not like your folks, or mine." He leaned forward, and his chair thudded on all fours. "Yeah . . . I vote relieved."

13
Get Real

After the Adams family took off, I went to bed, but I couldn't sleep. Midge curled at my feet and growled every time I flopped over. I couldn't stop thinking about Mrs. Kinney. Was she lying awake right now too? Was she really feeling relieved that Mr. Kinney wasn't lying beside her?

The only person I would have felt relieved to have out of *my* way—not counting Khrushchev or Castro, of course—was Wanda. She was the biggest obstacle to me fulfilling either of my summer goals. Mrs. Woolsey, who'd been our junior high art teacher, always chose Wanda's stuff for art shows. They were related somehow—Wanda's dad was Mrs. Woolsey's cousin, or something like that.

And Ray liked Wanda too.

If it hadn't been for Wanda standing between Ray and me, I could have imagined Ray and his sky-blue eyes waiting on the other end of a kiss worth writing about.

Last year Ray and I had English together, without Wanda.

The first day, Ray walked right in and sat next to me on purpose, even though there were lots of empty seats. Every day, I looked forward to English because I knew I'd be sitting beside Ray. We had fun too, trying not to laugh at Mrs. Erickson's overly dramatic readings. We discovered we both loved O. Henry short stories and Ray Bradbury, especially *Fahrenheit 451*. I even helped Ray with some of the reports we had to write for class.

But whenever Wanda was in a class with us, she made sure Ray didn't pay attention to anybody but her. I might as well have been going to school in Russia or Red China.

I would have been relieved to have Wanda out of the way—but because she moved, not because she got shot.

I hadn't liked looking for clues at the Kinneys'—not with Chuck, anyway. And I sure didn't look forward to prying information out of my dad. Maybe, I thought just before I finally drifted off to sleep, maybe I should rethink my big investigation. It sure would be a lot safer writing about steam engines.

Monday it rained so hard, I figured the pool wouldn't open. I got up early anyway and sat in the big living room chair, where I could watch the rain through our picture window. Water flowed in crooked lines down the glass. Midge, huddled on the footstool, was snoring away. "You know you still have to go outside," I told Midge.

She groaned.

"Okay, I'll go too." I got the leash and grabbed my raincoat and umbrella before heading outside for a rain-walk.

The gray skies and dripping rain made me feel like earth

was having a bad day. But Midge wagged her tail and trotted full speed ahead, leading me up the muddy road like she was on a mission. She stopped in front of the Kinney place and started barking. I tugged on her leash, but she kept it up.

"Here now," came a scratchy voice that stopped Midge's barking and made me look up to the porch. Mrs. Kinney stood in the doorway.

I stared at her. She wore the same dingy apron as before. Her faded cotton dress wouldn't have looked out of place in the Old West or on *The Beverly Hillbillies.* Her dirt-brown hair was carelessly pinned up, gray streaks flanking both ears. In my mind, I'd been picturing her barefoot, her unpainted toenails yellow and long. But seeing her sensible shoes again made me realize I'd imagined the part about her bare feet.

"You're Tree, ain't ya?" she asked. "Doc's youngest?"

I nodded.

Midge moved in closer, pulling me with her.

"The one what wants to be a writer?"

I was shocked that she knew that much about me. "Yeah?"

"Your daddy said as much. Your sister, Eileen, wants to be a nurse, I take it. Why don't you?" She narrowed her eyes, sizing me up as I stood in the drizzling rain.

I wasn't sure how I'd ended up on the wrong end of this interview. But she was waiting for my answer. "All I've ever wanted to do was write, Mrs. Kinney," I told her honestly. "Well, I guess I did want to be a horse trainer once. And a dancer. But not anymore. I want to write and get to the truth of things. It's like writing is something I *need* to do, whether I want to or not."

I stopped talking because I realized she probably didn't care why I wanted to be a writer. She just wondered why I didn't want to be a nurse like Eileen and Mom.

"Best get out of the rain," she said.

I didn't know if she meant I should get out of the rain or she should. But she stepped back and closed the door, shutting herself out of the rain and leaving me in it.

I walked Midge home. My first interview with Mrs. Kinney, and I'd messed up so bad, it would probably be my last.

I should have stuck with steam engines.

Mom, also known as Nurse Helen, came home to fix lunch. Eileen and I ate bologna sandwiches while Mom stuck a plate of leftover lasagna into the oven for Dad. She said half the people in the waiting room were talking about the upcoming Steam and Gas Engine Show, and the other half were speculating on the fate of Mr. Kinney.

I tried getting back to my journal, but I couldn't seem to produce anything except a chewed pen. Then I heard Mom and Eileen laughing hard. Their voices floated in from the family room as if traveling from another planet far, far away from mine.

I sneaked through the kitchen to eavesdrop.

"Try it over here," Eileen said.

They grunted like they were trying to lift the house. Then I heard a chair or a couch scoot across the tiled floor. Staying out of sight, I peeked around the corner and watched as they finished shoving the recliner next to the biggest window.

I liked the recliner in its old spot.

"Perfect!" Mom exclaimed. "You've got a great eye for this."

"Maybe I should be an interior decorator instead of a nurse," Eileen said.

"You can be anything you want," Mom assured her. "And that includes nursing."

Mom got that right. Eileen was so smart, she really could become anything she wanted to. Unless Einstein moved to town, Eileen would be valedictorian next year.

But my sister had chosen nursing. When we were little, Eileen dressed up as a nurse every single Halloween. Before settling on what I wanted to be when I grew up, I'd changed my mind dozens of times. Not Eileen. Changing her mind would have been like giving up.

I probably shouldn't have spied on my mother and sister, but I couldn't help myself. Maybe I wanted to find out what they did that made them so close. You only had to see them for two seconds to know they loved spending time together. When they walked down the street, people stared, people smiled. In her own way, Eileen was as beautiful as our mother.

I stepped back so they wouldn't see me, but I could still hear them.

"You wouldn't believe what Elizabeth wore to Curt's Café yesterday," Eileen said, after more scooting and grunting.

"What?" Mom sounded truly interested.

"I liked her silky blouse. Pastel blue with a tie-neck. But her skirt? It had to be two, maybe three, inches above her knee."

There was a *thud,* like something heavy dropping. "You're kidding!" Mom exclaimed.

"I kid you not. It may not have been as short as that red suede skirt we saw, but—"

"The skirt in *Bazaar?* Now, that was short." Mom's voice changed. "This way a bit. Hmm . . . no, let's try the table on the other side."

"Good idea," Eileen agreed.

No surprise there. My mom and my sister agreed on everything.

"You know who would look great in a short skirt like that?" said Eileen.

"Nobody," Mom said.

"Tree. I wish I had her knees."

I couldn't believe she'd said that. I stared down at my legs, pushing up my cutoffs for a better view of my skinned-up knees.

"Both of my girls have great knees." Something slammed against the wall. "And neither of my girls will be displaying them under short skirts."

"I know. But Tree could carry it off," Eileen insisted. "You know what else Tree would look great in? A red sweater dress with a wide belt. And kitten heels."

"Tree wouldn't wear kitten heels if you got her a litter of them."

"I know. And the only thing she'll wear to school are shifts and sack dresses," Eileen said.

"Because they're comfortable," Mom explained.

"She'd wear jeans to high school if they'd let her," Eileen

complained. "You should get her an A-line skirt. Ooh—I know! Remember those kick-pleat skirts we saw at the Jones Store in Kansas City? They look like straight skirts, but the pleat in front and back makes them comfortable. Remember? The woman said you could do the twist in that skirt."

Mom laughed. "I remember! I thought about Tree when she said that. Do you think she'd wear one if we brought it home?"

I backed out of the kitchen. I wasn't sure how I felt about what I'd heard. It always made me feel kind of lonely inside when I listened to Mom and Eileen talk. Sometimes I heard them laughing while Mom curled Eileen's hair behind the closed bathroom door. I never asked what they were laughing about.

Normally, I hated it when my mother and big sister tried to make me dress like them or act "ladylike." I had put up a fit when they told me their plans to have Eileen and me wear prairie dresses for the steam engine show.

But my ears were still ringing with what Eileen said about me. My sister thought I'd look good in a sweater dress. I knew she didn't want one because she said they showed every extra pound and imperfection.

Plus, Eileen wished she had my knees?

Just when I thought I had my sister all figured out, she went and said a nice thing like that.

And just when I thought I had my dad figured out, he claimed he didn't want to talk about things.

Maybe the whole world had flipped upside down.

14
Going in Circles

Before I could get caught eavesdropping, I slipped outside. If it hadn't been raining so hard, I might have gone for a long walk to clear my head. Instead, I grabbed my Hula-Hoop and my transistor radio and headed for the carport. Rain was pounding the metal roof, and the whole outdoors smelled like evergreens.

I took my hula stance and started the hoop. Our California cousin, Barb, sent Eileen and me Hula-Hoops months before anybody in town had even heard of them. It took me forever to get the hang of keeping the yellow plastic hoop twirling around my middle. But now I could keep it spinning all day.

By the time Dad came home for lunch, it had stopped raining. Still twirling my Hula-Hoop, I moved out of the way so he could get his car in. We hadn't talked much since Saturday, when I'd tried to ask him about the Kinneys.

I turned up "Duke, Duke, Duke, Duke of Earl." Great hula music. Plus, Dad really liked it. Most of my friends' parents hated our music, but not Dad. He kept his radio tuned to WHB, same as me.

Hatless, Dad climbed out of the car. He left his suit jacket hanging on the hook over the backseat window and slammed the driver's door closed. Then he stretched like his back ached. His white shirt looked wrinkled. He hadn't turned around to see me, and for a second I didn't think he was going to.

"Hey, Dad!" I tried to sound normal, hoping he'd forgotten about my Kinney gossip.

He glanced over his shoulder. "Hey, Tree." Then he walked into the garage. He didn't even ask how I was doing.

But half a minute later, he strolled out with Eileen's pink Hula-Hoop. "This might be just what I need for my aching back. I'm always after my patients to exercise more." He dropped the hoop over his head and wiggled. The hoop landed with a smack on the cement drive.

"Step into it, Dad." I stopped my hoop so I could demonstrate. "Hold it with both hands like this, to one side. Then start it spinning, moving your hips back and forth. Let your hips flow in a circle until you catch the rhythm."

"Got it." He stepped into the hoop, grabbed it, wiggled. The hoop did half a spin on his waist, then dropped. "Good exercise bending down to get the thing, I suppose."

"Try starting it counterclockwise." I wanted Dad to be able to make it work. But more than that, I loved that he tried. Especially now, with me. "Put your feet farther apart."

The song ended, and the top-of-the-hour news blared. I didn't pay any attention to it, but I did hear the word "Vietnam."

Dad's hoop almost made it all the way around his waist. He shook his head, breaking the rhythm, and the hoop plunked to the ground.

"Don't give up, Dad. You'll get the hang of it."

"Maybe." He sounded so down.

"You really did almost get it to spin that time. Don't worry."

"Hmm? What?" He picked up the hoop and tried again. "No. It's not my lack of Hula-Hooping skills I'm worried about."

I waited. Something was bothering him. I just hoped it wasn't me.

The radio started playing music again. I kept my hoop spinning and held my peace until the Beach Boys got halfway through "Surfin' Safari."

Then Dad broke. "'Advisor,' my eye! Twelve hundred 'advisors' sent to Vietnam? How can they call those young boys advisors? They're soldiers. Sent with guns over to a country where nobody wants them. And to people who wouldn't take their *advice* if they offered it, which they won't because they're trained to shoot and kill. I tell you what, Tree. Sometimes I think the whole world's going crazy." He shoved Eileen's Hula-Hoop around his waist so hard that it spun three times before crashing at his feet. "Most of those poor boys don't even have a clue where Vietnam is before they get there."

Dad sounded so depressed that I didn't want to tell him that *I* had no idea where Vietnam was, either. Except that it had to be far away from America. "They'll be okay, though, won't they? America's never lost a war, right?"

He picked up the Hula-Hoop and tried again. "This isn't like the big war your mom and I fought in. Or World War One, the war your grandfather fought in. Vietnam is nothing but hills and jungles and rice paddies . . . and dead bodies. We rushed in, and we haven't the vaguest notion of what that culture is like, what those people are thinking."

"Dad! You're doing it!" The Hula-Hoop circled Dad's waist, clicking against his belt buckle and wobbling over his wide striped tie.

"I've got it! I can Hula-Hoop!" He suddenly sounded more thrilled than I had been the first time I caught on.

One more reason to love my dad—not that he could Hula-Hoop but that he was so excited about it.

As soon as Dad left to make a house call, the rain started up again. I'd just turned on the TV when the phone rang. Nobody answered it, so I shut off the television and answered it myself. "Hello?"

"Tree, is that you?"

I was pretty sure it was Wanda on the other end of the line. Only I couldn't remember a single time when she'd called me, except maybe to get the language arts assignment, which she hadn't heard because she was too busy flirting with Ray. "Yeah, this is Tree."

"Good. Because I need to talk to you."

"Wanda?" It was definitely her voice—nasal, like a permanent whine.

"Duh," she said, as if I was the stupid one for not recognizing the voice of the Great Wanda right off. "I want you to know that I saw you talking to people at the pool Saturday and asking dumb questions about the Kinneys."

"So?"

"So," she continued, "I know what you're trying to do. And you're only going to be disappointed . . . and embarrassed."

"I don't know what you're talking about, Wanda," I lied.

"Right. Like it's not obvious that you want *my* job on the *Blue and Gold* next year?" She laughed, the way a grown-up would laugh at a little kid. "Don't get me wrong. Aunt Edna—Mrs. Woolsey to you—didn't pick me because she's my aunt. I—"

"She's not your aunt," I said.

"Then why do I call her Aunt Edna?"

"I don't know. So you can get on the *Blue and Gold* staff maybe?"

"Very funny, Tree," Wanda said, not laughing.

"Thank you. And I really should be going, Wanda."

"Not until I tell you why I called. Look . . . Tree, you are not a reporter. Even if you did write something about the Kinneys, nobody would ever read it."

I tried not to take in the words coming through the phone line. "Are you done?"

"Don't be that way, Tree." Wanda pulled out her syrupy sweet voice. "I think it's cute that you were trying to conduct interviews. Ray thinks so too."

Ray? I couldn't help picturing them together at the pool, their towels overlapping.

Wanda was still talking. ". . . so we both think now is the

time to burst your bubble. This way, you won't get shot down during school, with everyone looking on. We don't want you to have to go through that. Tell me you understand?"

"I understand, Wanda. Goodbye."

I hung up, and for a second my head fogged. I was an inch away from crying.

But only for a second.

I understood Wanda, all right. She'd never call me for my own good. Everything she'd said had been calculated for *her* own good. She didn't want me to write a great article about the Kinneys. Because if I did, Mrs. Woolsey—aunt or fourth cousin twice removed—would have to choose me for the *Blue and Gold*. And not Wanda.

I would write that article. I'd show Wanda, Mrs. Woolsey, and everyone else that I could do it. Wanda may have thought she'd warned me away from writing, but, man, was she wrong. That phone call made me more determined than ever to get to the truth and write something that even Mrs. Woolsey couldn't ignore.

Thank you, Wanda!

With new resolve, I went back to writing. Eileen hadn't come out of her bedroom when the phone rang, so I figured she was holed up studying. That left the kitchen table free. I spread out my notes and got comfortable on the breakfast bench.

I wanted to capture the first moment I saw Mrs. Kinney with the rifle. That one thing—the fact that *she* was the one with the gun—had turned out to be *my* secret. In spite of all the gossip going around town, nobody except Dad and me had seen her holding the rifle. And Dad still thought he was the only one.

I decided to approach things from a different angle. In English, we had to pick out figures of speech in novels. But my favorite assignment was to make up my own similes and metaphors.

Mrs. Kinney was as stiff and sinewy as the cottonwood beside her house.
She clutched her baby, a rifle, hers alone for now.
She was a faded dishrag, wrung dry but left twisted.

"Tree, are you still here?" Eileen stopped in the kitchen doorway. She had a giant textbook pressed to her chest. She could have been headed for school, hair combed, wearing a polyester shirtwaist dress with her initials monogrammed on the front pocket.

I was wearing cutoffs and a plain white T-shirt. "Um . . . am I here?" I glanced down at me. "Guess so."

"Did Mom leave already?" Eileen whined. "I think I hate the human circulatory system."

Now that she'd earned an early acceptance to Mizzou's nursing program, Eileen was all about testing out of beginning courses. At the end of summer she'd go to Columbia and take a giant test designed to weed out the dummies from the brains. Nobody who knew Eileen doubted that she really would study all summer, ace the test, and earn advanced placement in every course.

But Jack and I still couldn't see Eileen as a nurse. She

couldn't stand the sight of blood. And seeing other people sick made her sick. Maybe she believed she had to carry on the family tradition.

"Mom went back to the office," I informed the frustrated Eileen. "It's Monday, remember?" Monday mornings were the worst. Mom said the townspeople did too much partying on the weekend, and farmers did too much work. "Nurse Helen is already taking blood pressures, stabbing people with needles, sewing up gashes, and mopping up blood—you know, nurse stuff."

Eileen groaned. "Drat! How am I supposed to keep veins and arteries straight all on my own?"

"Good posture," I replied, straight-faced.

She looked at me as if she'd never admired my knees. "Grow up, Tree."

"Dry up, Eileen. And blow away."

I slid out of the kitchen booth so I could lift the bench seat and look inside. I took out the last three *Kansas City Stars*. I would have loved to read what Randy Ridings was writing, but I'd have to wait until Friday for the *Hamiltonian* to come out.

I scanned the *Stars*, but I couldn't find anything about the Kinney shooting. Kansas City probably had enough of its own shootings to report.

An hour later, I'd outlined everything I knew about the Kinneys. But I had too many holes in my story. And writing about the shooting seemed hopeless until I could say for certain what had happened before the gun went off.

"Something wrong, Tree?" Eileen had come back into the kitchen. She ran herself a glass of water, then leaned her back against the sink to drink—exactly like Mom.

"I'm trying to write an article about the Kinney shooting," I answered.

"Yuck."

I should have known she wouldn't understand.

She took a sip of her water. "Go on."

"That's just it. I can't go on until I know exactly what happened."

"Doofus, why don't you just ask Dad?"

"I tried. Dad said he didn't want to talk about it. He didn't want 'gossip' in his house."

"So go talk to him at the office."

"Funny, Eileen."

"I'm serious. . . . Okay. When did you try talking to him?"

"Saturday after I got home from work."

"Well, there you go."

I wasn't getting this.

She continued. "Lesson one: Never ask Dad for anything after dinner. (a) He'll be too tired to talk about it. And (b) that's when he reads the newspaper and gets upset over the news."

I'd never thought about it, but Dad did get upset reading the paper, especially about Vietnam. And he did read it after dinner. "So you think he might have a different reaction if I asked him in the daytime?"

"And at the office, since he doesn't want gossip at home. There are all kinds of gossip at the office, Tree."

Eileen had a point—two points. Dad loved it when we visited him at the office. Since he and I had always been able to talk, night or day, I never even thought about the best time to ask him about the Kinneys. "You, Eileen Taylor, are a genius." I walked over to my sister and hugged her. Her water spilled.

"Tree!" She brushed at her dress as if it were on fire.

"Sorry." I slid my shoes back on.

"Where are you rushing off to?" Eileen demanded.

"Where do you think, ding-dong? I'm going to see Dad."

15
Nuclear

The clouds parted and the sun broke through as I pedaled across the railroad tracks.

"Hey, Tree!"

I turned so fast, I nearly went down.

Randy Ridings hurried over to see if I was okay. "Sorry. Didn't mean to cause a wreck."

"Might have made a good story for the paper, though," I said.

"Not if my dad had anything to say about it," he muttered. "Can't report anything negative. We might hurt somebody's feelings."

I was pretty sure he was talking to himself. "I thought your dad retired."

"So did I. Here." He helped me straighten my crooked bike basket. "Hey, stop by the office later. I've got a couple of new writing quotations for you. They were in the *Caldwell County Advertiser.* I saved them. You be careful now, Tree."

I thanked him. And as I pedaled to Dad's office, I thought about Randy and his dad. I wondered if the *Hamiltonian* really would change, if Randy would write what he felt he had to. And if his dad would understand. I hoped so.

I was leaning my bike against the big maple out back of the doctor's office when I heard a familiar holler.

"Hey, cowgirl!" Tommy Lebo and his mom were walking toward their car. They must have come from Dad's.

"Hi, Tommy!" We exchanged waves.

Nobody except Tommy called me cowgirl. All because of something Sarah and I did a lifetime ago. Tommy's dad owned the farm next to Sarah's, which was how he came to witness my most embarrassing moment.

One Saturday, Sarah and I roamed her farm until we got bored. We stood on the fence, watching cows in the near pasture. My favorite, Blondie, lay in the grass, while grasshoppers jumped knee-high.

"Want to ride Blondie?" Sarah asked.

"Sure!" I wondered why we hadn't thought of it before.

"You can go first," Sarah offered.

Blondie didn't budge, even when I had to take a run at her to get up on her bare back. I could barely get my leg over her bony spine. My legs stretched so wide that I understood how cowboys got bowlegged.

Then it happened. Blondie's back legs straightened first, nearly pitching me over her head. Then the front legs wobbled, bringing her to a stand. And off she ran.

"Hold on!" Sarah cried, racing behind us.

I grabbed what little mane I could and closed my eyes as

that cow tore around the pasture. Finally, Blondie tired herself out and plopped back down.

Tommy and Sarah caught up with me. I slid off, my knees buckling as I landed.

"You should be in the rodeo!" Tommy exclaimed.

I tried not to show how scared I was. "Does Blondie always run off like that when you ride her?"

Sarah shrugged. "I don't know. I've never ridden a cow."

"Me neither, cowgirl," Tommy said. He never let me forget it.

I waited until Tommy and his mom drove away, then circled behind the white-board building that had been my granddad's home before he died. I was only three, but I think I remember his big hands, his wire-rimmed glasses, and the way he said my name, like it made his day to see me. Maybe my memories came from pictures and stories about Granddad Pete, but I always thought he liked me best.

Dad's office still looked like a home. Patients rang the bell before entering through the front door. They found their own way to the waiting room and waited, sometimes for hours, before filing into Dad's office, first-come, first-served.

Nobody except Eileen and me used the back door. I'd always known that even when the gravel lot overflowed with cars and the old waiting room magazines were being fought over, I could see my dad whenever I needed him.

I buzzed—two long, one short. From inside the exam room, I heard Dad's Doc Taylor voice telling someone to go to the nurse's office.

A minute later, Dad waved me in. "Everything okay, Tree?"

I nodded, and he shut the door.

"Too wet to mow. Did you come to get weighed?" He moved over to the scales.

Eileen dropped in once a week to weigh herself, but she instructed Dad not to tell her how much she weighed, only if she'd gone up or down. If the answer was "up," we all kept our distance for a day or so.

"Sure." I stepped on the scale.

Dad lowered the measuring stick to touch my head. "Five-five. And still a hundred and ten. Sounds about right for you, Tree."

He was in such a good mood. Eileen was right about daytime and the office visit.

"Dad?"

"Mmm?" He scribbled my stats on a wall chart next to Eileen's secret chart, which was covered with a blank sheet of paper.

"I wanted to talk to you about Mr. and Mrs. Kinney."

He stopped writing and hung his head.

I forged ahead. "Is Mr. Kinney still in the hospital?"

Dad turned to face me, but he didn't answer.

"And Mrs. Kinney? She doing okay?" I asked.

"Why do you care so much all of a sudden, Tree? This couldn't have anything to do with the little interviews you've conducted at the pool, could it?"

That was the problem with doing anything in a small town. Sooner or later, everybody knew about it. Usually, sooner.

"Or," Dad continued, "the article you're writing?"

I should have figured that if Wanda knew about it, Dad would too. "That's what I wanted to talk to you about on

Saturday," I said. "See, I'm pretty sure that if I can write a great article about the Kinneys, I can win a spot on the *Blue and Gold* staff."

"You know, if you have to write about people's misery, Tree, why don't you tackle Gary Lynch?" His voice was even but tight. "I just got back from seeing him. That boy never leaves his room, his bed, his dragons. Dozens of dragons—dragon bedspread, stuffed dragons, dragon knickknacks. That's his entire world. Lots of misery there, Tree. Or you could write about the soldiers dying every day in Vietnam." His eyes narrowed, like he was trying to see through me. "Did you ever say two words to Mrs. Kinney before this happened?"

Guilt shot through me like a fiery arrow. "I know. I'm sorry. I should have."

"Is there anything else, Tree? Because if not, I have patients waiting."

I turned to go. Only I couldn't. I just couldn't go back home like this, with my secret dragging behind me, sprawled between my dad and me. "Dad?" He was writing on the growth chart. "I saw her holding that rifle."

His head snapped around so fast that I took a step back. "What did you say?"

I swallowed. "I saw Mrs. Kinney . . . holding the gun." There was no backing down now. "That morning. Before you took the gun away from her, I—"

"What?"

My heart was pounding so hard, my ears hurt. "I stayed back, like you told me to. Only then I saw her carrying that gun, and I got so scared—scared for *you*—I didn't know what

I was doing. Honest, Dad. It was like my bare feet ran on gravel without me."

His face turned the color of red licorice. I saw veins throbbing in his neck. "And where did your bare feet run?"

"To the cottonwood beside the Kinney house."

"You were spying on me?"

"I was scared for you! She had that rifle, Dad. I was afraid she'd shoot you."

He took three deep breaths and turned his back on me.

I braced myself for a nuclear explosion. I waited. "Dad?"

Nothing.

I couldn't stand it. Anything was better than this silence. "Dad, I didn't mean—"

"Go home, Tree." His back was still to me.

I started to say something. "I—" Then I gave up.

I had to wipe away tears with the back of my hand to see my way out. Shutting that office door felt like closing something huge. Something life-changing. Something I could never get back.

I climbed on my bike and rode fast, but not home.

What had just happened? And how could my dad be so mad about it? So what if I'd followed him when he told me not to? Big deal! Was it my fault I saw a crazy old woman holding a rifle? And yeah—reporters do write about misery, when it's news.

Dad wasn't being fair. I wasn't his little obedient kid.

Not anymore.

I was going to write my article with or without him.

16

Progress

I rode back the same way I'd come. As I coasted past the *Hamiltonian* office, I heard loud voices. Randy and his dad were shouting at each other. I dragged one foot and came to a stop just outside. I wasn't sure why I'd stopped—not for any quotes Randy had saved for me. Maybe I wanted to hear someone else's dad yell for a change.

Just stepping inside the newspaper office did me good. No place on earth smelled like the *Hamiltonian* office, with its mix of fresh ink and sweat and old newspaper. Every time a teacher assigned a career report, I interviewed Randy or his father or Carol, who'd worked there almost as long as Mr. Ridings. I'd even tried to get on as paperboy, although the once-a-week job didn't pay much. But the job went to Randy's nephew Larry, even though Larry had rotten aim. Our paper always ended up in the bushes.

Nobody was manning the front desk. And the shouting continued. "Dad, you shouldn't even be here." Randy's voice sounded like too tight fence wire.

"I've been coming here since before you were on the earth, Randy. And I'm not stopping until I know *my* paper won't be run into the ground by slander and unsavory—"

"Slander? I quoted the man word for word! He shouldn't make speeches if he doesn't want people to read what he says."

"And I've been on the phone half the morning with him, smoothing his ruffled feathers so he won't pull his advertising."

"That can't be our problem. I'm going to print the truth, Dad. People deserve to know what—"

"Balderdash! People don't want to read about ugly things."

I agreed with Randy. I thought I'd always want the truth, no matter what.

"Everybody take a deep breath." The woman's voice had to be Carol's.

Carol must have succeeded in calming the men because their voices got too low for me to hear.

That gave me time to think. Dad didn't understand why I wanted to write about the Kinneys any more than Randy's dad understood why he had to write the truth. Suddenly, I wanted to talk to Randy. He'd understand. He wouldn't think I was stupid for wanting to know what had really happened at the Kinneys'.

I checked the bulletin board, which was filled with little notes. Paper littered the office—folders piled on every surface, newspapers stacked in all corners. The whole town would go up in smoke if old Mr. Ridings's cigar ever dropped an ash in there.

Finally, Randy stormed out of the back office and walked

straight to his desk. He flung his suit jacket over the back of his chair, and I saw that his white shirt had sweat marks under the arms. Randy was only a few years older than Jack, but already he had to smooth his straight black hair over a growing bald spot. He picked up a stack of reports and sprawled into his desk chair. "Tree? Didn't see you there. Can you come back later? I don't know where I put those quotes." He looked down at the papers in his hands, shuffled them.

"Actually, I wanted to talk to you about something else."

"Pretty busy right now." He didn't look up. "Steam engines are cutting-edge news around here. Never mind that the mayor wants to move the voting age to fifty. Never mind we've had a shooting in town."

"Mr. Kinney's?" Like there was any other shooting in Hamilton.

Randy looked up then. "Sorry, Tree. And I'm sorry for any ranting and raving you overheard. Nothing but war between the generations."

"There's a lot of that going around."

He raised his eyebrows but didn't ask. After a moment he sighed and said, "So, what's on your mind? And don't tell me it's steam engines or I'll toss you out on your ear."

"Nope. It's about Mr. and Mrs. Kinney."

"I'm listening." It was hard to believe he was listening because he kept flipping through pages that looked like write-ups on tractors.

"Well, I thought I'd write about it—the shooting—for the *Blue and Gold*."

"Didn't know you'd made staff. Congratulations, Tree."

"I haven't. Not yet, anyway. I thought if I wrote something good . . ."

Randy finished for me. "You'd earn your spot."

"Yeah. Something like that."

"Not a bad plan." He scribbled on what looked like a picture of an old car.

"My dad doesn't agree."

"Ah. Dads again." Randy leaned back in his chair. It squeaked. "And your dad's the one with all the answers about the Kinneys, right?"

I shrugged.

"I haven't been able to get a word out of your dad, either," Randy admitted. "Not that *my* dad would want me to print anything about the shooting. After all, what kind of a person wants to read about blood and guns? They'd much rather read about tractors and steam engines." He stopped talking, then looked me square in the eye. "Tree, go for it. You want to be in the newspaper business? You go for the news."

"I want to, but—"

"You're too young for *buts*. Get that story. Get it any way you can."

Carol stuck her head out of the back office. "Randy, we need you on this. I've got three steam engine owners, and they all want front row at the fairgrounds."

Randy got to his feet. "I've got to go. I can't think past the steam engine show. We do extra inserts and two papers that week." He let out a one-note laugh that had zero funny in it.

"My dad's right about one thing. Around here, there is no bigger story than the steam engine show."

"Thanks for listening, Randy."

He lowered his voice. "I wasn't kidding about going for the news, Tree. Something about the Kinneys doesn't smell right. Never has. The sheriff stonewalled me when I tried to talk to him. And your dad won't even talk to me." He looked back to where Carol had disappeared and where his dad must have been waiting. "Tell you what. You get that story, and you write it up for me."

"For *you*?" I couldn't believe it. Was Randy giving me an assignment?

"No promises. You get what you can, and we'll see." Randy Ridings was giving me a chance to write something for the *Hamiltonian*. "Let me get this blasted steam engine show behind me. Then bring me what you've got . . . preferably when my father isn't around." He paused, like he was thinking of something. "Dad's leaving town right after the steam engine show. He won't be back for three months. Perfect timing for your deadline, Tree."

"I'll do it. You'll see."

He grabbed his stack of papers off the desk. "Good. Things are going to change around here. Might as well start now."

"You'll have it on July Fourth!" I called after him. That was the day of the steam engine show.

Randy turned back and grinned. "That just may be the only thing I'll be looking forward to that day."

"Randy!" Carol shouted.

"Coming."

I didn't say a word to Eileen when I got home. I was on a mission. I was going to give Randy Ridings the best feature he'd ever seen: "The Truth about the Kinney Shooting." Hamilton deserved to know the truth, even if a generation of fathers disagreed.

17

Tree, Girl Reporter

I changed into clean jeans and a button-down blouse. I wasn't going to wait another minute to research my article for Randy.

Next to my dad—and Mrs. Kinney—Sheriff Robinson had more firsthand information than anybody. Randy hadn't been able to get anything out of him, but I thought I might have better luck. I'd seen things even the sheriff hadn't seen. I looked up the number and dialed.

Someone picked up on the first ring. "Hello. This is Bev."

"Is this the sheriff's office?" I asked.

"Yessiree. Can I help you?"

"This is Tree Taylor, and—"

Bev didn't let me finish. "Tree? This is Mrs. Berger, honey. How the heck are ya?"

"Fine, Mrs. Berger. How are you?"

Mrs. Berger had been my dad's teacher when he was in grade school.

"Truth be told, my arthritis is acting up. I'll have to get in to see your daddy one of these days. Whaddya need, sugar?"

"I was hoping I could talk to Sheriff Robinson."

"Didn't you hear? Leo's quit policing. For good this time, or so he says."

"But I just saw him the other day."

"Well, he's not going anywheres, sweet thing. And he didn't quit exactly. He retired."

A million questions popped into my head. Had he planned to retire? Or was he retiring because of the Kinney shooting? "Could I at least talk to him, Mrs. Berger?"

"Sorry, honey. He's home packing his rod and reel. Going up north on some fishing trip. No phone."

"So we're not going to have a sheriff in Hamilton?" First the shoe factory. Then the picture show. And now the sheriff? There wouldn't be anybody left in town by the time I graduated.

"Now, I didn't say that," Mrs. Berger said. "We're getting us a new sheriff. Comes in tomorrow. A young feller. Officer Duper."

"*Officer* Duper? Not *Sheriff* Duper?"

"That's exactly what I asked. Told him we'd always had us a sheriff. But he said he preferred to be called Officer Duper of the Hamilton Police Department."

The police department of one.

She lowered her voice. "I'm supposed to answer the phone that way. 'Officer Duper's office, Hamilton Police Department.' Time I get all that out, the poor soul on the other end of the line's bound to hang up."

I couldn't think of anything else to ask her. "Well, thanks for the information. Could I call back tomorrow? Maybe Sheriff—I mean, Officer—Duper will talk to me."

"Sure thing. I hope nothing's wrong at your place." She waited to see if I'd fill her in.

"No. We're fine. I'm writing an article and wanted to ask some questions."

"You call back anytime, Tree. Nice talking to you, honey. Tell your mama and Doc hey for me."

I hung up, feeling like I'd struck out. But it wasn't going to stop me. I was just getting started.

I dialed Sarah's number, and she answered the phone. "Tree? Is the pool open again?"

"No—at least, not that I know of. Any chance you could hitch a ride to town and go with me to talk to Mrs. Kinney?"

"About time you went. And no. Mom is nuts. All of a sudden, she's having a giant yard sale this weekend. She's got me making signs and clearing out the basement and the attic." I heard her mom shouting in the background. "Sorry. Gotta run. Call me if the pool reopens."

No problem. Walter Cronkite never had a sidekick when he was interviewing someone.

I checked myself in the mirror and forced my thick, wild waves into a ponytail. Immediately, strands of hair tugged at my forehead. Eileen warned me that wearing my hair up would make me go bald. Tough. I wouldn't have minded losing some of my too thick hair. Dad's hair.

The air smelled like clean earth, and the temperature must have dropped twenty degrees. A bobwhite called from the thicket across the street: *bob-bob-white.* One lone bird. The others stayed in hiding, which meant it would likely rain again.

As I got closer to the Kinney house, my feet slowed. I should have written up questions for Mrs. Kinney in advance. Or asked Randy how to do interviews.

I glanced across the street and spotted the DeShon boys digging in the mud with their bare hands. I stopped a safe distance from them and watched as they piled mud into a sloppy mound. They had identical eyes, hollow, small, set too deep into their heads, like somebody had shot BBs into their bony faces and called them eyeballs.

The boys would be heading to kindergarten and first grade in the fall. I pitied their teachers.

Eileen used to babysit the DeShon boys. Once, she asked me to stand in for her because she had a date with Butch. I got Sarah to help. Eileen promised us the boys would go to bed early, and we'd get paid for watching TV. Ha! Those boys never went to bed, and I doubted they slept—ever. One of them—I thought it was Larry, but I couldn't tell them apart—slugged me with a baseball bat when I tried to make his brother stop coloring the kitchen cabinets purple.

"Whatcha making?" I asked.

The one I thought was Larry answered, "Mud pies." He glared up at me like I'd threatened to steal his baked goods.

Their mother hollered out, "Tree? Come in a minute."

I wanted to tell her I didn't have time, that I had an assignment. I glanced at the Kinney house, then had a thought. Maybe I could get more background information before talking to Mrs. Kinney.

A crooked screen hung on the house's peeling doorframe. The screen was too big, and somebody had tried to staple it to the frame, creating a big screen bubble.

Peering through the tiny wire squares of the screen, I got familiar glimpses of the DeShon home—an overflowing laundry basket, an overturned tricycle, a pile of diapers, toys scattered as if rained there, and a tiny, loud television. Canned laughter filled the house. I felt like I should knock, even though Mrs. DeShon was the one asking me in. I knocked.

Footsteps, bare feet, squeaked on the wood floor. A baby cried. Somebody swore—the "d" word for the structure that keeps water back. I'd forgotten they had a new baby. Dad had gotten the call in the middle of the night. I asked Mom once why babies were always born at night. She said they weren't, although she agreed it did seem like it. Then she added, "Besides, that way your dad can deliver the baby at home. People around here don't like hospitals, and they hate hospital bills."

If somebody couldn't pay Dad, he didn't make them. Instead, patients kept us supplied with jams, jellies, fruits, veggies, and whatever else they had. We didn't have the money for a new roof, but we always had plenty of pies, deer meat, and pickles. And we didn't have to worry about Midge getting sick because the vet would take care of her for free. Dad had delivered both of Doc Snyder's kids.

Finally, Mrs. DeShon stumbled to the door, her baby hoisted on her hip. Glancing past my shoulder, she must have caught sight of her boys. "You stay out of that mud, hear? Don't you go getting dirty! We got to go to town."

The boys didn't make a move to stop baking.

Their mother looked back to me with the same deep-set

eyes as her boys'. Strands of two-color hair, brown roots, blond otherwise, stuck to her head. "Is your dad home?"

So that was why she wanted me? "He's at the office."

"Dang." She started to walk away.

"Wait! Mrs. DeShon? Could I talk to you for a minute? I'm . . . I'm writing an article about what happened at the Kinney house." I waited for her to ask who'd want *me* to write an article.

But she didn't. She cracked open the screen door and signaled for me to follow her inside. "That was a bad business. We heard the shot, of course. Woke the baby. Scared the boys." She shoved clothes and toys off the couch and sat down. "We was the ones—Robby was—to call the sheriff."

"That must have been pretty scary."

She shook her head. "Nah. We're used to it." She might have read confusion on my face because she nodded, like she was agreeing with herself. "Them two wake us up all the time. We can hear them fighting over the TV."

Now we were getting somewhere. "They fight over TV?"

Mrs. DeShon looked at me like I had cooties. "No. They're so loud, we can't hear *our* TV."

"I get it. Do you know what they fight about?"

"Everything. Him, mostly." She felt her baby's diaper and made a face. "Come to think of it, she never does her share of shouting. Nope. It's him. Yelling at her for wasting money planting flowers. Then screaming at her for not watering them. He threw a hissy fit once and ripped out all her roses." She grabbed a diaper from the laundry basket, plopped her baby onto the floor, and knelt beside it . . . him, or her.

"I feel for that woman. I really do," Mrs. DeShon continued. "No kids of her own. Just that nasty man for a husband. I made Robby go over to their house once, it got so bad."

"What happened?"

I watched as she unpinned the diaper and held the pins in her mouth. Even I knew you were supposed to clean up the baby when you took off the old diaper, but she didn't bother. She just scooped off what she could with the old diaper. Then off with the old and on with the new.

I decided right then that I would never have kids. Especially not babies. And absolutely not boy babies. Gross.

She waited until the pins were out of her mouth. "Robby knocked on their door. Mrs. Kinney peeked out, and my Robby said she didn't look so good. He asked her if she was all right. She said she was fine. But he called your daddy anyways, and Doc come down to check on her. I don't know what happened after that."

Mrs. DeShon picked up her baby and held him close. "If you ask me, Old Man Kinney shooting himself was about the nicest thing he ever done. I hope they keep him in the hospital a long, long time."

I thanked Mrs. DeShon for talking to me and told the boys bye as I left. The interview, or whatever it was, had taken a lot out of me. But I'd learned four things, and the minute I was out of the house, I pulled out my little notebook and wrote:

The Kinneys argue and fight a lot, and Mr. K does all
    the shouting.

Robby DeShon was the one who called the sheriff. Ask
   Sheriff what R said.
Mr. Kinney ripped out Mrs. K's rosebushes.
Dad got called in to look at Mrs. Kinney.

I felt pretty good about my background interview. Now I
was ready to talk to Mrs. Kinney herself.

18

Straight from the Horse's (Mrs. Kinney's) Mouth

I needed a strategy. I couldn't just show up on Mrs. Kinney's doorstep and ask her if her husband had shot himself or if she had shot him. I could ask, but I'd probably get the door slammed in my face.

I raced home and found Eileen at the kitchen table, catching air-conditioning while she studied. "Eileen, do we have any cookies?"

"Mom made macaroons yesterday." She pointed to the top of the fridge.

I loaded a paper plate with cookies and marched straight to the Kinneys' front door and knocked three times. While I waited, I glanced back at the step where Mrs. Kinney and my dad had sat, the rifle between them.

The door creaked, and I jumped like a rabbit.

Mrs. Kinney peered out, looking ten years younger than when she'd stumbled out carrying that rifle. She'd trimmed her hair, and it looked less gray. *She* looked less gray. "May I help you?"

"Cookies?" I said, like an idiot.

"Excuse me?"

I held out the macaroons. "Mom wasn't sure if you liked coconut." I didn't know why I said that. It would have been true if Mom had been thinking about Mrs. Kinney when she made the coconut cookies. "We love macaroons at our house. Even Midge, our dog, can't get enough. I thought you might like them, with Mr. Kinney in the hospital and all. Well, some of them. Eileen may have eaten some already. Maybe not, though. She's always on a diet." I shut up and wondered if Randy had ever started an interview with macaroons.

"That's mighty kindly of your mother. You be sure to thank her for me." She started to shut the door.

"Mrs. Kinney, wait!"

The door stopped just shy of shutting. Bony, crooked fingers snaked around the doorframe like the door was a bass fiddle and Mrs. Kinney was about to play it.

"Do you think I could talk to you for a minute?" My voice eked out so thin, you could have used it for varnish.

"Well . . ." She seemed to be considering the question. "Why don't you come in for a spell, Tree?" She held the door open until I moved inside. "Let's have us one of your ma's cookies. Won't spoil your dinner none, will it?"

"Nah. I mean, thanks. I'd love a macaroon."

Mrs. Kinney disappeared into the kitchen—I could see the sink from where I stood, barely inside the door. I looked around her front room and tried to take it all in. I was prepared to use Dad's memory hooks so that later I could write about what was in the room. Dad was always teaching himself new things—how to speak French or Swahili, how to find constellations. And new memory systems. You could give my dad a list of fifty items, and he could repeat every item back to you, in the same order. Even a year later, he could list all fifty. The system had something to do with mental hooks.

But as I scoped out the Kinneys' front room, what struck me were the things that *weren't* there. There were no pictures. No photos. Nothing at all on the walls. No television and no radio. No magazines or books that I could see.

What did they do all day and night? Sit and stare at each other?

I still hadn't taken a seat. I eyed an old couch shoved against the wall, behind a coatrack. Sarah's family used to have a couch like that—gray and made out of rough material that scratched when you sat on it and left funny patterns on your legs if you wore shorts. The arms of Mrs. Kinney's couch looked frayed. Sarah's mother covered the arms of their couch with little towels.

None of the furniture in the room matched. One coffee table leg had been glued together. There were no overhead lights, just short lamps on tables and a three-way pole lamp by the big chair.

The last place I looked was down. Because the last thing I wanted to see was Mr. Kinney's blood. But there was no blood, just narrow wood slats where there might have been a rug before.

"Here you go." Mrs. Kinney came back with two macaroons on two napkins. "Sit yourself anywheres you like." She handed me a cookie, then took the worn wooden rocker.

I chose the straight-backed chair next to hers. Mine didn't rock, and it sure could have used a pillow. I couldn't help wondering if this was Mr. Kinney's chair. Might have explained some of that grouchiness. "How's Mr. Kinney doing?"

"Now, that there is a good question." She bit into her coconut macaroon.

I followed her lead and bit into mine. "Will he be coming home soon?"

"I reckon not."

We listened to each other chew for a while.

"Coconut." Mrs. Kinney smiled at her last bite before popping it into her mouth. "Some folks call coconut trees the tree of life."

"Really?" That wasn't the way I heard it.

"You can cook with it, use it on your skin or hair. Some around here puts it into livestock feed. Them Vietnamese make ropes out of coconut fiber. Reckon that's where they get that tree-of-life name—using coconut for so many things."

I nodded. I'd have to remember to tell Dad about coconut ropes in Vietnam . . . if he ever spoke to me again.

Mrs. Kinney nodded toward the other side of her chair, at a half-made basket, round on the bottom and unfinished on top. "That there basket's got coconut for a base."

"Cool. Are you making that for the steam engine show? The ladies at church are making all kinds of things to sell for the missionaries overseas. Eileen and I are dressing up as prairie girls. My friend Jack says he'll go as Jesse James, but he might be kidding. Will you be going?"

"Well, I don't rightly know. Haven't given it much thought. Alfred doesn't hold with community shindigs." A faint smile crept across her lips. "Reckon now I just might give it some thought."

Neither of us said anything for way too long. "How do you know so much about coconuts, Mrs. Kinney?"

"I read. When I was your age, I wanted to be a librarian."

I glanced around but didn't see a bookcase. A knickknack rack tucked into the far corner had shelves, but no books— just three glass figurines huddled like the Cozad kids on a cold night.

Suddenly, I wondered if that rifle was still in the house.

"I know what you're thinking, Tree." Before I got a chance to pray that she didn't really know what I was thinking, she went on. "Nary a book in sight, eh? Alfred's never cottoned to books. I check out everything from encyclopedias to mysteries from the library and hide every single one of them under my bed. Might ought to rethink that too, I reckon. Your daddy passes me them old copies of *National Geographic* time to time."

Another long silence passed. Mrs. Kinney may have felt it too because she returned to coconuts. "Did you know that a body's got a ten times better chance of dying from a coconut falling on his head than from getting killed by a shark?"

I took that as my cue to exit.

19
Ain't Got Jack

The second I stepped outside, the skies opened. Rain slapped the ground in slanted sheets. Across the road, the DeShon boys were throwing mud pies at each other.

Before I reached the sidewalk, I was soaked to the bone. I ran home in the pounding rain, dashed to the bathroom, tore off my wet clothes, and wrapped myself in a towel. Then I headed for my bedroom to change.

Mom stopped me in the hallway. She was still wearing her nurse's uniform: white stockings, white shoes, white dress, and a white nurse's cap. "Looks like you got caught in the rain."

"Yep."

"I have to start dinner. But I'm glad I ran into you. You need to try on the outfit Eileen and I got you in Chillicothe last week. It's on your bed."

"Okay. Thanks, Mom." She acted so normal. No way Dad told her about our fight.

On my bed I found a hideous pink-and-white-striped shorts-and-top outfit that I'd never wear in public. I put it on but didn't bother glancing in the mirror. I didn't need to. Jack would have cracked up if he'd seen me in pink.

Mom called to me and demanded I show her the outfit, so I trudged to the kitchen.

"Tree! You look darling!" She turned to Eileen, who was poring over a medical book. "Eileen, don't you think Tree looks cute in that outfit?"

Eileen glanced at me. "Nice." Then she went back to her studies.

I retreated to my room. But even in my own bedroom, I felt self-conscious about the Eileenesque cutsie-shorts outfit. I probably looked eight years old in the thing. I plopped on my bed and tried to brush the tangles out of my wet hair. I wanted to take some notes on my first, brief interview with Mrs. Kinney. I wasn't sure what to think of her. Next time, I told myself, I'd have questions prepared.

Without warning, my bedroom door burst open. The sound sent chills through my heart. My mind flashed back to Saturday. The gunshot. The door slamming. Dad flying out.

Mom stood in the doorway. "Tree?"

I dropped the brush. It bounced off my bed and clunked to the floor. "What? What is it?"

I had no idea what was wrong. But I knew something bad had happened. Something very bad. In the span of two seconds, dozens of terrifying possibilities flashed through my head, a slideshow of horror. "Is it Dad?"

I knew that Eileen was studying in the kitchen, and Mom was standing in front of me. So something must have happened to Dad—Dad, who was angrier at me than he'd ever been.

"No, it's Jack," Mom said.

My head buzzed. Mom went blurry. Images flashed through my mind at the speed of light. Jack . . . shot. Jack . . . in an ambulance. Jack . . . hunched over the wheel of his car. Bloody. Jack . . . in a hospital, hooked up to tubes, the way Grandmother Taylor had been her last trip to the hospital.

"Tree, he's okay. Did you hear me?" Mom had me by the shoulders.

"Wh-wh-what?" Did I? Did I hear her?

"Jack's all right, honey."

"He is? Honest?"

"Yes. I'm sorry I scared you. I should have told you that first."

She should have. But Jack was okay. That's what mattered. That was all that mattered.

"I knew you'd want to know." She let go of my shoulders. "Donna just called. There's been a robbery."

"A robbery?" I'd never heard of a robbery in Hamilton. Kids took cars at night sometimes and went joyriding. But they always returned the cars, and the owners rarely knew anything was wrong. "Where? What's it got to do with Jack?"

"It was at the IGA, in the meat department. I guess an armed robber—"

"The robber had a *gun*?"

"Tree, listen for a minute. I'll tell you everything I know—everything Donna knew, anyway."

I nodded and bit my tongue, praying she'd get on with it.

"Okay. A man with a gun—I think Donna said he wore a mask—stormed into the IGA and demanded money from the cash register. But there wasn't much there. So he said he wanted everybody's watch and wallet. But there weren't many customers in the store, thank goodness." She stopped and sighed, like she didn't want to tell me the rest.

"Mom, please!"

"He went back to the meat department and told them he wanted all of *their* money from *their* cash register."

"There's no cash register in the meat department," I protested, picturing the whole thing, with Jack in the middle. Jack, with his long apron and the silly white hat they made him wear.

"The robber didn't know that, honey. And when they told him they didn't have a register in the meat department, I guess the robber didn't believe them."

"What do you mean?" I could tell we were getting to the bad part. I wanted her to spit it out, not piece it out the way Donna passed along gossip.

"He went behind the counter—the robber, that is. Shirley was there. He grabbed her in one arm and waved the gun around in his other hand, threatening to shoot her."

Shirley had worked at the IGA forever. She had to be a hundred years old. I waited, my heart not beating, the blood stuck in my veins.

"I can't imagine what Jack was thinking," Mom said. "He came up behind them—behind the robber—and he . . . he stabbed him with the butcher's knife he had in his hand."

I gasped.

"Shirley got free. The robber reached for her again. And Jack tried to stop him. They struggled, and—"

"Mom, is he okay? Is Jack okay?" I was shouting. I caught a glimpse of Eileen standing behind Mom. I hadn't seen her come up. I could barely see Mom anymore because of the tears that wouldn't stop.

"I told you, Jack is all right," Mom insisted. "He got cut, but Donna said he refused to go to the hospital. Maybe I should call your dad." She said this last part like she'd just thought of it.

"Did the robber get away?" I hoped he wouldn't come back and try to get even with Jack. What if he wanted revenge?

Mom looked at Eileen. Then she faced me and whispered, "No, Tree. The robber didn't get away. He . . . he died."

"What?" I didn't think I'd heard her right.

"He's dead. Jack killed him."

Before I even knew what I was doing, I was on my bike. Pedaling faster and faster. I needed to get to Jack. He was injured.

And he'd killed somebody. How was he going to live with that? I knew him. He would never get over taking someone's life.

Halfway up Main Street, the rain picked up. Giant raindrops slammed my face, stinging my eyes. I had to keep blinking to see across the railroad tracks.

Pulling into the loading dock behind the IGA, I spotted the sheriff's car next to Jack's. Out front, maybe a dozen people huddled under the awning.

I dropped my bike and dashed for the back door. It opened into the meat department. Right away I saw Jack talking to Sheriff Robinson.

"Jack!" I broke into a run and didn't stop until my arms were around him. I couldn't stop crying.

"Ah, Tree," Jack said. "Not you too?"

I let him go and stood back to see for myself that he was okay. I looked for a stab wound. His apron was smudged, but no bloodier than usual.

"I'm fine, Tree. Settle down, okay?"

"Looks like Donna is faster on the draw than we are." Sheriff Robinson was holding his cowboy hat in both hands and turning it.

I stared up at Jack. "What does he mean?" I glanced around, studying the meat room floor for signs of struggle. There was blood on the cutting blocks, but nowhere else that I could see. "What's going on, Jack?"

Jack rubbed the back of his neck. "I should have known. It was Donna. She called and asked for the millionth time, *What's new at work, Jack, honey?* So I made something up. I didn't think she believed me. I was teasing, for crying out loud. But she must have called the whole town."

Sheriff Robinson gave me a tired smile. "Sorry you got worried, Tree. We've been trying to call Donna and tell her what happened—what *didn't* happen, more like—but the line's busy." He looked back to Jack. "I'll take a drive over there."

"Again, Sheriff, I'm really and truly sorry. Man, I can't even believe all the trouble from one measly phone call—"

"Well, now you know. Don't mess with your mother." Sheriff Robinson slipped his hat back on. "Then I reckon I'll be headin' up north for my date with those bass. Your mama caught me just in time. I was walking out the door."

"Sorry about that," Jack said. "Good luck fishing."

The sheriff nodded to us and left through the main entrance.

The second he was gone, I turned on Jack and slugged him as hard as I'd ever hit anybody. "Don't you ever do that again!"

"Ow!" Jack rubbed his arm.

"I mean it! I thought you were dead! Then I thought you killed somebody! And all the time, you were just—" I couldn't finish. The mix inside of me felt violent, like atoms breaking loose, ready to explode into the universe in some new kind of bomb.

"Tree, I'd never want to upset you. You know that. I'm really—" He stopped, frowned. Then he burst out laughing. "Where on earth did you find that getup? You look like a melting candy cane."

I looked down at the hideous outfit sticking to my skin. Then I slugged Jack again, harder, and stormed out of the IGA.

As I pedaled home in the rain, I shook with anger, and with something worse than anger—fear. I'd believed every word about the robbery because it would have been exactly like Jack to try to save somebody and get hurt doing it. *That* was the truth in his story. It could have happened. In an instant, he could have killed . . . or been killed.

That was a truth I never wanted to face.

20

Cold Wars and Roses

I had never been this mad at Jack. And it wasn't just the way his prank had scared me to death. He'd changed the way I looked at things. Before, I'd never been afraid of the future, but now I understood a secret about "tomorrow," and I blamed Jack. I knew how quickly and completely everything could change.

Jack's fake story had even made me confused about journalism. What if I heard a story about somebody, and then I wrote about it, thinking it was the truth. Only it wasn't. People would believe what I wrote. They would believe me.

At home, Dad took the lead in how we handled each other. There was no mention of our office blowup or the Kinneys. We didn't talk about much of anything. We were polite. I told him about Jack's fake robbery, and he almost reacted like normal Dad. But underneath the normal, I felt a chill. I wondered if that was how the Russians and Americans felt *their* cold war.

I hated feeling so far away from Dad. But at least I wasn't grounded. On the other hand, if I'd gotten to pick between a cold war and being grounded, I'd have chosen grounded.

I knew I needed to visit Mrs. Kinney again. Only this time, I'd be prepared with more than a plate of macaroons. I wanted more background information, so I could ask her specific questions. I wished I could have talked with Sheriff Robinson, but maybe he had clued in the new sheriff before going fishing. Or maybe the new sheriff had gone to the hospital to talk to Mr. Kinney. Rumor had it that he was in St. Joseph Hospital, forty-five miles from Hamilton. It would be great to hear what Old Man Kinney had to say about the shooting. I phoned the sheriff's office.

Mrs. Berger answered on the first ring and reported that *Officer* Duper was in the office. But when he heard it was me on the phone, just a kid, he told Mrs. Berger to explain that he was much too busy to talk to a "minor."

The rain continued into Wednesday. I actually wished I knew a reverse rain dance to make it stop so I could get out of the house and go back to work. I couldn't mow our lawn or the office lawn, both my chores. But I did take advantage of the time off. I wrote.

I settled into my writing nook in the living room and opened to the writer's quote for the day:

If I don't write to empty my mind, I go mad.
—Lord Byron

I thought Lord Byron really did go mad. But I might have gotten him mixed up with some other poet.

At any rate, I was beginning to understand what he meant. My mind was a messy attic, with snippets of my interviews and different rumors jumbling in my head. The sounds of birds chirping and a gun blast mixed with human voices, all talking at the same time.

I put pen to paper and tried to describe the DeShon house. Soon as I'd written that, I could see Mrs. DeShon. Her words came out of my head and formed on the lines of my notebook paper. And I felt a little less crazy.

After a while, I changed gears and read the front page of the *Kansas City Star*. I tried to find the *who, what, where, when, why,* and *how* in each news story. I waded through a long article about leaders in Cambodia and Laos accusing the United States of sending spies into their countries, just because they were Vietnam's neighbors.

After that, I dug out Agatha Christie's *The Murder of Roger Ackroyd* and decided to reread it. Since I already knew who committed the murder, I read to learn about mysteries and getting to the truth. I paid attention to the way the detective got answers out of people.

It was after noon when I finished writing my interview questions. Then, armed with an umbrella and a Bic, I ventured down to the Kinneys' again. There were more puddles than road.

This time, Mrs. Kinney opened the door before I knocked. I think she smiled, but it came and went too fast to swear to it.

She took my dripping umbrella and glanced around for someplace to put it. "I'll set it in the kitchen."

I kicked off my muddy shoes and crossed to her rocking chair, where I spotted two finished baskets and one just started. "Wow! You definitely have to show these off at the steam engine show." The weaving looked tight enough to hold water.

"I don't know about that," she said as she came in from the kitchen. She picked up the yellow basket. "But I think I got it right with this here one. My grandma used to make Easter baskets like she learnt from her ma. She was a Dodge, like me before I married. I read a book on where names come from. Dodge started from a fella in Gloucestershire in 1206. That's in England. Right close to Wales. I used to dream about going there."

I took the basket from her. "This is so cool." The bottom was a scooped-out coconut, but the top had straw woven together.

We took our usual seats. Rain pounded the roof. "I'm starting to hate rain," I said.

"Don't move to Cherrapunji. Or Waialeale."

"Huh?"

"Rains five hundred inches a year in Cherrapunji, India. Waialeale's in Hawaii." She pronounced it "Hawai-ya." "Rains three hundred thirty-five days a year there." She said this while rocking and looking at her feet instead of at me. I got the feeling Mrs. Kinney wasn't used to talking to kids. And maybe not to grown-ups, either. In a way, she reminded me of Penny.

"Have you been to India and Hawaii?" I asked.

"Me? I've barely been to Hamilton." She rocked a few times, still studying her shoes. "But I dream about going to Hawai-ya."

"It sounds beautiful." I put my hand into my pocket, where I'd stuck my notes with the questions I wanted to ask her. Only I couldn't figure out how to get from Hawaii to the shooting.

"You ought to go there," she said. "To Hawai-ya. You being a writer and all. They got some good newspapers. The *Hawaii Tribune Herald* started a new weekly for the Kona District just last year. That's on the Big Island, where Captain James Cook was killed in 1779."

"I'm not a writer yet," I said, probably blushing but liking the way she called me one.

We sat in silence, the only noise the *squeak, creak* of her rocker.

"You sure know a lot of facts," I said, trying to get us talking again. "I have trouble remembering dates and numbers. Dad remembers everything, except where he left his hat. He has a memory system. How do you remember all those facts and numbers, Mrs. Kinney?" Dad would love her weird facts. I wondered if she'd given him any.

She frowned and let her rocker ease to a stop. "I reckon remembering them facts is better than remembering things best forgot." She glanced over at the coffee table.

The flimsy table was marred by a dozen drink rings. My mom would have killed Eileen and me for not using coasters. In the center sat a clear globe of a bowl. Rose petals floated on top of the clear water. They looked totally out of place in the gray room, like Dorothy's ruby slippers in a drab and barren Kansas.

"Are the roses from your bushes?" I asked.

"I got no more roses," she said. And that's when I remembered what Mrs. DeShon said about Mr. Kinney yanking out the roses in a fit of temper. "Somebody brought these here for Alfred. But I like them where they are."

We stared at the petals.

"Do you miss him, Mrs. Kinney?" It was the first real question I'd asked about her husband. And it wasn't even on my list. "I mean, if you don't mind me asking."

"I don't mind the askin'." She seemed to be considering her answer, though. Finally, she said, "His absence is duly noted. That's a true thing, that is."

21

Pedal to the Metal

Since the non-incident at the IGA, Jack had phoned me a dozen times. I had Eileen and Mom tell him I was still too mad at him for scaring me. But the truth was, as Mrs. Kinney put it, Jack's absence was duly noted.

Somehow, Jack managed to sneak two "anonymous" notes into my bike basket:

```
Friendship is unnecessary, like
philosophy, like art. . . . It has no
survival value; rather it is one of
those things that give value to
survival. -C. S. Lewis
```

The second came from Walter Winchell, the voice of news radio:

```
A friend is one who walks in when
others walk out.
```

I had to admit the quotes weren't bad.

Just after supper the phone rang, and I forgot and answered it myself. "Hello?" We were supposed to say, "Taylor residence," in case it was a patient for Dad. But I forgot that too, like I did most of the time.

"Good. Tree, don't hang up," Jack said. "I know you're mad at me. But how would you like me to give you a driving lesson?"

I didn't answer. But I didn't hang up. I'd been after Jack—and Eileen and Mom and Dad—to teach me to drive. We wouldn't get to take driver's ed until sophomore year, but I didn't want to wait till then to get the feel of the wheel. Sarah had been driving trucks and tractors all over her farm since she was ten.

"Just think, Tree," Jack continued. "It will give you a chance to yell at me face to face."

"That's true," I conceded. "And you're going to let me drive Fred?"

"Fred is willing. I can be there in ten minutes."

"Five," I said, just to be contrary.

"Deal."

I changed into jeans and a clean red T-shirt and ran a brush through my hair. Five minutes later, Jack pulled up. Mom and Dad were playing croquet in the side yard.

I dashed out of the house and waved to them. The rain had stopped for good, and our dry ground had soaked up most of it. Sunshine burst through wisps of clouds as the sun made a grand appearance before setting. "Going for a drive with Jack!" I shouted to my parents.

They waved back at me.

I slid in and stared straight ahead.

"Before you officially have a cow," Jack began, "I've got to say that I'm not the one you should be mad at." He pulled onto the road. "This was Donna's fault, Tree, and you know it. Still, I'm sorry you flipped out." He reached across the gearshift and tapped my shoulder about where I'd slugged *his* shoulder. "I'd have done the same for you."

He rolled along at a snail's pace, neither of us saying anything. I'd already come to the same conclusion. If Donna hadn't bugged him for gossip, or if she hadn't called the whole town, none of it would have happened.

"So," I said, "are we going to talk all night or drive? Punch it! Pedal to the metal!"

Jack grinned. So did I.

I wished Dad and I could get over things the way Jack and I always did.

"First, there's something I want you to see." Jack turned onto Main Street. When he got to the bank, he slowed down.

"What?" I didn't see anything.

He tilted his head toward the bank, motioning me to look up.

Then I saw it. On the roof sat a sign, like a stop sign, only white. I couldn't read it from where I sat. "What's it say?"

"Haven't you seen our new police officer's specially made parking sign? It says, 'For police department vehicles only, by order of Officer Duper.'"

"No way!"

"The guy hadn't been here twenty-four hours when he brought out that sign. He moves it from the sheriff's office, where nobody ever parks anyway, to the café, where spots can fill on a Sunday after church. Wherever Duper goes, it goes."

"So you moved it to the top of the bank?" I was trying hard not to laugh.

"Did I say that? I just thought it looked cool up there, and I wanted to show my best buddy how Hamilton welcomed the new fuzz."

I filled Jack in on my visits to the Kinney place and how I hadn't gotten much for my article but that Mrs. Kinney made cool baskets and knew weird facts about places she dreamed of going. I told him what Randy Ridings said about letting me write something for the *Hamiltonian*. Jack filled me in on how the IGA had returned to normal—boring. And how Donna had taken him seriously and was making a Jesse James getup for the steam engine show, and how he didn't have the heart to tell her he'd been kidding, especially after the IGA disaster.

Jack drove to the reservoir outside city limits. It was the perfect place for a driving lesson, although the sun had already gone down, making it harder to see. The reservoir looked like a mini-lake, with winding trails around it. Hardly anybody ever drove out there.

"Do you remember when our dads used to bring us out here to the spillway?" I asked. A concrete slope directed water down so the reservoir wouldn't overflow. We used it as a water slide.

"That was the best place to cool off before they built the pool," Jack said. "I haven't thought about the spillway for years. Wonder why we stopped coming."

"Don't you remember? Water moccasins. One slid right over my leg." We'd seen black snakes and king snakes at the reservoir. But water moccasins are poisonous.

"Man, I can't believe I forgot that! Eileen screamed louder than you did. I thought I'd never get over seeing that snake wiggle over your leg." He shivered.

"Tell me about it." I could almost feel that slimy snake on my leg again. For a second, I flashed back to Jack and the imaginary robber, and how things could change in an instant, and what if that water moccasin had opened its mouth and sunk its fangs into my leg.

Jack stopped the car and turned off the engine. "Your turn." He walked around the front of the car.

I scooted over and let Jack take the suicide seat. "One question."

"Shoot."

"Why do they call where you're sitting the 'suicide seat'?"

"Yeah, well, it's also called 'riding shotgun.' So shut your face and drive."

We moved the seat up. I had no trouble starting the engine. But I was concentrating so hard on the little diagram on the gearshift that I forgot about the clutch. The car shrieked when I tried to put it in gear. "Sorry," I told Jack. Or Fred.

Finally, I got the car into first without killing it. We jerked forward. Then rolled ahead. But just when I was getting used to first, Jack told me to shift to second. And the whole mess started all over again.

Half an hour later, we'd both had enough. We swapped seats, and Jack started the engine.

"Thanks, Jack. I hope I didn't hurt Fred." I patted the dashboard. "Do you think I'll ever get my driver's license?"

"In your lifetime?"

"Funny," I said, not smiling. I rolled down the window. Music came in with the breeze. "Do you hear that?" I strained to make out the song. "That's Jan and Dean, or we're not Jack and Tree."

"Cool!" Jack cried. "And it's not even Saturday." He looked over at me, and his grin widened. "You feel like dancing, Tree?"

"Always."

He spun Fred around and drove up the hill to the other side of the reservoir.

Just over the hill I spotted a circle of lights, like an alien spaceship. The music grew louder the closer we got to the lights. "What's going on out there?"

"Tree Taylor, I think it's about time I let you in on a secret."

22

Rock-'n'-Roll!

A dozen cars were parked in a circle, front ends pointing in, forming a big round grass dance floor in the center. Each car had the windows open and the radio tuned to WHB, Kansas City's rock station. "Surf City" blared out of every speaker while couples danced in a ring of headlights.

Jack pulled Fred into the circle and turned off the engine, but not all the way, so he could play his radio too. The dial was already on 710, so our Jan and Dean joined everybody else's.

"This is the coolest thing I've ever seen!" I exclaimed. I knew the dancers, kids from Jack's class, and Eileen's. The guys wore jeans and T-shirts. But the girls were dressed cool—full skirts, some housing even fuller petticoats underneath, sleeveless tops with big buttons and wide belts.

Several of the kids waved at us—well, at Jack.

"Ready?" he asked, one hand on the door latch. The song ended, and the DJ cut in with something about Dick's Used Cars in Liberty, Missouri.

"Wait. I can't dance in front of all these people."

Liz Cavenaugh had on a red skirt with a hidden pleat in front and back, exactly like the one Eileen told Mom I'd look good in. Her red sneakers matched the skirt. I glanced down at my old jeans and my plain T-shirt. And why had I worn my yellow rubber flip-flops?

Liz and her boyfriend, Kent, jogged up to Jack's window. They were holding hands and didn't let go, even when Kent leaned in. His gaze rested on me. "You robbin' the cradle these days, Jack?"

I wanted to disappear under the floorboard.

But Jack came to the rescue. "Tree could dance the socks off all of you. I was lucky to get her to agree to have me as a dance partner."

Kent frowned at me. "Right, man."

I had no business being here. I stared out the windshield, hoping to see at least one person from my class. "Wait a minute. Jack, is that Butch? And Laura?"

It wasn't like I hadn't heard about Butch and Laura, but seeing them together creeped me out. Butch Hamlet was the only guy my sister had ever dated seriously. Eileen was the prettiest girl in her class, and everybody loved her. But she never went out with anybody more than once or twice.

Except for Butch. She'd had a crush on him since grade school. Last year they started going together. He made it official—gave her his class ring and told her they were going steady.

But Eileen wasn't with him tonight. And Laura the Life-guard was.

"Yeah," Jack said. "About that—"

"What's he doing with Laura?" I demanded.

"Dancing. They come here and dance. That's all."

"Why didn't he bring Eileen?"

"Tree," Jack said, "I love your sister. You know that. But . . . well . . . have you seen her dance?"

He had a point. Still . . . "So that's it? They dance. But where do they go *after* they dance?"

"You'd have to ask them about that. But don't do it here. Here is for dancing."

Suddenly, "Heat Wave" shouted at us from every car. I loved that song.

Jack hopped out of Fred and reached in for me. "Come on, Tree! You love Martha and the Vandellas."

I stayed where I was. "Yeah. But not with all these people around."

"So pretend they're not. We're missing it, Tree!"

I thought for a minute and figured I'd already made a fool of myself by showing up here. I might as well enjoy it. I slid out and ran into the dancing ring while Martha belted out: ". . . like a heat wave, burning in my heart. I can't keep from crying, tearing me apart."

A few voices shouted something to Jack, but I shut them out. There was nothing but the music now. Now was for dancing.

Jack took both of my hands, and, like we'd done on umpteen Sunday nights, we danced. I got into it so deep—spinning, bridging, underarm turning—I didn't even notice another dancer until the song ended.

When I looked up, Jack and I were standing in the center of the circle, and I was shoeless. Nobody else was dancing. My heart pounded, but not from dancing. I knew they were going to tell me to leave. I was too young. I didn't belong here.

Then somebody clapped.

And before we knew it, cheers burst out all around the circle. Hoots and hollers and applause. Even Kent. Especially Kent. "Take a bow, cats! You weren't kidding about Tree dancing us into the ground, were you, old man!"

Several of the girls—not Laura—rushed up to me.

"Tree, that was so cool!"

"Far-out, girl!"

"Was that the watusi you did at the end?"

Before I could get a word in, Suzi exclaimed, "You have to teach me how you do that thing when you spin under and come up swinging!" Suzi was Hamilton's homecoming queen.

"Where did you learn to dance like that?" Liz asked.

Before I could answer—and I wouldn't have had a clue how to answer—another song started, and Jack whisked me away.

Then another. And another.

Jack wouldn't let anybody else dance with me. Only him. Which was fine with me. We danced every song as if we were on *American Bandstand*. Meanwhile, lightning bugs flashed all around us, and stars shone overhead. A train wailed in the distance. I could smell grass, and water, and perfume.

Jack and I twisted. We did the mashed potato. We jived

and jitterbugged. I'd never gotten so much applause in my whole life. Even Eileen hadn't gotten this much when she did piano recitals.

"Wipe Out" came on, and I was dancing by the first note.

Not Jack. "Tree, it's late. I'd better get you home before your dad sends Officer Duper out looking for us."

"No! I love this song, Jack!" I was so jazzed I could have danced *on* the reservoir.

But he was already halfway to the car.

I hated leaving, but I followed him.

Instead of heading back by the spillway, we took a different road out, past the main reservoir. It would have made a fine lake if we hadn't needed to drink it.

"Right over there." He pointed to a worn path near the water's edge.

It reminded me of pull-over spots on highways so drivers could stop and get a good view or take pictures. It was a pretty spot, but no better than anywhere else around the water. "So what's down there?" I said.

"That, my dear Tree, is a place you should never let those young rascals in your class take you once they get their licenses."

"Why not?" I pictured water moccasins looming over the edge.

"Because that's where *some* people go to watch submarine races."

"Submarine races? Right. Like they're ever going to see a submarine."

"Exactly. So don't let anybody take you there looking for any. Got it?"

"Ah." Suddenly, I did get it. I knew about making out, and "going all the way," at least in theory.

"What time is it anyway?" I asked, changing the subject and settling safely into the suicide seat.

"After eleven."

"You're kidding!"

"When's your curfew?"

Good question. I didn't actually have a curfew. I'd never needed one. Eileen was supposed to be in by ten on weekdays, eleven on weekends. "I'm going to be in trouble, aren't I?" *Again.*

"Sorry, Tree."

I shook my head, reliving the sensation of dancing in the headlights, while stars floated their shapes above us. "Don't be sorry. Whatever they do to me, tonight was worth it."

The porch light shone as we drove up to my house. Giant moths flopped against the glass dome.

"Want me to go in with you?" Jack offered.

"I think it will go better if I face the music alone." I grinned, knowing he'd get the music line. "Thanks, Jack."

He drove off, and I took a deep breath before going on in. I opened the front door, expecting my parents to be waiting there, arms crossed, lecture at the ready.

Midge rushed up to me. She jumped on me, like she'd been worried.

Apparently, she was the only one.

Half-expecting a trap, I checked the kitchen blackboard, where we left notes for each other. I had to flip on the light to read it:

TREE —
WE POOPED OUT EARLY. TURN OFF
THE PORCH LIGHT.
LOVE, MOM

Unbelievable.

I wasn't quite sure how I felt about being so ultra-trustworthy, with such worry-free parents. I got ready for bed, then cuddled up with Midge. I closed my eyes and let the headlight circle take over my mind. Music still played in my head, and my insides danced as I lay still, remembering, tasting the night again, the way the breeze stirred laughter and music. Words broke through my night-dream like unwanted car commercials on station WHB—*suicide* seat, riding *shotgun*. Then the music exploded back, bringing with it streamers of fireflies and stardust.

I fell asleep as visions of the reservoir danced in my head, with only the shadow of a water moccasin swimming below.

23
Nowheresville

Thursday was supposed to be Dad's day off, although he usually ended up going into the office half a day. Some Thursdays he and Mom went to Kansas City shopping. But that morning I'd heard them talk about visiting Mr. Kinney in the hospital.

That gave me an idea. Maybe I could write a better article if I talked to Mr. Kinney instead of Mrs. Kinney. I'd had more than a couple of false starts trying to write about Mrs. Kinney. Whenever I tried to record my conversations with her, I'd start thinking about the real person, the way her eyes sparked when she cracked open her door and saw it was me. And I didn't really want to write anything that could take away that spark.

But Mr. Kinney was a different story. If I could talk to him, maybe he'd spill everything about what had really happened, all the details about the shooting. I could still deliver the truth of it to Randy, and I wouldn't have to get it out of Mrs. Kinney.

I put on a green dress that only a mother would love. And since it was my mother who loved it, I thought it might help my case. When they came out in their dressed-up clothes, I was waiting. "I'm ready," I informed Mom.

Mom looked too good for a hospital. She wore a pillbox hat, like Jackie Kennedy, a straight black skirt, and a short jacket with fake diamond buttons. "Ready for what?"

"To go to the hospital. To see Mr. Kinney."

"I don't think that's such a good idea," Mom said.

"How come?"

Eileen must have heard us from the kitchen. She left her studies to join our discussion. "Why would you want to go to the hospital and hang out with sick people? Gross." She shuddered.

"Really, Nurse Eileen? Better hope none of your patients are sick, then."

"You don't even know Mr. Kinney, do you, Tree?" Mom asked.

"He *is* our neighbor."

Dad had been trying to tie his tie in the hall mirror. Mom walked up to him and took over the tie tying. He frowned over his shoulder at me, and I knew he'd seen through my bogus request. "You're not coming, Tree. And that's that."

That *was* that. I'd gotten dressed for nothing. And my best chance of observing Mr. Kinney close-up? Gone with the wind.

The minute Mom and Dad closed the door behind them, I tried calling the sheriff's office again. Maybe he'd have Mr. Kinney's story by now. Mrs. Berger informed me that Officer

Duper could be found at the railroad tracks reclaiming his parking sign. I could tell she was laughing.

I changed clothes, and for the rest of the morning, while Mom and Dad were at the hospital, and while Eileen memorized the digestive system, I wrote.

The quote for the day was pretty neat:

In my beginning is my end.—T. S. Eliot

I wasn't sure I understood it, but I turned to a clean page in my notebook and started over. This time, I discovered that the hardest part was not making things up. Like I'd talked to two women who volunteered in the church nursery with Sarah and me, and they told me stuff about Lois Dodge before she got married. Only I couldn't remember their exact words, and I didn't want to make anything up. And when I tried to record my DeShon interview, I could have guessed which DeShon boy said what. But the truth was, I couldn't tell those boys apart. I wondered if real newspaper people had the same problem.

The rain kept coming off and on, and the pool stayed closed. D.J. and Sarah both called and told me to knock off the rain dances. Sarah reported that her mother hadn't started sewing her costume for the steam engine show yet—she was too busy with the yard sale. While emptying junk from the attic, Sarah had found a bonnet in an old trunk. She sounded as stir-crazy as I felt.

I got so desperate, I phoned Penny. Her sister answered

and hollered for Penny to come to the phone. I heard two clicks and figured they were on a party line, which meant that several houses shared the line and any of them could listen in.

"Hello?" Penny sounded scared, even on the phone.

"Hi, Penny. This is Tree."

"I know."

This wasn't going to be easy. Sarah and I could talk forever without thinking about it. "So, what are you up to on this rainy day?"

"Reading."

"Yeah? Cool. What are you reading?"

"*Fahrenheit 451.* I know we read it in school, but I'm re-reading it."

"Great book."

The line went silent, except for a cough that didn't come from either of us.

"Okay, then." I couldn't think of a single thing to say. "So, see you later?"

"Okay. Bye."

That afternoon I visited Mrs. Kinney again. We had a little routine going. She grinned, and I grinned back as she opened the door. We took our appointed seats, and I checked out how her baskets were coming along.

"Your mama called to ask if I wanted to visit Alfred in the hospital," she said, getting up from her chair. "As you see, I declined."

"How come?"

"Don't reckon I'll be seeing Alfred again." There was not a note of regret in her voice. I thought of Jack's word, "relieved." She sounded relieved.

This was the perfect opening for me to hit her with the hard questions Randy would have wanted answered. Did Alfred say he'd never see her again? Or was she the one who said it? And what about that gun in her arms on the porch that morning?

She came out with my hot chocolate. I took a sip and set it on the rickety table. She'd sprinkled nutmeg on the whipped cream. "Thanks. I love nutmeg on top."

She sipped her chocolate. "Nutmeg is poisonous if you give it in a shot. But it's just right on whipped cream on a rainy day."

Then, before I could ask her about Alfred, she was sharing weird facts about Wyoming (she'd always wanted to see a rodeo), France (she'd dreamed about seeing the *Mona Lisa* painting), and Yosemite Falls in California, the highest waterfall in the U.S. (she'd dreamed of going over it in a barrel). "I love big bodies of water." Her eyes narrowed as if she could see the ocean from her rocker.

"You should come to the pool . . . if it ever stops raining," I said. "It's just a small body of water, but it's pretty when the sun hits it . . . if the sun ever shines again."

"Can't swim a lick."

"Lots of people who come to the pool can't swim."

"That so?"

I'd been thinking about Wanda when I told Mrs. Kinney about nonswimmers coming to the pool.

"Anybody in particular you'd be thinking of, a non-swimming person?" Her tiny eyes stayed fixed on me.

"Wanda," I admitted. "She's my age. And she wears a bikini."

"That why this Wanda comes to the pool, you reckon?" Mrs. Kinney asked. "So's she can show off that there bikini?"

I shrugged. "Maybe. I think she comes because she hopes Ray will be there."

"Ah. This Ray—you reckon he comes for the same reason? Hoping Wanda will be there?"

"No!" I answered too fast. And too loud. "I mean, I don't think so. *She's* the one chasing after *him*. I don't think it's the other way around at all."

"You reckon this Ray fella's got more sense than to go for a gal who can't rightly swim?"

"I do. I think he's got a whole lot more sense than that."

Mrs. Kinney frowned, like she was taking in this information. Then she nodded, slowly. "I'll bet you're a good swimmer," she said.

"Not bad."

We finished our hot chocolate. I hadn't meant to talk to Mrs. Kinney about Wanda. Or Ray. I didn't think she'd tell anybody what I'd told her, though. Only that made me wonder if she felt the same way. Did she trust me not to tell anybody what she told me? Not that she'd told me much of anything so far.

Mrs. Kinney carried our cups and saucers into the kitchen. When she sat down again, she launched into facts about swimming and countries that held the Olympics.

I asked her half a dozen questions about the Olympics. But I just couldn't bring myself to ask a single question about Mr. Kinney or that gun.

24
Unreal

On Friday when the sun finally came out, I couldn't wait to go back to work. I got ready earlier than I needed to and dressed in my green swimsuit, with white shorts. My quote for the day was one I got out of a school library book of quotations:

Next to doing things that deserve to be written, nothing gets a man more credit, or gives him more pleasure than to write things that deserve to be read. —Lord Chesterfield

I wasn't so sure the quotation had anything to do with me. I couldn't claim to be getting pleasure out of writing about the Kinneys. But I'd promised Randy I'd hand over an article at the steam engine show, July Fourth. And pleasure or not, I would. I settled into my writing chair by the picture window. Something crinkled in my pocket—a note. I knew *I* hadn't put it there. My "anonymous" note writer could have stuck the note into my pocket when my shorts were in my pool basket. Or Jack could have done it Sunday.

The message was typed.

```
I may sometimes differ in opinion from
some of my friends, from those whose
views are as pure and sound as my own.
I censure none, but do homage to every
one's right of opinion.
-Thomas Jefferson
```

I tried to connect Jefferson's words to my writing. Maybe he—and Jack—meant that if I ended up writing something people disagreed with, it would be okay. I had a right to my own opinion.

I wished Dad would read the quote.

In a stroke of brilliance, I copied Jefferson's words into my notebook, then left Jack's note out on the coffee table in hopes that Dad would read it.

Plopping back into my writer's chair, I heard another crinkle. After checking my remaining pockets, sure enough, I found another note:

```
Believe nothing against another, but
upon good authority; nor report what
may hurt another, unless it be a
greater hurt to others to conceal it.
-William Penn
```

After rereading the note, I decided it was saying I shouldn't gossip. But it made me think about the Kinney article I'd promised Randy. William Penn was like Randy's dad. Neither of them wanted to report anything that might hurt another person, unless they had to. I guess that's how I was starting to feel about Mrs. Kinney.

By then, the whole house had started getting ready. While I scribbled in my notebook, I got the feeling Dad was watching me. He ran his electric shaver over his morning stubble like always, sitting on the floor of the narrow hallway, so we had to step over him. With his back to the wall, his feet drawn under him, knees high, he had a clear view of everything that went on in our house.

I fought hard not to make eye contact with Dad. I did not want him to ask me what I was working on. I didn't know if he knew I'd been talking to Mrs. Kinney, but I doubted Hamilton kept many secrets from Doc Taylor.

I had always loved the hum of the razor as it moved up and down Dad's cheeks and over his chin. He claimed he shaved in the hall because long ago he'd given up on getting a decent turn in the bathroom. True, even that morning Mom and Eileen were vying for the shower. But I believed Dad shaved in the hall because he'd found the perfect spot to spy on us.

Finally, he clicked off the razor and pulled out a bottle of Aqua Velva from his dopp kit. He poured some of the liquid into one hand, rubbed his palms together, then slapped his cheeks. The scent of minty aftershave filled the living room. It was what blue would smell like if blue had a smell. It made me think of Ray Miller's eyes.

I knew every move Dad would make from now until he left for the office—the hunt for his bag and hat, his goodbye kiss to Mom, "hidden" behind his half-raised hand, the wild patting of his shirt pocket to make sure he had his glasses, then the goodbye call-out to Eileen and me.

"Bye, Tree," Dad said, his hand on the doorknob.

Right on cue, I said, "Bye, Dad."

And I wondered if he wondered what I was really thinking as much as I wondered what he was really thinking.

I got to the pool early and couldn't believe everybody except Sarah was already there. Guess I wasn't the only one suffering from cabin fever. "What's happening, guys?"

Nobody paid me any attention. They were crowded around a newspaper, spread out on the counter.

"What a fink!" Laura exclaimed.

"Wouldn't you know she'd be the one to complain?" Mike said. "She's a kook."

"Did you see how she signed it?" D.J. said.

Laura looked, then spit out the words: "'A concerned mother'? That'll be the day. What a phony!"

"What's going on?" I shed my shirt and moved closer.

"Didn't you see the *Hamiltonian* this morning?" D.J. asked.

"Ours never comes this early. Why?" I eased in to see what had them so upset.

D.J. shifted the paper my way. "Read it and weep. I could get fired over this."

Fired? I snatched up the paper. On page one was a letter to the editor circled in red ink. The only times I'd seen letters to the editor in our paper were when the mayor was up for re-election. Even then, Jack said the anonymous letters came from the mayor's wife. Maybe Randy really was taking over at the office.

I tried to digest what I was reading, but it wasn't easy because of all the shouting and cursing going on in the basket room.

> Dear Fellow Hamiltonians,
>
> I'm sure it comes as no surprise that we are being cheated by our own Hamilton swimming pool. The goof-off kids that run that pool sneak around and close it before they're supposed to. Check the regulations and you'll see for yourself. Pool is open noon to nine. Yeah, right! The other night it wasn't nine when they kicked my poor children out. My kids love to swim. I'm writing this for them. Nothing is more important than our children. I go to all the trouble of getting them to the pool, and we deserve to find it open. We owe it to our children to make sure them lifeguards keep the blamed pool open and quit cheating our children. And if they can't do that, I say we fire the lot of them!
>
> Signed,
> A Concerned Mother (Connie Cozad)

I stared at the letter—the very negative letter—to the editor. Where was old Mr. Ridings when we needed him?

25

One Cool Cat

I skimmed the letter again. It was so ridiculous. "You can't believe anybody's going to take that woman seriously."

"I've already gotten three calls from board members." D.J. hiked up his faded swim trunks. "King-sized flak session for yours truly."

I glanced around at the others. "But that's crazy!"

"Apparently, the board doesn't think so," Mike said as he turned to D.J. "Did they say anything about firing lifeguards, or just you?"

"Just me. Thanks for asking, though, Mikey."

Laura raised her eyebrows at Mike. Apparently, all of her anger had floated away with this revelation. "Well, I should get on out to my lifeguard stand."

D.J. and I frowned at each other because Laura never went on duty a second before she had to. Even then, he had to push her out. I moved to where I could watch her stroll to the lifeguard stand. Then I understood.

Butch.

Butch Hamlet was standing on the other side of the fence, right behind Laura's stand.

I was definitely going to have to keep an eye on those two, for Eileen's sake. But right now, I had a bigger problem—D.J.'s pool career. "What are you going to do?"

Before D.J. could answer, Sarah hopped over the counter, waving the *Hamiltonian*. "Did you guys see this? Isn't she the woman who leaves her kids here to fry? What does she think we are? Babysitters?"

"You got that right," I agreed.

"She's a lying creep!" Sarah slammed down her paper. "We can't let her get away with this!"

D.J. sighed and dabbed zinc oxide on his nose. "The board's not going to believe me over a 'concerned mother.'"

Again, I thought about the power of the press, how words in print became truth for readers—even if the press got it wrong.

"Don't know what I'll do if they can me," D.J. said.

I'd heard about guys out of college and out of work ending up in Vietnam. "Well, it's not fair!" I protested.

"Hey!" A snotty junior high girl pounded the ticket counter. "Are you guys going to open up or what?"

"Have a cow, why don't you?" Sarah muttered.

D.J. hustled to the counter. "Better get to work. Some concerned citizen might write the *Hamiltonian* about not opening on time."

Sarah and I hit the baskets, but my stomach hurt with worry for D.J., worry about sneaky Laura and cheating Butch, and frustration over my looming deadline for the *Hamiltonian*. Not to mention the ongoing cold war with Dad. Sarah said I was turning into a worrywart.

D.J.'s problem seemed the most urgent, so I decided to focus on it and worry about the rest later. As I took in baskets, I thought about how I could help D.J. I could go to the board and tell them the truth about their "concerned mother." But if they wouldn't believe D.J., why would they believe me?

"Thank you, Tree."

The thank-you startled me back to earth.

Penny Atkinson smiled at me. I still felt crummy about our stupid, almost silent phone conversation. I watched, just as stupidly, as she walked away, pinning her number onto her polka-dot swimsuit.

"Penny, wait up!"

She turned and frowned, like she was afraid she'd done something wrong.

I leaned over the counter, not sure what to say to her. "Um . . . hi?"

Her frown lines deepened. I read suspicion there. "Hi," she said.

"I mean, thanks for saying thank you," I said, because I couldn't think of anything else. "Most people don't bother."

She nodded.

"Well, that's all. Have fun swimming."

She nodded again and headed toward the pool.

"Penny turning in her froggy-dos?" Sarah asked.

I glanced in the basket and saw that, yes, she'd worn the

canvas slip-ons she wore every day to school. Big deal. I wore the same tennis shoes.

I put up Penny's basket. Then I joined Sarah. Today, she'd tried something different with her hair. Two very short braids stuck out from the sides of her head like furry fingers.

"We can't all be the fashion goddesses you expect us to be," she said, reading my mind. She gave me the fish eye. "So what did Penny have to say?"

"She thanked me for taking her basket. Have you noticed that nobody ever thanks us?"

As I said this, two little girls shoved a basket onto the counter. The bigger girl barked, "Here. Take this."

"See what I mean? I don't think I've ever had two people say thank you in the same day."

Sarah pretended to wipe away tears. I threw a towel at her.

For my supper break I hit up the snack bar for a frozen Milky Way and sat on the picnic table facing the pool, my feet on the bench. I was peeling off the wrapper when the table moved. I looked over, and up, right into the dreamy sky-blue eyes of Ray Miller.

"Shouldn't you be snarfing something better than that for dinner?" he asked.

Please, God. Let me be able to form words. "I know. I ordered barbecued ribs and a juicy sirloin, but they were all out of asparagus. So I went with this."

He grinned. "That explains it."

"So, what are you doing here?"

"Felt like swimming. I guess I could have gone to the

track or the football field, but there's no water there. So I came here."

"That explains it."

There was nobody around except us. "Where's Wanda?" I tried not to sound all that interested.

Ray shrugged. I wondered if he was trying not to *look* all that interested. He eased himself onto the table and sat beside me.

I took in a deep breath to calm my racing heart. Big mistake. All of my senses took in the unforgettable scent of Ray Miller—earthy, manly, like cigars, though I couldn't remember ever smelling cigars.

Somebody went off the board and landed a cannonball that reached our table. We dodged, and our knees touched. I shivered and hoped he'd think it was because of the splash.

"Man, I love that song!" Ray exclaimed.

I tuned in to the snack bar music. "Ahab the Arab" was playing. I'd liked it too, the first couple of times I heard it. But it was kind of hokey.

Ray grinned at me like he was waiting for me to agree with him.

"Ray Stevens sure has a wild way with lyrics." I tried to sound enthusiastic. "I'll bet you liked 'Jeremiah Peabody's Poly-unsaturated Quick-Dissolving Fast-Acting Pleasant-Tasting Green and Purple Pills.'"

"I loved that one! Although I've never known anybody who could actually say that title." He moved to the beat. No rhythm, but he sure looked unbearably cute. "What do you listen to?"

"Just about anything on WHB." I had to look away. Every time I risked meeting those eyes, seeing those lips, I couldn't think of anything except my second summer goal. Ray's lips were full and perfect, with a curve on top, like the start of a heart.

Suddenly, I realized he'd asked me another question. "Sorry. What did you say?"

"I was just wondering what kind of music you like best. Which singers? What groups?"

Great question. "I love the Beach Boys, of course. Jay and the Americans. Chubby Checker—you gotta love Chubby Checker because without him, we might not have the twist, right? The Shirelles can be good. Sam Cooke. Roy Orbison. In the right mood, I love Brook Benton's blues and James Brown. Or Pete Seeger, Woody Guthrie. Man, do you know Smokey Robinson and the Miracles? But I'm really getting into the Beatles. There's everything classic in their music. 'Love Me Do' is genius. They're going to be around forever. They're that deep. If I'm in the right frame of mind, I like the Drifters and Dylan too." I stopped talking. Jack and I could argue about music for hours. But maybe this was more than Ray wanted to know.

"I guess you really love music."

I nodded.

"And dancing," he added.

Did the whole world know about Jack and me dancing at the reservoir? On second thought, nobody else had said any-thing, not even Laura. Jack promised me those dances were a well-kept secret. "How did you know I like to dance?"

"I saw you. At the sock hop. After the Gallatin game last year?"

"The game where you scored two touchdowns," I reminded him.

"Don't change the subject. Where did you learn to dance?"

The whistle blew.

"Saved by the whistle." I hopped off the picnic table and pitched the remainder of my candy bar. "Thanks for the dinner company. I hate eating alone."

"Anytime."

Anytime? I walked away and hoped he couldn't tell how loud my heart was beating. I could almost hear it: *Second goal, second goal, second goal.*

"Hey, Tree!" Ray called after me.

I turned and kept walking backward.

"Did I tell you how good you look in that green swimsuit?"

I smiled and felt the heat rush to my head. Then I waved and jogged on in.

I would never take off my swimming suit. I would wear it rain or shine, dry or wet (even though wet suits are gross), for the rest of my life.

26

Hazy Crazy

It took me over an hour to finish replaying my seven minutes with Ray. I wandered around the basket room, forgetting if I was taking a basket or returning it. Sarah covered for me, for once.

Finally, I managed to turn my attention back to poor D.J. After all, he was the best boss I'd ever had. True, he was the only boss I'd ever had, if you didn't count my lawn-mowing or babysitting customers. Or the summer I counted pills for Dad.

D.J. could lose his job because of one ridiculous letter. The mighty power of the pen . . .

The rest of the day, as I took baskets and handed them back mindlessly, a funny thing happened inside my head. Rhymes formed all by themselves.

Dad and I had always loved to rhyme. When I went with him on house calls, we played rhyming games in the car. I'd give him a word and challenge him to come up with ten rhymes in twenty seconds. Or he'd make up the first line or two of a funny poem, and I'd have to come up with the next two lines. While he doctored his patient—I never got to go in with him, even in the freezing cold—I'd write it down. Dad had dozens of our poems stuffed into Buddy's glove compartment.

I thought about Penny's thank-you and how rare that was. And Sarah's question, "What are we, babysitters?" The Cozad kids were there as usual. And as I kept my eye on them, I imagined myself sitting in Laura's lifeguard chair.

And just like that, my rhymes took the form of a poem, "Ode to a Lifeguard."

In between baskets, I jotted down the lines, although I didn't need to. Rhymes stayed in my head forever. I probably could have repeated by heart every poem in Dad's glove compartment.

"Okay. What are you writing?" Sarah eyed the paper I'd been scrawling on.

"Probably nothing. But if it pans out, I'll make you guys copies. I'm hoping it will cheer D.J. up."

"He could use it. We all could."

"D.J. said he was the only one who could lose his job, though," I reminded her.

"Doesn't mean he's the only one who needs cheering up."

Something in the way Sarah said it made me look up. "What do you mean? Is something else wrong? Are *you* okay?"

She shrugged. "I don't know. I guess."

"Spill."

She wouldn't look at me. "I think . . . well, my dad's in money trouble."

"Farmers are all having a rough time. Most of Dad's patients are farmers. He says some are planting grains besides wheat and corn, hoping to turn a profit. Others are taking out loans to buy cattle or pigs." I knew it was a tough year because Mom and Dad still hadn't made plans for that new roof on our house, but the freezer overflowed with deer meat and the pickle shelf was full. I didn't tell Sarah this, though. I had no clue whether or not her dad's bills were stuffed into the unpaid-bill drawer of Dad's desk.

"But Dad's not trying anything new. He's not even plowing the back forty. And this giant yard sale I've been slaving for . . . It just doesn't feel right. Dad auctioned off his newest tractor last week. And there was a guy out to our place looking to buy a John Deere. *And* Dad put an ad in the paper offering to sell off his pigs, if the price is right."

"Did you ask him or your mom about it?"

She shook her head. "Wouldn't do any good. They don't tell me anything." She gave me a weak grin. "Maybe your new role as worrywart is rubbing off on me, Tree."

"Sure. Blame me. Everybody does."

We got busy all of a sudden. My mind flipped back to rhyme and stayed there until closing. By the time I left the pool, the entire poem was permanently etched inside my brain.

As I biked home, I recited my poem to the moon and the stars, imagining the day when I would be a lifeguard.

Ode to a Lifeguard
O woe is the life of a lifeguard who sits on her throne
    all day.

Noble is she who sits and stares while all around her play.
On her throne of steel and wood she sits to gaze away
At life below. Her sweating brow makes sure it stays
> *that way.*
And woe is the life of a basketgirl. Orders, she gets plenty!
Two said thank you. One said please. That's out of 120.
It hurts my heart whene'er I hear that someone is
> *not pleased.*
Unfair claims of "closing early" bring me to my knees.
I have sat wrapped in my towel on many a chilly night
Pitying children Mother left to get them out of sight.
I could continue in retort to words which made me bitter.
I'm a philosopher and noble guard . . . not a babysitter.

Soon as I got home, I typed it up on Dad's typewriter. I'd taught myself to type when I was nine—using all my fingers and not looking at the keys.

I had to redo it twice because of typos. But when I was finished, I read it over and felt pretty good about it. I wondered if Mrs. Woolsey would consider a poetry section in the *Blue and Gold.*

The next morning, I read my ode again. In the light of day, I hated it. How could I have thought about sharing it with D.J. and the pool gang? The line about the lifeguard making sure life stayed that way? Totally scurvy.

I must have been dumbstruck from seven minutes with Ray.

But reluctant to throw away even bad writing, I shoved it

into the game cupboard, where I stashed everything that didn't have a better place to go. At least I hadn't made a fool of myself by showing it to anybody.

Saturday afternoon, Penny was first in line when we opened the pool, so I had time to talk with her. During breaks, I'd go out, and we picked up where we'd left off. She'd seen Officer Duper's parking sign on the slide at the park, at the pitcher's mound at the ball field, and peeking through the window of the dentist's office.

No wonder Officer Duper didn't have time for me.

Penny laughed so hard when she reported the parking sign being found by the school janitor on the stage, standing at the microphone as if ready to give a speech, she could barely get her words out. And she cracked up when I told her some of Mrs. Kinney's weird facts—like that African elephants can swim twenty miles a day, using their trunks as snorkels. Or that the blue whale's belly button is eight inches wide.

I couldn't remember hearing Penny laugh at school. But it turned out that not only could she laugh, she could also make me laugh.

Still, even with all the talking we did, I felt she was only offering me the tip of the Penny iceberg. She could change the subject so fast, I wouldn't have time to figure out why. And even when we laughed together, she sometimes cut off the laughter as quickly as it started. She seemed to keep an eye on everybody who came near us. It was like she expected somebody to sneak up behind her every minute of her life and shout "Boo!"

"Don't look now," Penny whispered late in the afternoon, when I'd used my ten-minute break to work on my tan. We were sitting on her towel, facing opposite directions.

"Why?" I couldn't resist turning around.

I wished I had resisted. Wanda and Ray strolled in together.

"They might not have come together," Penny said. "She could have grabbed him in the parking lot."

"Why should I care?"

Penny didn't answer, and I felt like a dip for snapping at her.

"Yeah, you're right," I said. "She definitely grabbed him in the parking lot."

"I can see the claw marks on his arms," Penny added.

"Skid marks on the sidewalk."

"Poor Ray."

We laughed together.

Her laughter broke suddenly, and she scrambled to her feet. "I have to go."

I glanced at the pool clock. "I've got two more minutes of break, Pen. Don't leave me here alone. You can stay that long, can't you?"

"No." She tugged at her towel, the one I was sitting on. When it didn't come out from under me, she let it drop. "Keep it." Then she raced to the locker room, ignoring Laura's whistle.

Penny's stepbrother strutted up. It took me a second to recognize him. His long hair had been shaved to a crew cut.

"Fancy hairdo, Chuck," I said.

He ignored the comment and jerked his head in the direction of the disappearing Penny. "What scared the mouse?"

I didn't like the way he called Penny "Mouse" all the time. After a while, she probably started to feel like a mouse. "You got me. I don't know why Penny ran off like that."

He yawned and scoped out the pool area. "So, Tree . . ."

"That's my name. Don't wear it out." I laughed.

He didn't. "What were you and the mouse talking about?" His words came out covered in thick syrup, as if sliding out in their own time.

I shrugged.

"You two aren't talking about me behind my back, are you?" Chuck's smile looked forced to me. "Really, what were you talking about?"

I got to my feet and folded Penny's towel. "Nothing much. I'd better get back to work, Chuck."

"Work? I didn't know you worked here."

I nodded toward the basket room. "There. I'm a basketgirl." I'd never realized how silly that sounded. I handed him the towel. "Give this to Penny, okay?"

He jerked the towel from my hands, nearly toppling me. "All right, Tree the Basketgirl."

I walked away, with the eerie feeling that he was watching me.

Sarah was waiting when I got back to the basket room. "What were you talking about with Charles Atkinson? That *is* Penny's stepbrother, right?"

"Nothing. I just gave him Penny's towel. Did you see her split like the place was on fire?"

165

"I thought you said something that ticked her off. Maybe it was Charles. I don't think they like each other much. He's kind of creepy, don't you think? But he's awfully cute."

"I don't know."

"I think he has a crush on you, Tree."

"Gross, Sarah!" I threw a basket at her. "How about you work more and talk less?"

She grew quiet all of a sudden. She bit her lip and eased the basket into the right slot. People all around me were changing moods faster than a Missouri weatherman.

"Sorry I snapped," I said, taking the next basket.

"Doesn't matter," she muttered.

"Well, something's wrong," I said. "You've been acting kind of crazy all day. Is it the farm? Did you talk to your dad?" Maybe she and her family had worse money troubles than she thought.

Sarah shrugged and wouldn't turn to look at me.

"That does it!" I dragged her to the corner of the basket room.

"The baskets are going to pile up," she said, still not looking at me.

"Let 'em." I held on to her shoulders and waited for her to look up.

"Okay. After work yesterday, I went home to a store instead of a home."

"I don't get it."

"My parents had put tags on the furniture, Tree. Everything is up for sale today. Okay—not everything. Not the antique stuff Mom got from Grandma. But everything else.

166

When I left this morning, people were walking all through our house, buying lamps and junk. I know my parents really need money, but how are we going to watch TV without a couch?"

I did not like the sound of this at all. "You have to make them talk to you, Sarah."

"I tried. Believe me."

"What did they say?"

"The usual—that I didn't need to worry. But I kept pressing them until they promised to talk to me after the sale tonight. And they said I shouldn't talk to anybody about it until they've had a chance to explain things to me."

"Explain what?" I asked. "I don't get it. Half the town already knows about the yard sale."

"Exactly. So why am I supposed to keep things secret?" Sarah demanded.

I had no answers for her. "I don't know. But I think I hate secrets."

27

What's the Tale, Nightingale?

Sunday morning I made our whole family late to church. I wanted to keep sleeping so I wouldn't have to worry about Sarah. But I couldn't stop wondering how the big talk with her folks had gone. It would be hard to have to sell off your own furniture and belongings.

Finally, Eileen dragged me out of bed and practically stuck a dress on me, a stupid plaid I never would have worn if I'd been in my right mind.

Sarah was already in the Sunday School room when I got there. She hadn't saved me a seat next to her, and our teacher had already started talking. I'd have to wait until Sunday School was over to find out if she'd had the big talk with her parents.

The second our class ended, I rushed over to her. "Sarah, what did they say?"

She swallowed hard. "I'll tell you about it later. We're going to be late for church."

"There's no way I'm waiting until after church." Maybe *she* could wait, but *I* couldn't. By the end of the service, I'd be a basket case. I was already imagining a million awful reasons why her parents would put everything up for sale. Maybe something was wrong with Sarah, and they needed money for her . . . polio, tuberculosis, or leukemia—like Gary Lynch. Or maybe her parents were getting a divorce. Or her mom was pregnant, or—

Her eyes were red. I couldn't remember a single time when Sarah had cried. She claimed farmers never cried. Even when she broke her arm on the teeter-totter, she didn't shed a tear.

"Tell me! What's going on?"

Sarah took in a deep breath. "Dad sold the farm."

"What? He can't—"

"He and Mom finally told me last night. That's why they've been selling off everything. That's why they had the stupid sale."

Sarah loved the farm. I could not imagine her living in town . . . although I hated myself for imagining it right then. Sarah and me walking home together after school. No bus to catch. She could come to ball games and be on school committees.

"I know it will take some getting used to," I said. "But it won't be so bad. You might even come to like living in town. You and I can hang out more and—"

She frowned up at me then, her mouth a hard, straight line. "No, Tree. We're moving."

"I figured. But maybe you can find a house on our end of

town. Wouldn't that be cool?" I put my arm around her. "Pretty soon, we can drive ourselves to the country. It's not like the country won't be there, right?"

"Tree, you don't get it!" She jerked away from me. "We're moving. To Kansas."

"What? *Where?*"

"Kansas. Uncle Thomas, Mom's older brother, runs a hardware store in Iola, Kansas. Dad's going to work for him. They've got it all figured out. And they never even asked me."

"Kansas?" Of all the places in the world . . . We hated Kansas. We'd grown up hating Jayhawks. I knew more Jayhawk jokes than knock-knock jokes.

"They've known for months they were going to sell, and they never said a word. Even Mack knew. But they let *me* go on thinking I'd be coming back to school here. I guess I should have figured it out without them telling me. There were enough clues—not planting, selling off the tractor, stock. And the yard sale! I should have seen it coming."

Me too. Some investigative reporter I turned out to be. All I could do was shake my head. I'd be losing my best friend. I would never be as tight with any girlfriend as I was with Sarah. We'd grown up together, walked hand in hand into every classroom on the first day of school, celebrated every last day of school with chocolate ice cream and three cherries. I'd never missed a single one of Sarah's birthday parties, and she'd never missed one of mine. We trick-or-treated together every Halloween and hunted eggs every Easter. Sarah was too big a part of my life. She *couldn't* move away.

Eileen appeared and whispered, "You two. Mom says to come and sit down."

I slid into our pew, my regular seat. Sarah's family always took the pew behind us. All I could think about during the service was that Sarah wouldn't be there from now on. She'd be sitting in some strange pew in Kansas.

After church, two people cornered Dad for free medical advice. Then when we tried to leave, we couldn't get through the little congregation, still congregated outside on the lawn. People were pointing up and laughing.

There on the roof, propped against the steeple, stood the latest reserved parking spot for Hamilton police vehicles.

As soon as we got home and ate our traditional pancake lunch, I excused myself, grabbed my notebook, and headed outside to try to write. I wanted to record everything Sarah and I had ever done together.

Mom caught me at the door. "Hold on. I need you to run something down to Mrs. Kinney for me." She left, then came back with a folder of papers labeled "Federated Church Missionary Society." "Tell her this is the information about our projects for the steam engine show. She's welcome to attend our meetings too."

"Okay." I piled the folder on top of my journal and walked to the Kinney house.

Mrs. Kinney looked surprised when she opened the door. "Tree, can't say I was expecting you today, Sunday being a family day and all."

"I know." I handed her the file. "Mom asked me to give you this. She said it tells you what they're doing for the missionaries. And there's information about the Steam and Gas Engine Show too."

"Mighty thoughtful of your mother. Thank her for me."

She stood in the doorway, the screen held open by her elbow. "Would you like to come in a spell, Tree?"

I thought about it. Part of me did, and part of me didn't. "Thanks, but I was planning to write this afternoon." I patted the journal in my hand.

"Ah, then that's what you'd better do. I imagine writers need to write most when they're feeling the deepest. They can put their emotions on paper. I get the feeling something's bothering you."

"How'd you know, Mrs. Kinney?"

"It's written all over your face, Tree."

I grinned. "That's what Jack always says." The grin died on my lips. "Sarah, my best friend, is moving to Kansas. She told me in church this morning."

"Well, I'm right sorry about that. It's not easy losing a best friend."

Telling her about Sarah made it too real. My throat tightened, and I felt tears coming on. "Well, I'd better go."

I walked back home as far as the end of our property. Dad had anchored an old porch swing to the ground. I eased onto it, never positive the swing seat would hold. With a touch of my toe, I swung low in the shade of the willow. I closed my eyes and breathed in horse and strawberry atoms and tried not to think about the fact that my best girlfriend wouldn't be with me next year. I knew how moving away worked. You say you'll stay best friends. But letters stink. Phone calls are too expensive. And pretty soon you run out of things to talk about.

Midge barked at me from the backyard, but I couldn't let

her out. She'd want to sit on my lap. And if I shooed her off, she'd go hunt chickens. Finally, she wandered back into her dog palace—with windows put in by Dad, a rug donated by Mom, glamorous walls decorated by Eileen, and my best pillow for a bed.

A horn honked. I looked up expecting to see Jack whiz by in Fred.

Instead, a dark green pickup pulled up with Wayne Wilson behind the wheel. He stopped in front of me, took the cigarette from his mouth, and blew a string of smoke. His black hair was slicked back on both sides, forming a ducktail. Wayne had just turned sixteen and gotten his license. Already he had a reputation for drinking and smoking. But he'd always been okay to me.

"What's happening, Wayne?" I shouted.

He gave me a chin wave. "All is copacetic, Little Tree."

Ray Miller leaned forward. I hadn't seen him in the passenger seat. "What's happening with you, Tree?" he hollered past Wayne.

"Not too much," I answered.

"Heard you made the scene at the reservoir," Wayne said.

So much for the well-kept secret. "I guess."

"Heard you danced the socks off your elders." Wayne said this while taking another puff on his cigarette.

I sneaked a glance at Ray's face and could tell by his wrinkled brow that he had no idea what Wayne was talking about. I had to change the subject fast. "So what are you guys up to?"

"Just drivin' around." Wayne shoved up the sleeve of his black leather jacket and turned his wrist to check his watch. A chunk of gray ash fell to the ground. "I gotta split, though."

Ray and Wayne exchanged words I couldn't hear. Then Ray climbed out of the truck, and Wayne drove off, honking again.

When the dust settled, there stood Ray Miller, his dark hair windblown. He wore a cool madras plaid shirt with faded cutoffs and loafers, no socks. And he was standing in the middle of the road—*my* road—grinning at me.

28

Foxes

"Lost?" I called out to Ray, hoping my voice wouldn't shake the way the rest of me was.

"I just decided I didn't want to go where Wayne was headed," he answered.

"Should I ask?"

"Some things are best left unsaid." He hadn't moved from his spot in the road.

"You could get run over out there," I warned.

"That would stink."

I scooted over. "I can't guarantee this swing will hold us both. But I'm willing to risk it if you are."

Ray ambled over and sat beside me. "They don't call me Ray the Risk-Taker for nothing."

"So you pay them to call you Ray the Risk-Taker?" I breathed in his Ray-ness.

"Of course." He nodded at my notebook. "Don't tell me you're studying. Trying to get an edge on freshman year?"

"Not likely." I held the notebook to my chest so he couldn't see anything.

"What are you working on?"

I didn't answer right away. I could have said I was writing about Sarah, although I hadn't written a word yet. But I didn't want to talk about Sarah's horrible news with Ray. What if I broke down and cried like a baby?

Ray narrowed his sky-blue eyes at me. "Either tell me what you're writing or tell me what dance Wayne was talking about."

I chose the lesser of two evils. I spilled the whole story—about how I started out trying to write an article on the Kinney shooting, about my writers' quotes, about the interviews with Mrs. Kinney going nowhere, and how I'd promised Randy Ridings I'd have an article for him the day of the steam engine show. "Okay. Let me have it," I said when I was all done. "Go ahead—laugh." I braced myself. But I was afraid I'd burst into tears if he really did laugh at me.

"Why would I laugh? You're a good writer."

"How would you know?"

"Tree, I've known you since kindergarten, in case you forgot."

Like I'd ever forget anything about Ray Miller. "I really want to get on the *Blue and Gold* staff next year." The second I blurted it out, I wanted it back. *Wanda.* Ray and Wanda. Wanda said they'd talked about how "cute" it was of me to dream of being on the *Blue and Gold* staff. The last thing I needed was for Wanda to know I was still gunning for her job. "Don't tell . . . anyone . . . okay?"

"Okay. But I think you'd be great."

"You do?" *Great,* not *cute?* Was Wanda lying about that?

"Are you kidding? You're a natural! You should go for it, man. Is that why you're writing about the Kinneys?"

I nodded. "And for the *Hamiltonian* too, maybe. Randy said if I could get to the bottom of the Kinney story, he'd run it in the paper."

"Way to go, Tree."

"I don't know. It seemed pretty cool at first. But now that I'm getting to know Mrs. Kinney, I'm not so sure." I pictured her in her doorway, looking sad for me because I'm losing Sarah. "Mom says Mrs. Kinney has had a pretty hard life. I don't want to make it worse."

"Huh. I never thought about that."

"Me neither, until I started talking with her."

"You'll figure it out."

I doubted it. But the fact that he thought I would made me want to grab him and kiss him right there. "Thanks."

"You should write about the Steam and Gas Engine Show, Tree. Wayne's into old Model Ts and Model Rs with flywheels. He knows all about that sh—that stuff." He glanced over at the strawberry patch. "Is this your garden?"

"Dad's mostly. Mom's too."

"Your dad's a pretty all right guy, isn't he?" Ray gazed around and seemed to take in more than strawberries.

"He's pretty cool . . . for a dad."

"I've been in Doc's office a few times."

"You should always get your shots from my mom if you get a chance. She's painless."

He grinned. And, man, did he have a great grin close-up like that.

"Wayne needs to go to your dad's. Doc got *me* to stop smoking."

"You smoked?" Soon as I said it, I wanted another chance for a first reaction. I'd sounded like he'd just told me he used to be an ax murderer. "I mean, so you used to smoke, huh? What did Dad say to make you quit?"

"That's just it. Nothing."

"I don't get it." I shifted on the swing. The metal clinked and squawked, then settled.

"I had to get a physical so I could play football. So your dad takes his stethoscope thingy and listens to my heart. When he slides the earpieces down around his neck, he frowns, all intense. I'm freaking out. 'What, Doc? What's wrong?' He doesn't answer. He takes my wrist and, like, checks my pulse. When he's done, he shakes his head. I'm begging for him to shoot straight, to give me the honest truth on what's wrong with me, right? But he doesn't say a word. He listens to my heart one more time and asks, 'You don't smoke, do you, Ray?'

"Of course, I deny it all over the place. I'd only started smoking a couple of weeks earlier. I couldn't believe smoking had already hurt my heart so much that Doc could pick up on it."

"What did he say when you said you didn't smoke?"

"He looked all puzzled and troubled and told me to be sure I never took up cigarettes. But I'm telling you, I never touched another smoke after I left the office that day. It was about six months later I got to talking to Eric—you know Eric. He's a junior. Probably going to be quarterback this year."

I nodded.

"Eric said the same thing happened to him. Then he realized he'd gone into Doc's with a pack of Lucky Strikes rolled up in his shirtsleeve. So did I! Doc saw it and played it just right from there."

"Okay. Just so you know, he's not really my father. The gypsies left me on their doorstep thirteen years ago."

"Are you kidding?" Ray shoulder-bumped me. "That was about the coolest thing any parent ever did. You lucked out getting Doc for a dad."

I realized that I didn't know a thing about Ray's parents, which was pretty strange. I could have told you what almost everybody's dad did. My dad probably knew him. Dad knew everybody. Or at least, everybody knew him. "What does your dad do?"

Ray stopped smiling. "Drinks."

I wished I hadn't asked.

He leaned down and picked a gone-to-seed dandelion. He handed it to me with a big smile. The dandelion was perfectly round, with all the white fuzzy parts intact.

"For me? How totally groovy!" I said it sarcastically. But I also meant it. Ray Miller had given me a flower—yes, gone to seed, but still. I took a deep breath and blew until all the fuzz was gone.

"Did you make a wish?"

"I forgot. Is it too late?"

He slid a little closer. "It's never too late to wish, Tree."

"Tree!"

Ray and I scooted apart as if we'd been making out in broad daylight.

"That's Eileen, my sister," I explained, as if everybody didn't know her.

He turned to the doorway, where Eileen stood in her white short shorts and pink top. "Eileen is a fox," Ray muttered.

Here I'd been thinking that, maybe, a guy was actually starting to be interested in me, not my sister. "She's going steady with Butch," I snapped, sharper than I meant to.

"Butch is a mover—I hear he gets around, if you know what I mean. Have you seen that Caddy he drives?"

I shrugged.

"Besides, you didn't let me finish. I was going to say that Eileen is a fox, but not as foxy as her sister."

"Tree! I mean it! Dinner is ready. Mom says to get in here right now!" Eileen had a big fat mouth.

"Flake off, Eileen!" I shouted back, knowing I'd pay for it later, but not caring one little bit.

Ray stood up. "I gotta split. I'm unloading crates tonight."

"That's a drag and a half. On a Sunday night?" I felt the weight of unfair humanity bearing down on Ray, the guy who had called me foxier than my sister. I was ready to take on the cruel world single-handed.

"That's when the trucks come in. Anyway, you better go too. Later?"

"Later." But my heart was screaming, *Sooner is much better than later! Goal Number Two can't wait much longer.*

29
Lay It on Me

It was our turn to go to the Adamses' house, but they came to ours instead because they were varnishing their basement, where the piano was, and the fumes might have killed the musical quartet.

It didn't take the fabulous four long to get going with their unique version of "It Had to Be You," followed by "Stardust." They weren't that bad. And when they lit into "String of Pearls," Jack and I had to jump up from our game of Wahoo and dance.

"You two," Eileen scolded, like she was the adult. "Do you have to dance all the time?"

"We do," Jack answered.

But having her ask about dancing reminded me that I hadn't told her about seeing Butch and Laura dancing together, and at the pool.

I could tell Jack knew what I was thinking. He shook his head, but I couldn't keep this secret from my own sister.

"Eileen, what if you found out something . . . bad . . . about Butch?"

She eyed me like I'd eaten the grapes off the wallpaper. "That's a dumb question. I know everything I need to know about Butch, including the fact that he's coming by for me any minute. He knows everything about me too. That's the way it works when you're in love. You're honest with each other."

"Right, right. I have no doubts you're honest with him." Although I'd have been shocked if she'd told him about that Liquid Sunshine bottle in her wastebasket. "But what if you heard he wasn't so honest with you?"

"I'd know someone made it up out of petty jealousy."

"But what if they had evidence—like, that he was seeing someone behind your back?" I cringed, expecting Eileen to topple the table, then bite my head off.

She advanced her marble on the Wahoo board before smiling over at me like a patient aunt with a screw-loose niece. "Your turn, Tree. Oh, and as for your little hypothetical, I'd remind you that what we don't know doesn't hurt us, and people should mind their own business. Are you going to play or not?"

She knew.

Eileen knew that her supposed steady was cheating on her! It wasn't a secret at all. Did he know she knew? Did she know he knew she knew? My head grew dizzy with questions.

I managed to take my turn, but I couldn't think straight. When did the truth matter, and when didn't it? I could almost understand why Eileen made Dad keep her weight secret. Or how I knew better than to mention Eileen's bottle-blond hair. Mom and Dad had secrets too. Dad hated Mom's chili, but pretended to like it. Mom smoked in the bathroom, and he pretended not to know.

But how could my sister be okay pretending not to know that Butch cheated on her?

A horn honked.

"Butch!" Eileen checked herself in the mirror and dashed out the door.

Jack and I followed, even though she tried to close the front door on us.

Butch stayed behind the wheel but waved to Jack. "Hey."

"Hey, yourself," I muttered.

I guess you could call Butch decent-looking—big brown eyes (not as big as Jack's), lean build (no muscles to match Ray's). Eileen got in his Caddy and scooted as close to him as was humanly possible. When he put his arm around her, I went back into the house.

Jack and I cleaned up the Wahoo game. I gathered marbles while Jack folded the board and put it back into the box.

He walked the game over to the game closet. "Top shelf?"

"Right." I folded the card table and slid it into the hall closet.

Jack called from the living room, "Tree, what's this?"

He held up my typed poem, "Ode to a Lifeguard."

"I forgot about that. It's just something I wrote after that woman complained that we closed the pool early."

"So can I read it?" He looked like he was already reading it.

I shrugged. "I don't care. It's pretty awful, though. Then let's go outside. I want to see if Cassiopeia shows up tonight." I waited at the door while Jack finished my silly poem.

"I really dig this, Tree. Did you show it to D.J.? I was afraid they'd bump him from being manager after that letter got printed. The woman sure did a number on him."

"I know. It really shook him up. I'm hoping things have blown over. And no, I didn't show the poem to D.J. or anybody else. It's not any good. It sounds like those rhymes what's-his-name makes up before a big fight."

"Cassius Clay, that boxer?"

"Yeah. He's pretty full of himself."

"Bragging in rhyme is great PR," Jack said. "Nobody would know who he is if he didn't drive them crazy with those rhymes of his—'I'll battle and rattle his bones.'"

"Well, this ode sounds like his crazy rhymes."

"Are you kidding? This is classic!" Jack insisted.

Jack wasn't the best judge of writing. Music, yes. Writing, no.

"The band's stopped playing. You'll have to go pretty soon. Let's get outside."

Not only was Cassiopeia clear as could be, but the Milky Way striped the night like a carpet of stars. We walked across the road to get away from the lights shining through the windows. Crickets and cicadas were singing. Lightning bugs flirted with each other. A dog barked so far away I couldn't tell whose dog it was.

"I could never live in a city, could you?" I asked.

Jack took his sweet time answering. "I could if I had to. But I know what you mean, Tree. I'd miss this."

I stared up the road, where the Kinney house lay in darkness. I couldn't make out the shape, but it didn't seem scary now. I didn't miss Old Man Kinney frowning down from the porch. "Jack?"

"Hmm?"

"I think I need to talk to you about something. But you have to promise not to say anything about it."

"Do I ever, Tree?"

I knew I could trust Jack. But I wanted to make sure this wasn't the Butch-and-Laura kind of secret that people just pretended to keep secret.

Jack must have sensed I needed more from him. "I won't say anything if you don't want me to. What's up?"

"It's about the Kinneys."

Jack didn't jump in and ask questions. He waited on me.

"That morning, when the gun went off, I was there."

"You were there?" he said, too loud.

"Shh! Not *there* there. I was outside, here, trying to write. I heard the gun go off. It sounded so close."

"Man, Tree! Were you scared?"

"I didn't have a chance to be scared. Next thing I knew, Dad came tearing out of the house. He ran up the road and told me to stay put."

"Which you didn't." It wasn't a question. Jack knew me.

"Which I didn't. Dad didn't see me follow him, but he knows now. It was a pretty bad scene when I told him."

"I can imagine. Could you . . . did you see anything?"

"Not inside the Kinney house. Not where the gun went off. . . . But I could see Dad and Mrs. Kinney on the porch."

"Go on."

"Right after Dad got there, Mrs. Kinney stood in the doorway of the house. Dad was at the bottom of the steps, staring up. Then she came out on the porch carrying that rifle and—"

"Wait a minute. Mrs. Kinney was carrying the rifle? Tree, are you sure?"

I gave him a look that said I was sure, all right. "Dad turned his back on her and sat down on the top step. I was scared to death she'd shoot him in the back."

I felt Jack's big hand on top of my head. I couldn't see his face, just a shadow, like a silhouette. But it felt safe having his hand there.

"She sat down next to Dad. They sat on the step together, staring straight ahead. It was creepy."

"I'll bet," Jack muttered.

"Dad went and looked inside the house, then came back out and sat beside her." I stopped then. Jack had grown so intense—his body stiff, his gaze never leaving my face—that I started to get nervous. I'd always been able to trust Jack. But he was older than me. And sometimes older people thought they had to go back on their word and talk to parents. Eileen did it all the time.

"Tree, why did you stop? What aren't you telling me?"

"I don't know," I said, backtracking. "Maybe I imagined some of this."

"I know you, Tree. You imagine plenty. But you didn't imagine this."

"Well, you can't tell anyone, Jack." I looked up at him and wondered if he could see my face any better than I could see his. The moon was down to a sliver, so the only light came from stars.

"I said so, didn't I?"

We were quiet for a while. Then I went on. "Right before Sheriff Robinson showed up, Dad slid the rifle out of Mrs. Kinney's hands."

"You're sure?" Jack asked. "He did that before the sheriff got there?"

I nodded. "Then when the sheriff came, and after he took his own look inside the house and talked to Mr. Kinney, who screamed at him, he asked Dad what they ought to do about it. And Dad said, 'Accidents happen.' Only the deal is, Jack . . ." I took a breath, then let it out. "I don't think that shooting was an accident. And I'm pretty sure *Mrs.* Kinney did the shooting."

Jack waited.

"I told Randy Ridings I'd get to the truth and write it all up for him before the steam engine show. I promised. And he said he'd publish *my* article in the *Hamiltonian*. Only now, I'm getting to know Mrs. Kinney a little, and I don't know. I don't know what I'm going to do."

"Did Mrs. Kinney tell you she shot her husband on purpose?"

I shook my head. "But I didn't ask her."

I still couldn't see his face that well, but I could tell he wasn't shocked by anything I'd said. Eileen would have been. She'd have been horrified. Mom too. They'd both have been furious with me for going behind Dad's back and then as much as calling him a liar.

And still, Jack didn't say anything.

Finally, I was the one to break the silence. "Jack, I think my dad got it wrong . . . on purpose."

30
Heavy

Jack and I traipsed back to the house. I hadn't planned on talking to him about Mrs. Kinney, but I felt better for it.

When we opened the front door, I heard shouting coming from the kitchen.

"Frank, you don't know what you're talking about!" Bob Adams said.

Jack and I exchanged frowns. Our parents never argued. Well, maybe about whether Glenn Miller was better than Tommy Dorsey or whether the Cards could win the Series. But never like this. Besides, Bob Adams was the most easygoing man I knew. He didn't say much—maybe a result of having Donna for a wife. And when he did talk, he always sounded like he was finishing up a joke you just missed.

"Come on, boys," Mom pleaded. I could tell she was trying to smooth things over, like she did when Eileen and I fought.

"You're naive!" Bob insisted. "If we really are sending our

boys over to Southeast Asia, then there's a dang good reason for it and—"

"*If?*" Dad cut him off. "Open your eyes, Bob! We *are* sending soldiers. And we're dropping bombs on innocent people!"

"Innocent?" Bob fired back. "They're all Commies over there! If we let them take over Vietnam, other countries will fall like dominoes."

"Who made us the world's policeman?" Dad demanded.

"Somebody's got to be!"

Dad said something I couldn't catch.

But Bob wouldn't let him finish. "The whole thing will be over in two years, tops. McNamara says we're winning. You want us to quit? Americans aren't quitters. At least *I'm* not!"

"Bob!" Donna finally took over. "I've had enough out of you two. You should be ashamed." She kept talking, and at least it stopped Bob and my dad from continuing their shouting match.

It shook me up to hear our dads so angry. I whispered to Jack, "Why are they fighting? They never argue."

"This is different, Tree," Jack said quietly, like he was listening for more rants from the kitchen. "Vietnam matters."

Jack cared about what went on in Vietnam? "You've never said a word to me about Vietnam."

"I didn't say anything because I didn't want to argue with you. I figured you thought the same way your dad does about Vietnam."

"But why do they care so much? Why do *you*? It doesn't really have anything to do with us, does it?"

"Yeah, it does, Tree!" With that, he left me and headed for the kitchen.

But Bob was already storming out, aiming for our front door.

"Bob, please," Mom pleaded. "Don't go like this."

"Let him go, Helen." Dad stayed where he was.

Mom and Donna trailed after Jack's dad, trying to get him back, have another drink, play another song.

"Bob! You're acting like a little boy!" Donna must have given up pretending that she could fix everything. She tied her net scarf around her head and tucked sheet music under one arm.

Bob didn't stop or turn around. Without a word, he brushed past Jack and me. His cheeks were the color of cherry Kool-Aid. I was afraid he'd have a heart attack.

Jack ran outside after his dad.

Donna stood in the doorway a few seconds, watching them. Then she turned to Mom and shook her head. "Boys . . . they can act like two-year-olds. It'll be all right. I'll talk to Bob. Don't worry. He'll be fine. Then no more politics!" She stomped out to their car, where Jack and his dad were loaded and ready to go.

"Well, that was fun." Mom turned to Dad, who'd crept out into the hall. "I'm going to bed, Frank. Are you coming?" It wasn't a warm invitation.

Dad passed. "Not yet. I've got something I want to work on."

"Another letter to our senators?" Mom sounded like she was accusing him of something, though I couldn't imagine what. I thought it was great that Dad wrote to our senators. And not just senators. He'd written every president since FDR, sometimes to congratulate them on a vote that helped put people to work on roads and highways or to encourage them to vote no on funding things he didn't like.

"Get to bed, Tree," Mom said.

She disappeared before I could argue with her.

Dad headed for his den, but I stopped him. I didn't care if he was still mad at me. "Dad, what's it really about? Vietnam? Are we going to war?"

He frowned at me. "War? Yes, I think we're getting there, Tree. And it's a war we can't win. Even if we win it, we won't be proud of ourselves. It's not like Germany attacking and taking over the world and us getting in to help our allies. Bob's right about one thing. It's tough to quit. And I'd hate to see Communism spread. But this is a civil war, and we're trying to worm our way in where we don't belong."

He changed directions and plopped onto the couch. Mom and Eileen had picked it out, and it was fancy, but not very comfortable. I sat beside Dad. He and I had done a lot of talking on that couch. Only not so much lately.

He slumped, resting his head on the back of the sofa. "I get so tired trying to talk to people who think I'm un-American just because I don't want to see our boys die over there."

I hated to think anybody would consider my dad un-American.

He squinted up at our beige ceiling, streaked with shadows from the single light still on. "Do you want to know what the newspaper said on Friday, when four U.S. *advisors* were killed near Saigon?"

I nodded.

"'Over twenty of the enemy were killed, and our casualties were light today.' What does that even mean? 'Light'? I'll bet it didn't feel *light* to those four families. Or to the Vietnamese families, either. And even that tiny report was buried on page thirteen."

"But why, Dad? Why would we go there if we don't have to?" I really wanted to know. It had to be important to make my dad fight with his best friend, to keep Jack from even mentioning it to me.

"People are afraid," he answered at last. "They're afraid of Communism, especially after finding those missiles in Cuba pointed at us. And there's no doubt about it, Tree. Communism is nasty business. If Communists ever attack us, I'll lie about my age and sign up to fight for America.

"Only that's not what's going on in Vietnam. The Vietnamese are fighting themselves, and we have no idea who to support. But that doesn't stop us from sending bombs and weapons. It'll take decades for that country to recover." He looked down at me, his face tired and saggy. "I'm afraid you're going to be hearing more about Vietnam, honey. A lot more." He got up.

"Are you going to bed?" I wanted him to stay and talk to me longer. It felt like the cold war between us had thawed. Did I have Vietnam to thank for that?

"No. I can't sleep yet. I need to *do* something. Talking isn't getting me anywhere. I can't get anybody around here to listen—except you, of course." He almost smiled, but his lips wouldn't turn up. "So I'm taking a page from your playbook: I'm going to write."

A stream of warmth shot through me like hot chocolate on a snow day.

Dad had always written—not only letters to politicians but also poems for our birthdays and funny Christmas letters. He was secretary for the American Medical Association in Missouri, and they kept reelecting him because his reports were the only things worth reading in their newsletters.

But he said he was taking a page from *my* playbook. Like *I* was the family writer.

After Dad left, Eileen got home from her date and went straight to bed. She'd missed the whole fight. To make things worse, Midge chose to follow Eileen and sleep at the foot of her bed. The traitor.

Any other time, I'd have called Jack to see what he thought about everything. But something kept me from doing that.

I finally dragged myself to bed, where I found another typed note waiting for me. It would have been so great if whatever words I was about to read would answer every question, solve every problem. But I knew better. I unfolded the paper and read:

```
Nothing weighs on us so heavily as a
secret. -Jean de La Fontaine
```

Now that was the truth. I wondered which of my many secrets Jack was thinking of when he copied the quote. But my brain felt too tired to work it out.

I clicked off my light and crawled between the sheets, but I couldn't sleep. My mind refused to shut down. It had felt great having Dad talk to me as if we'd never fought. But I couldn't get over seeing him fight with his best friend.

My thoughts turned to *my* best friends. Sarah wasn't mad at me, but she was leaving me anyway. We'd been best school friends our whole lives. And now she'd be in Kansas.

And what about Jack? He wasn't mad at me, either. But he'd sided with his dad, and I'd sided with mine. What if Vietnam got in the way of *our* friendship? The thought made me hate that whole country for stirring up things here in Missouri.

And talking with Jack had helped, but it sure hadn't solved the problem of what would happen to Mrs. Kinney if I wrote the truth about her. Or what would happen to me if I didn't.

Then there was Penny. I really liked talking with her, but she was so skittish, so secretive.

My mind even traveled to the Lynches and the Quiet House, filled with dragons and pain.

The only bright spot in my whole week had been Ray. So I closed my eyes and pictured Ray and me sitting on the swing, talking and laughing. It wasn't much to hold on to. But as I lay on my bed alone and in the dark, it was about all I had.

31
Kind-of Friends

When Penny didn't show up at the pool on Monday, my new worrywart nature set in. The way she'd lit out when she saw Chuck the other day—something hadn't felt right. I was pretty sure she and Karen weren't close, either. As far as I knew, Penny didn't have a single friend . . . except maybe me.

After I got off work, I went straight to Mrs. Kinney's. I didn't plan on asking her any of the questions on my list, and I wasn't really sure why I wanted to go there. I just did.

"What's on your mind, Bo Peep?"

We'd settled into our chairs with our nutmeg hot chocolates.

"Bo Peep?"

"Well, you look like you lost your sheep and don't know where to find them."

I supposed she was right about that. "I guess I'm still upset about losing Sarah. We've been best friends since we were babies, Mrs. Kinney. Her dad sold their farm without even telling her. And *Kansas!* How can they move to Kansas?"

"That's a real shame." She sounded like she meant it, like she understood.

"Did you ever have a best friend?" I asked.

She sighed. "Once. Leastwise, I thought she was a best friend. Seems kind of silly now. But I remember how it was, like the whole world crumbled."

"What happened?"

She rocked a few times in her rocker before going on. "Arlene. Lived next door. Well, the farm next door, anyways. Didn't have no kindergarten like you got now. If I got my chores done, I'd walk to Arlene's, and we'd play. My, we used to laugh. Made mud pies, like the DeShon boys 'cross the street. Jumped in mounds of hay. Or just roamed the hills together."

"That sounds like fun. Sarah and I used to jump from the barn loft into a giant haystack." I tried to imagine Mrs. Kinney and Arlene jumping with Sarah and me. It made a funny picture. "What happened to Arlene?"

"School. Come time for fourth grade to start, and Arlene, she changed, I reckon." Mrs. Kinney stopped, and her gaze went past me and on to something I couldn't see. "That first day, I sought her out to sit next to, being's how we always did sit together." She shook her head. "Arlene acted like she had no idea who I was."

For a minute, I thought Mrs. Kinney might have forgotten I was there. She kept staring out into space.

I cleared my throat. "That was mean of Arlene." I wanted

to say more. I could see the hurt still there after so many years, fresh enough to make her eyes water.

She shifted in her rocker and brushed imaginary dust from her skirt. "Well, Bo Peep, is Sarah the only one troubling you today?"

I wondered how she knew. I had a whole flock of sheep bothering me, including Mrs. Kinney herself and the article I was supposed to write about her. But Penny was at the top of my "lost sheep" list. "Okay. There's this girl at the pool."

"Giving you trouble, is she?"

"No. Not like that. But there *is* one like that," I added.

"Wanda." It wasn't a question.

"Yeah. But this is a different girl and a different story."

I noticed the tiny whipped-cream mustache on her lip. I pointed to my lip, and she got the signal and used her napkin.

"So this other gal, she a friend of yours?"

"Kind of, I guess. She's in my class and comes to the pool. She and her brother and sister have come over to hang out with Jack and me a few times. But I can't shake the feeling that something's wrong. Like she's scared all the time and filled with secrets."

"This gal got a name?"

"Penny. Penny Atkinson."

"I know of her. Seen her in the hardware store when I was there with Alfred. At the library, time to time."

"She said she'd seen you before." I stopped there and didn't add the part about how Penny had said Mrs. Kinney did whatever Mr. Kinney wanted. "Thing is, I'm kind of her only friend, and I'm not much of a friend."

"That must happen to you a good bit, being a kind-of only friend." She grinned, and I thought she was saying that I was *her* kind-of only friend.

I smiled back. I couldn't imagine being her only friend, though. "What about your neighbors, Mrs. Kinney? You've got Mrs. Overstreet." I would have guessed that Mrs. Overstreet dropped by all the time. She sure did at our house. Once, after Mrs. Overstreet's fourth "emergency" visit to our house that day, Dad explained to Eileen and me that Mrs. Overstreet was a hypochondriac. Eileen happily informed me that meant Mrs. O. only thought she was sick. Mom and Dad were afraid to play croquet after dinner because Mrs. Overstreet might spot them and waddle up for a talk about her latest ailment. Dad believed Mrs. Overstreet would send him to an early grave, while going on to live to be a hundred herself.

Mrs. Kinney sighed. "I don't think Mrs. Overstreet considers me a friend. She still thinks of me as the little waif in the back row of her eighth-grade English class. She likely remembers how I used to read books during her lectures, instead of listening to her."

"I'll bet she's forgotten all that," I said.

Mrs. Kinney shook her head. "It doesn't appear she's forgotten a lick of it."

"Then amnesia must be the only ailment she doesn't suffer from."

We both chuckled a little.

I tried to think of her other neighbors. Probably not the DeShons. "What about Gary and Mrs. Lynch?"

"Gary? That poor boy. Can't say I've had the pleasure of

his acquaintance, though I've thought on him quite a bit. On my downest days, I remember that young'un, who can't never get out and see the world. Oh, not that I've seen much more. But I travel in my mind." There was a glint in her eyes, like a candle being lit.

"My dad said I should think about Gary when I start complaining."

"And do you?"

"Not enough," I admitted.

"But you done thought about this Penny?"

"I guess. We talk at the pool. I've even talked to Penny about you."

Her expression flattened. "Have you, now?"

"Just that you and I have been getting to be friends," I added quickly. "You'd like her. I think she'd like to meet you." It was just something to say. Penny and I had talked about Mrs. Kinney, but neither of us ever talked about Penny meeting her.

"Can't imagine why she'd want to meet me," Mrs. Kinney said. "But I guess I don't see how it's a problem if one kind-of friend meets up with another kind-of friend. Bring her by next time. I've got plenty of nutmeg."

As I said goodbye, I was already imagining getting the two quietest people I knew together. And as I walked down the Kinney porch steps, I wondered what I'd gotten myself into.

32
Time Travel

Penny didn't show up the next day, and I still hadn't heard from Jack since the Vietnam argument.

Mrs. Lynch surprised us by coming to the pool—without Gary, of course. It was only the second time I'd seen her there. "Hey, Mrs. Lynch!" I called.

"Hello, Tree. My mother's in town for the day, so I thought I'd take advantage and show my support for my swimming pool."

"That's nice of you. How's Gary?"

She grinned. "Thanks for asking, sweetheart. Did you know my boy will be turning nine on Thursday?"

"Well, tell him happy birthday for me. Are you having a birthday party for him?"

The smile disappeared. "I wish I could. Gary's condition makes him catch every germ any visitor might carry without even knowing it. But I'll bake him a cake. And I wouldn't be surprised if he gets another visit from his Secret Dragon."

I remembered what Dad said about Gary loving dragons. "He has a Secret Dragon?"

"He does. For about a year now, somebody has been dropping off a dragon every now and then—a toy, a book about dragons, a T-shirt with a dragon on it."

"Who is it?"

"Wish I knew. I'd like to thank him." She squinted sideways at me. "Don't suppose you've caught your daddy with a stuffed dragon in his pocket? He's high on my suspect list."

"Can't say as I have." But it would have been like my dad.

Mrs. Lynch didn't stay long, but she spent the whole time swimming, not sunning.

I thought about the Secret Dragon. It was kind of nice knowing about a good secret for a change.

That night, before I could change my mind, I called Penny. Someone picked up after the fifth ring.

"Hello?"

"Hi. This is Tree Taylor. Is Penny home?"

"Yeah."

"Could I talk to her, please?"

"Yeah." There was the hint of a laugh.

"Is that you, Penny?"

"Yeah."

Great. Another one-way call. "So I get a chatty conversation, like the last time I called you?"

"Yeah."

"Thought I'd see you at the pool today."

"Didn't feel like swimming," she said.

"Okay. Well, I had this idea. And you might not feel like doing it, either. But you know Mrs. Kinney, right? I told you I've been visiting her. Turns out she's really nice. But lonely. And I'm the only one who visits her. . . . Are you still there?"

"Yeah."

"So I was thinking, maybe you'd like to go see her with me tomorrow? I get off early. We could meet up at the pool. Or at my house. She'd really like to meet you." That part was a stretch, but I was pretty much talking to myself anyway.

"Yeah. Okay."

"Yeah? You'll come? I get off at three. Will that work?"

"Yeah."

We said goodbye. At least I did. Then I went to sleep, wondering again what I was getting myself into.

The next day Penny didn't come to the pool, so I figured she must have finked out on me. But when I got home, she was waiting outside. We walked straight to Mrs. Kinney's and knocked.

Mrs. Kinney opened the door, wide this time. "Hope you don't mind hot chocolate in the summertime, Penny," she said.

She'd dragged out another chair from somewhere, but Penny took the couch. For a few minutes, the only sounds in the room were our slurpings as we drank our hot chocolate.

I tried starting a conversation about swimming. I tried talking about the steam engine show. But I ended up talking to myself.

"So," I tried again, "guess who I saw at the pool yesterday."

They didn't guess.

"Mrs. Lynch. Gary's mother."

"Ah," Penny said.

"That poor young'un," Mrs. Kinney said.

"She said Gary's birthday is tomorrow. He can't even have a party because kids would give him germs. That's why he can't go anywhere, either."

"Now, that's a real sadness," Mrs. Kinney declared.

I tried leaning back in my chair, but the chair had no lean to it. "I wish we could do something for Gary. Maybe we could come up with something to give him for his birthday."

"We could give him books?" Penny ventured.

"Great idea!" I exclaimed, a little overly enthusiastic because she had actually said more than two words. "Only I don't know how much he can read."

"Maybe his ma reads to him," Mrs. Kinney said.

"Right!" I said. "But she works from home. I'm not sure what she does, but Dad says she works all the time when she's not seeing to Gary."

"I'll bet he's got a good mind," Mrs. Kinney said.

Now I clammed up because I didn't know where she was going with that one.

But from the look on Penny's face, she understood what Mrs. Kinney meant. "You're right. When all you can do is live inside yourself, your mind has to get big enough to handle it."

Mrs. Kinney nodded. "Yep. That's what I'm saying. I go all sorts of places in my own head. I hope that little fella can travel inside his."

"Then that's it," Penny said.

"I reckon you're right, Penny," Mrs. Kinney agreed.

"Wait—you've lost me," I said.

"Mind travel," Mrs. Kinney explained. "We'll make it so Gary can travel in his mind."

From there, we tossed out ideas like crazy, popping them off right and left. Mrs. Kinney may have moved like a turtle, but her mind hopped like a hare. She came up with five ideas to every one of mine.

We finally settled on getting Gary to Camelot, where King Arthur and the Knights of the Round Table—and plenty of dragons—lived.

"His birthday is tomorrow," I said, wondering if we really could pull off this plan. "Eileen saw a musical called *Camelot* at the Kansas City playhouse, but there isn't a city called Camelot, right?"

"I got pictures of Essex in England and Cadbury Castle in Somerset," Mrs. Kinney offered. "That's as close as we'll get to what them Arthur legends talk about. Only my pictures are mostly tore from magazines. I wish they was bigger."

"We can make them bigger," Penny said.

"How?" I asked.

"If we had poster board, I can copy from a magazine picture. Then we can color it in. I could start now if we had everything."

"I can write up some of my facts on that area," Mrs. Kinney said. "I suppose Gary's mama could give everything to the boy, let his mind do the rest."

I stood up. "I'll go get poster boards and markers right

now. And I can stop by Dad's waiting room and see if any of the magazines have anything we can use."

"Penny and I will get started here. Tree, you go and hurry back, now."

I found markers at home and took time to call Jack to tell him what we were doing. He had to work or he would have come to help too. Then I biked to town for poster board. I bought six, which was all I could balance on my bike basket. Then I stopped by the office and flipped through old magazines. I found stuff about England and castles in two *Look*s and also the newest issue of *Life*.

On the way back, I passed the *Hamiltonian* office. Randy was smoking out in front. I gave him a chin wave because my hands were full with my overflowing bike load.

"How's that article coming along, Tree?" he called.

I pretended not to hear. I didn't want to think about it. Not now.

He hollered something else to me. It sounded like, "You'll get me in hot water one way or the other!" But I was already too far past him to ask what he meant.

When I got back to Mrs. Kinney's, I knocked and heard her shout, "Come on in!" She and Penny were down on the floor, Mrs. Kinney printing facts about dragons and Penny drawing dragons and castles.

The three of us worked the rest of the afternoon and through the evening. I ran home and brought back sandwiches for us. Mrs. Kinney and I colored in Penny's pictures, which were so good.

"Penny, these are even better than the magazine photos," I told her.

"Anybody can copy," she said.

"I sure can't," Mrs. Kinney said.

"It's getting dark," I said, stretching out my cramped back muscles. If I was this stiff, I could only imagine how Mrs. Kinney's back felt. "We'll have to finish up tomorrow morning before I go in for work."

Mom and I drove Penny home, and on the way, Penny and I took turns describing our birthday project.

"I think this is wonderful, girls. You should be very proud of yourselves," Mom said.

"It was Mrs. Kinney's idea," Penny explained.

"Well, she should be proud too."

Mom didn't ask Penny for directions to her house. Unlike Dad, Mom always seemed to know where she was going.

"You should hear some of Mrs. Kinney's weird facts about dragons, Mrs. Taylor," Penny said. "The English dragons were supposed to be fire-breathing and mean. But Chinese dragons were wise."

"I'm giving Gary that book about King Arthur, the one Aunt Vin sent me last year," I said. "The only thing we're missing is music. Eileen bought the forty-five of 'Puff the Magic Dragon' last month. You think she'd let me borrow it and her portable record player tomorrow?"

"I'll just bet she would," Mom said.

Mom proved to be right. Eileen gave us her blessing and her record player, along with "Puff the Magic Dragon." Mom called Mrs. Lynch and worked out the details. Mrs. Kinney, Penny, and I finished everything by noon, but we still had to deliver our gift. So I called D.J., and he said I could come in late. He didn't expect a crowd because storm clouds threatened pouring rain at any minute.

We must have looked like an odd trio walking to Gary's dark house. I carried Eileen's precious record player, with "Puff" ready to go. Penny and Mrs. Kinney were loaded down with posters and sheets of fun facts about dragons and Camelot.

Penny rang the bell with her nose and got a classic *dingdong* in return.

The second Mrs. Lynch opened the door and saw us, tears burst out of her. "This is . . . well, it's beautiful. I can't believe you went to so much trouble. I will never forget this. And neither will Gary."

We helped her get everything inside, but we didn't go in.

"Did Gary's Secret Dragon stop by?" I asked.

Mrs. Lynch grinned. "This morning before dawn, I found a giant stuffed dragon sitting on the porch. Gary went absolutely crazy. I told him he had another surprise coming, so he's been excited all day." She hugged us, one by one. "Thank you. I . . . well, just thank you."

We didn't say much as we walked away from Gary's house.

We were almost back at Mrs. Kinney's when Penny said what I'd been thinking. "I wish we could be there when Gary goes to Camelot."

"Well," Mrs. Kinney said, walking up her porch steps. "I reckon we can go there with him . . . in our minds."

33
Teed Off

The phone woke me Friday morning. Mom answered it, but I couldn't get back to sleep. Then it rang again. And again.

They couldn't all be Donna.

I stumbled into the kitchen. Mom, still in her robe and slippers, was on the phone.

I slid into the booth and drank my orange juice. Mom always had juice set out for each of us. That's how I could tell who was already up. Dad's juice was gone. Eileen's still sat at her spot. She could sleep through anything, even a barrage of phone calls.

Mom hung up and took a seat across from me in the booth. "Nice of you to join me, Tree."

The chill in her words made me rack my brain for what I must have done wrong. *Took out trash. Cleaned the bathroom. Put away my clothes.* Besides, Mom already said she was proud of me for giving Gary a great birthday. Maybe I was just imagining the chill in her voice.

"I guess you've noticed we've had quite a few calls this morning," Mom said.

"Yeah. What's the deal? Is Donna on a roll?" I chuckled. By myself.

"No. But half the town seems to be. The half who get their *Hamiltonian* in the morning, that is."

I had no clue what she was talking about or why I was about to be blamed for it.

"Why didn't you tell me you're a poet?"

"What?"

"A poet with social commentary."

"Mom, you're acting weird."

She narrowed her eyes. "The paper? Your poem?"

"My poem? What—" I stopped. A creepy feeling inched up my spine.

"Now it's coming back to you, is it? Well, here you go. Donna was kind enough to drop by with her paper. Front page, Tree. Congratulations." Her tone was anything but congratulatory.

I took the paper from her, and there it was, right in the middle of page one: "'Ode to a Lifeguard' by Tree Taylor." I had to admit that seeing my name in print like that nearly took my breath away. They published my poem? They published *my* poem! On the front page! I had a byline.

"Do you have anything to say, Teresa? As you can guess, this took me by surprise."

"Mom, I didn't send this to the paper. I just wrote it after that woman wrote the letter complaining we closed the pool early."

"That woman? As in Mrs. Cozad, who called around seven, right before *Mr.* Cozad called and asked to speak to your father? And, let's see, that was a few minutes before a friend of Mrs. Cozad called and launched into me without so much as a hello. I believe she said—right before she hung up on me—that she'd be nominating me Worst Mother of the Year."

"That's ridiculous!" I protested. "I'd nominate you Best Mother of the Year any day."

Her expression didn't change.

"What's Tree done now?" Eileen had sneaked into the kitchen in her frilly nightgown.

I got up from the booth to let her slide in. "I didn't do anything, but thanks for asking." I turned to Mom. "I never sent that poem to the newspaper. I didn't even take it to the pool. The only person who's even read that poem is—" I stopped because it was all coming clear now.

Jack!

I tried calling Jack at home, but he'd already left for work. I tried him at work, but he couldn't come to the phone. Or wouldn't.

He must have given my ode to Randy. And that's what Randy meant about me getting him in trouble. His dad would not have liked my social commentary.

I was not looking forward to going in to work. The board had probably been getting more calls than we had. What if my ode got D.J.—and all of us—fired?

I biked to the pool, then shoved my bike against the tree

where I always left it. As I hopped the counter into the basket room, I braced myself for whatever hassles I'd caused with my stupid poem.

I could have killed Jack for sending it to the paper without even asking.

Laura, Mike, D.J., and Sarah were all waiting for me with the front page of the *Hamiltonian* spread out on the pool counter, held securely in place by two baskets.

I opened my mouth to apologize when they burst into applause. D.J. grabbed the paper and shook it over his head. "Tree, my ace!"

Sarah shouted, "Three cheers for the best writer in Hamilton!" Her smile stretched her face. It tore me in two because this was the Sarah I wouldn't have to cheer me on next year.

"Hip, hip, hooray! Hip, hip, hooray!" They all joined in.

I had officially entered the Twilight Zone.

I got so many pats on the back I nearly toppled over. "So we're not in more trouble because of my lifeguard poem?"

"Are you kidding, kiddo?" D.J. said. "Phone's been ringing off the hook! We aren't the only ones who know the truth. We've gotten calls from a dozen mothers who witnessed those kids shivering and wrapped in towels. And they didn't just call us. They called the board. And the mayor himself! I am officially the man!"

"You always were, D.J.," I agreed, more relieved than I'd have thought possible.

"And you, Tree?" He bowed, like I was royalty. "You are the golden girl."

"Fine as wine!" Mike chimed in.

I wasn't entirely sure what a golden girl fine as wine was, but it sounded good. I returned the bow.

As the day wore on, I got a lot more comments about my poem. Most kids thought it was pretty cool. Adults were harder to figure out. A few glared at me as I took their baskets. Several said things like, "I saw your piece in the paper," and left it at that. Two of my old grade-school teachers, Miss Tomlin and Mrs. Cox, said they always knew I'd be a writer.

Maybe I'd have to forgive Jack after all.

I felt a little bad when the Cozad kids were dumped off at the pool, though. So I bought them each a candy bar and kept a close eye on them.

Later, when Penny walked up to the basket counter, she crinkled her lips, like she was trying to hold in a smile. "Here." She handed me a copy of "Ode to a Lifeguard," which she'd secured between two sheets of plastic. She'd punched holes around the edges of the plastic sheets, then stitched the newspaper inside, using brown yarn. "I thought you might want to hang on to this. It's really good, Tree."

I took the gift from her. "Wow! This is great. My mom probably burned our copy. Thanks, Penny."

Late in the afternoon, Ray dropped by as I was taking my break. He followed me to the snack bar, and we both bought peanuts. We took the same spot as before. On *our* table. I loved the sound of that.

Thank heavens I'd kept my vow and was wearing my green swimsuit.

The first thing Ray said after we'd settled in was, "I think your letter to the editor was awesome. And funny."

We sat and talked way past my break, but I didn't think D.J. would complain. Not today.

Ray brought up music again. Then we switched to talking about school and when we could get our driver's licenses. I told him about Sarah moving to Kansas, and he said he was sorry—for her, and for me.

I tried to focus on every word he said so that later I could replay our conversation in my head. But how could I focus on anything except his full lips? And his eyes. Plus, his arms, all bronzed from the sun, and hunky from all that lifting and unloading.

I had to get a grip. "Have you seen *Dr. No* yet?" I asked. "I heard it was unreal."

"Saw it right after it came out. A bunch of us went to the Cameron drive-in. You should have come."

I would have if you—or anybody—had asked me. That's what I was thinking. But after rewriting in my head, I said, "I've read a couple of James Bond novels and really liked them."

"I didn't know he wrote books. Anyway, *Dr. No* was one fine flick! You ought to see it."

"I love movies, and I love drive-ins," I said. *Hint, hint.*

"You should come with us next time. Hey! Maybe you should write movies instead of books . . . and poems."

We both cracked up, and I hoped my face didn't turn red. Or if it did, I hoped he'd blame the sun. It felt great to be laughing with Ray Miller, sitting on our table, and—

"Ray! There you are!" Wanda, barefoot and bikini-clad,

tiptoed over the gravel toward our picnic table. "Come on! We didn't come to the pool to sit in the shade. *Snap! Pop!* You don't have much time before your shift." She held out her hand.

Ray hopped down off our table and walked over to her. "See you, Tree," he said.

Wanda latched onto Ray's arm as if she'd fall without it.

I was sure she was ignoring me, but she turned back. "Tree, I almost forgot. I read your little poem in the paper."

"It was great, wasn't it?" Ray said.

"Bet that got you in trouble, huh? *Snap.*"

"Not really," I answered.

"I'm surprised," Wanda said. "It's the kind of writing Aunt Edna—Mrs. Woolsey—calls 'inappropriate.' She says we have to respect our readers. I ran into her this morning and told her you had no way of knowing that. Anyway, it doesn't matter." She waved with her free hand, while clinging to Ray with the other.

So Mrs. Woolsey hated my poem? Great.

I couldn't remember which author wrote the quote from a few days earlier:

A writer needs to write something that pleases himself because he can never please everybody else.

I hadn't understood it then.

I did now.

34
Casualties

For the first time I could remember, not counting when we all had the flu, the Adamses and the Taylors did not get together on Sunday night. I didn't ask whose decision it was, but I didn't like it.

As the week wore on, life got back to normal. At the pool, the only thing anybody wanted to talk about was the steam engine show. At home, Eileen moved on to the respiratory system. Mom experimented with chili recipes and worked on our prairie dresses. Dad barbecued hamburgers on the grill, and we ate as if nobody had ever threatened to nominate Mom for Worst Mother of the Year.

I kept writing, clinging to my latest writer's quote, which was from Epictetus, who Eileen the Know-It-All said was a Greek philosopher:

If you wish to be a writer, write.

I started recording Mrs. Kinney's odd facts about faraway places. She'd come up with the great idea of taking Gary to different places in his mind each month. We'd settled on Romania for July because she knew a dragon story from there. Plus, she said Romanians used to believe it was dangerous to sleep with your mouth open because your mouse-shaped soul might escape. And tickling used to be outlawed in Romania. I was getting quite a collection. Nothing Walter Cronkite would have bothered with, but at least I was writing.

Then on Saturday, everything changed.

It was the hottest day yet, and the pool had been packed all afternoon. Sarah volunteered for the evening shift, but I was itching to get back to kitchen air-conditioning.

Even the fast bike ride home did nothing to cool me off. The house was quiet, except for the banging of pots and pans. I headed for the kitchen, eager to feel that cold breeze on my hot face.

Mom was washing strawberry pans from the garden. Her apron covered her navy pedal pushers and a sleeveless shirt that tied in front.

A bowl of fresh-picked berries sat beside the sink. I popped a couple into my mouth. "Hey, Mom. Don't mind if I snarf a few, do you?"

Mom didn't look up from her Brillo pad. "Why should I mind? Not that it would matter what I mind or don't mind around here." She was scrubbing the silver off her pans.

I took another handful of berries and moved over to the AC. I had to kneel on the booth seat and turn one of the vents down. The second that air hit my face, summer disappeared. My head froze. I'd waited all day for this.

A pan banged. Then another. Something was definitely going on.

"Um . . . Anything I can do, Mom?"

"I think you've done enough, thank you. And now, so has your father."

"Dad? Did he do something? Did I?" I backed out of the booth, hoping to make a clean getaway.

Mom harrumphed, then muttered, "Lucky me—two writers in the family."

The phone rang. When Mom made no move to get it, I did.

"Don't answer that!" She kept picking stems from the berries, twisting her spoon a lot harder than she needed to.

The phone kept ringing. Ten, eleven, twelve times.

"I'm never answering that phone again," Mom announced. "Never ever!"

I spied Eileen down the hall, slipping into her bedroom. She motioned for me to come.

I made my escape and tiptoed to Eileen's room. Maybe she could clue me in on Mom's weirdness.

My sister's room was exactly what you'd expect. Powder-blue wallpaper with silver-white flowers covered all four walls. Lace curtains, blue-and-white flowery bedspread, white shelves with figurines and trinkets she'd picked up on vacations. All clothing was folded in her dresser or hanging in her closet, even though Mom's inspection wasn't until Monday.

"What's up with Mom?" I asked, once safely inside. I started to sit on her bed, which was made, of course.

Eileen gasped like I'd just come from a round of mud

wrestling. Then she changed her mind. "That's okay. Go ahead and sit down." She plopped onto the bed next to me.

Midge jumped up and joined us. I scratched her ears and let her lick my nose.

I was in Eileen's room, by invitation. She was letting me sit on her bed with Midge. Whatever was wrong, it had to be bad. "They're getting a divorce." I said it but didn't really mean it. My parents were the last people who'd divorce. Still, Alicia's parents got a divorce, and she was in my class. Her parents had played bridge with ours. So it wasn't impossible.

"No," Eileen said. "But there was some serious yelling going on a while ago. Dad left the house. Said he needed to check on the garden."

"Ouch. What happened?"

Eileen reached under her pillow and brought out a copy of the *Kansas City Star*. "Butch came by an hour ago and gave me this. He said he didn't want his parents to see it. But he thought I should."

"What's in it?" I could not imagine anything that would fit the description of something Eileen should see that Butch's parents shouldn't.

Eileen handed the paper to me. "There." She poked at the third column, the letters to the editor section. There were three letters, one circled.

It was a poem: "The Casualties Were Light." And below it was the byline: "By Frank R. Taylor, M.D."

"Outtasight!" Dad had a byline in the *Kansas City Star*!

"Go on. Read it." Eileen dropped back onto her pillow.

I read aloud.

219

The Casualties Were Light
by Frank R. Taylor, M.D.

"The casualties were light today," it read.
In jungles deep, a sniper added one.
"And many of the enemy lay dead."
For him, the end of life had just begun.

Advisors and counselors advised you should die.
Their families and loved ones will never know why.

The poem went on for five stanzas, with the two-line "chorus" repeated after each verse. I could hardly finish reading it. My throat went dry. I pictured the scenes in Vietnam and the scenes at home, where families got the news that their loved ones had been killed.

Dad's poem made mine sound like a car commercial. I didn't think I'd ever been prouder of my dad, and not just because it was such a well-written poem.

When I looked up, Eileen was lying on her back, her arm crooked over her face so I couldn't see her eyes. I knew she wouldn't feel the way I did about Dad's poem. She cared what other people thought of Dad. She'd care what Butch thought, and he was the one who'd hidden the paper from his dad.

"Was Butch upset about the Vietnam stuff?" I asked.

She didn't take her arm off her face. "Oh, I don't know. He didn't come right out and call Dad a Communist."

"He better not!"

"He wouldn't. He doesn't care about politics. I was hoping

he'd ask me to the movies tonight. I thought that was why he stopped by."

"I'm sorry." I thought about *Dr. No* and Ray and wished again that he'd invited me along to see it. I wondered if he'd meant what he said about me coming to the drive-in with them next time.

I lay down on my back next to Eileen, my head on her second pillow. Midge curled between us, and her wagging tail smacked my cheek so I had to scoot over. "Remember how we used to go to movies when we were kids? Dad dropped us off every Saturday, and we wouldn't know what was playing until we got there."

"Usually a Ma and Pa Kettle film," Eileen muttered.

I laughed. She was right. "Or Jerry Lewis. Or a Western. Why doesn't Hamilton have its own picture show anymore?"

She stuck her arm in the air and waved. "Because bye-bye, shoe factory, I suppose. Or maybe one too many Ma and Pa Kettle adventures." She paused. "I really wanted to see *West Side Story,* but Butch hates musicals."

"I wanted to see *Dr. No,*" I complained. "But did anybody ask me? *No, Doctor.*"

Eileen laughed. We used to talk like this a lot. I didn't know when that stopped. I missed it.

"I've been talking to Ray at the pool lately," I ventured.

Eileen propped her head up on one elbow so she was looking right at me. "Tree! Ray Miller?"

"Yeah."

"Nice going, Tree. He's the cutest guy in your class, you know?"

"I've kind of noticed."

"So what are you guys talking about?" she asked, like she was really interested—no teasing in her voice.

"Music mostly. School some. Movies today."

"Ah. So he's *Dr. No*?"

"Yes."

She rolled back onto her back. "What is wrong with that entire sex?"

I was a little surprised to hear Eileen say the "s-e-x" word, even in this context. "You're asking me?"

"Boys," Eileen muttered. "Who needs them?"

"Exactly."

In the background, I'd been hearing the phone ring a dozen times. Mom still wasn't answering.

"Exactly!" Eileen sat up straight and punched her pillow. "Come on, Tree! We don't need men. We're going to the movies!"

"We are?" I couldn't remember the last time we'd gone to the movies together.

"Absolutely! You and I are going to see *West Side Story* tonight." She hopped off the bed and picked up her hairbrush. "Why not?" She took a seat at her dressing table, an item of furniture she chose when I chose a desk for my room, which was why Eileen did most of her studying at the kitchen table.

I was getting psyched, even though I didn't know anything about *West Side Story*. "Cool. But aren't you afraid somebody will see us out together, without dates on a Saturday night?"

"Nah." Then just when I was starting to get an all-new

picture of my sister, she added, "A musical at the Cameron drive-in? Trust me. Nobody will see us."

Still, it was neat going to the movies with my big sis. Definitely better than sticking around for the upcoming home show with Frank and Helen Taylor.

35
Do Your Own Thing

I loved drive-ins. Nobody yelled at you for talking, crunching popcorn too loud, or laughing in the wrong places.

Eileen held up a strand of hair and ran a comb from tip to scalp, teasing her poof back. "I'll ask Dad for the car."

I was getting psyched. "Buddy's the perfect drive-in car." We'd had our blue-and-white station wagon since the days when Dad drove us to the drive-in to see Disney cartoon movies.

"It'll start getting dark in an hour," Eileen said. "We should get going so we can get a good spot."

"And we don't want to miss previews." I would have loved a whole night with nothing but previews. Previews were like promises. Glimpses of the future.

"Then scoot!" Eileen commanded, but in a good way. "I have to change."

As I exited the queen's room, I heard the front door open.

I hustled up the hallway just as Dad eased the front door

shut behind him. "Dad," I whispered, in case he was still hiding out.

He was standing barely inside the door, like this wasn't his house and he wasn't sure he'd be welcome.

I crossed over to him. And without thinking about it, I hugged him.

We rarely hugged in our house. We loved each other plenty, and all that. It just felt funny to hug or kiss. My parents hadn't hugged their parents—maybe the lean-forward-and-pat-arms kind of hug if they hadn't seen each other for a while. My friends didn't hug their parents, either.

But I hugged my dad as he stood in the doorway. And I whispered, "I think it's a great poem, Dad. A really wonderful poem."

At first, I was the sole hugger, hanging on by myself. Then slowly, I felt Dad's arms wrap around me. "Thanks, Tree. I guess that makes two of us. But if I were you, I'd keep my opinion to myself."

I let go and ran over to the window to get my writer's notebook. I had to flip through pages to find the right one. "I have a quote for you." I showed it to him. "I forgot to write down who said it." I let Dad read it for himself:

If you can't annoy somebody with what you write,
I think there's little point to writing.

Dad laughed. "Well, we've certainly nailed that one, haven't we, Tree?"

Mom appeared from the kitchen in her apron. And her

scowl. "Nice you made it back, Frank. You missed a few phone calls. I stopped answering after an old woman, who neglected to give her name, suggested we move the family to Russia with the other Communists."

Eileen came bounding up the hall. She looked good enough to go on a date with Butch. She'd pinned up part of her hair and left the rest in a flip, like Jackie Kennedy. She'd changed into pink pedal pushers and a sleeveless pink mohair top, with a pink scarf around her neck. Her pill-bag purse matched her white sandals. She'd put on pink lipstick and blue eye shadow. "Tree and I want to go to a movie. *West Side Story* is playing at the Cameron drive-in." She casually tied a three-cornered scarf over her hair. "Can we borrow the car? We'll come straight home."

I caught Mom looking to Dad for the answer.

Dad grinned, and I was sure he was going to say yes.

"No," he answered.

"No? Why not?" Eileen demanded.

"You can't borrow the car because *I'm* driving all of us to the drive-in." He walked over and untied Mom's apron. "Come on. We'll get hot dogs there. We could all use a night out." The phone rang again. "Especially tonight."

Mom took her apron from Dad's fingers. She started folding it, and for a second, nobody said a word. I was afraid she was going to put the kibosh on the whole thing. Then she wadded up her apron and zinged it back into the kitchen. I heard it hit its target, the telephone. "Let's blow this firetrap!" she shouted. "Last one to the car's a rotten Commie!"

★ ★ ★

Fifteen minutes later, Dad pulled up to the drive-in ticket booth. He paid the carload fee and thanked the attendant, a wrinkled man whose fingers looked like rawhide sticks.

"Drive up front, Frank," Mom said.

Dad weaved past sedans and VW bugs crammed with big families. One row looked like couples only. I couldn't believe so many people had come to a musical.

"There!" Mom pointed to the second row, off to the right, a good place to see the screen but a long way from the snack bar.

Dad shut off the engine. He was almost too far from the speaker pole, where two clunky metal speakers hung—one for the front, one for the back. You needed the speakers if you wanted sound to go with the picture on the giant screen. Luckily, the cords stretched just far enough. Dad hung one speaker over his half-opened window and turned the volume knob.

The Beach Boys were in the middle of "Surfin' U.S.A." Dad started bobbing to the beat.

"I love this song!" I could hear the music streaming from dozens of speakers.

"No dancing, Tree," Eileen warned. She leaned out her window to haul in our backseat speaker. When she turned it on, it was scratchy. But it cleared up.

"You girls can watch from the roof if you want to," Mom offered. "I threw blankets into the back. You can probably see the screen better from up there."

Dad slipped his arm around Mom's shoulder. "Yeah. The windshield up here's liable to get pretty steamy."

"Frank!" Mom shoved him a little.

"Gross!" Eileen moved the speaker to the luggage rack and

227

tossed up blankets. "Tree and I can get food before the movie starts."

The speakers went silent. Lights faded across the parking lot.

"Previews!" I cried. "We can't go now."

"Tree," Eileen pleaded. "They're just previews."

"Shh!" No way I'd miss the best part of the night.

Eileen gave up as the screen exploded with the words *The Great Escape.*

"I've heard about this one," Dad said. "Bob claims it's going to be a great movie. Steve McQueen. World War Two."

I was relieved that my dad was still talking about Bob. I hoped that meant he was still talking *to* Bob, even after the Vietnam poem hit the paper.

I made myself quit thinking about anything except what was on the screen.

The previews were awesome. The only one that didn't look worth seeing was *Cleopatra,* although I liked Elizabeth Taylor. I loved her as a kid in *National Velvet.* Sarah and I watched that movie every time it came on TV. At least, we *had* watched it. Now we'd be in different states, and Kansas probably didn't even show *National Velvet* on TV.

I forced myself to put Sarah's move to Kansas out of my mind too.

Eileen and I agreed we *had* to see the next James Bond movie. Only, seeing Bond on the screen made me think of *Dr. No.* Eileen elbowed me, like she knew what I was thinking. I elbowed her back and made myself stop thinking about Ray.

Suddenly, the screen filled with birds. Speakers all over the lot squawked with the cries of flying creatures that chased school kids, pecking at their hair and arms. Big letters spread across the screen: Alfred Hitchcock's *The Birds.*

"That was the best preview I've ever seen!" I announced as soon as it ended.

Dad agreed. "We'll have to see that one for sure."

"Not on your life!" Mom protested.

"Me neither," Eileen said.

I stared at the screen, hoping for another preview. Instead, rinky-dink music started up, and cups danced across the screen.

Dad shoved money at Eileen. "Hot dogs, popcorn, Milk Duds, Coke. And whatever you girls want."

Eileen scooted out my door so she didn't wreck the speaker. "We should have gone earlier. Everybody will go now. We could miss the start of the movie."

Now that I'd seen the previews, who cared about the show?

I was trotting between cars, looking out for speaker cords, when obnoxious cackles caught my attention. It might have been because they were the loudest or maybe because I recognized something in that laughter. Or someone.

Two cars over, I spotted Wayne Wilson's green pickup. Around it, the ground was littered with hot dog wrappers, squished cups, and squashed cigarette packs. Smoke rose from the truck bed, where a dozen kids sat, some from Wayne's class, some from mine. In the center of it all was Wanda. And next to her, Ray.

I nearly stumbled trying to get away.

"Tree!" Eileen shouted when I caught up to her. "I've been standing here shouting forever. Can't you even drag yourself away from the dancing cups?" She turned and walked into the snack bar.

229

While we waited, she frowned over at me. "What's the matter with you?"

"I just saw Ray."

"Ray Miller?" She glanced around, like he might be in the room with us.

"And Wanda. And a bunch of kids from my class. They're out there in Wayne's pickup. I only saw them because they were laughing so loud."

"Tree, I'm sorry. Did they see you?" She paid the snack bar person and put Dad's change into her purse.

"I don't know." I took one of the food trays.

"Come again!" called the snack guy. I was pretty sure he was making a play for Eileen.

She ignored him and followed me outside. June bugs buzzed around the lights at the door. Crickets hopped on the cement. Eileen sighed. "I don't know what to say, Tree."

"I don't get it. He could have asked me to come along. I don't smoke. But I do laugh."

"Dad says smoking can kill you, and laughter cures," Eileen added. "So . . . their loss, right?"

"Right." But I knew neither of us believed it. Would Ray have been embarrassed having me hang around with his buddies? Was I *his* secret?

I led the way back to the car, weaving a little farther out so I didn't have to go by Wayne's pickup. "Sorry about taking the long way, Eileen." I turned around, but she wasn't there. "Eileen?"

The lights began fading again. The movie was about to start. Great. What else could go wrong?

I retraced my steps until I found her standing next to a VW, staring off at something. "Eileen, you're making us miss the movie."

She didn't budge. I couldn't see her face—it had gotten dark without the parking lot lights on. I shut my eyes to get them used to the dark. Then I opened them.

Eileen was crying.

"Eileen? What's wrong?"

Her hand went to her mouth, like she wanted to keep herself from screaming.

I stared where she was staring. Then I saw it—Butch's daddy's white Caddy. I could tell by the big wings in back. I could also tell that he had Laura with him—in the backseat. They were not watching the movie. They were making out, so slumped in the seat it was hard to tell where one began and the other left off.

I shuffled my box of food so I could take Eileen's arm. "Come on. That guy's—" I wanted to tell her the truth, that he wasn't worth it. That she was worth a thousand Lauras, ten thousand Butches. But I knew that wasn't what she wanted to hear. I just didn't know what she *would* want to hear.

Words. Sometimes words just weren't enough.

"We were about to come looking for you!" Dad took the food from us as we climbed into the backseat.

"Must have been crowded in the snack bar," Mom said. "Don't worry. You haven't missed much. Need catching up?"

"We're good." I glanced at the silent Eileen. "We've seen enough."

36
Be That Way

As soon as Mom's head dropped to Dad's shoulder and his arm snaked around her, Eileen and I escaped to Buddy's roof. By silent agreement, we pulled one of the blankets over us. The last thing either of us wanted was to be seen.

We didn't talk. I heard Eileen crunching popcorn. She must have heard me chomping peanuts.

We watched the movie. It didn't take long for a Romeo and Juliet kind of love story to unfold. There were funny parts too—Officer Krupke cracked me up. He made me think of our sign-toting sheriff.

But the best part was the music. I wished Jack could have been there—he would have dug the strings and horns. Then when the dancing took off, I figured if Jack *had* been there, we would have danced on Buddy's roof.

When all the characters rallied for the big finale, Eileen had to hold me down.

She climbed back inside the car before the lights came up. I tossed the blankets, then followed her.

"How did you like it?" Mom asked, once we got settled in.

"I loved it!" I answered.

"Me too," Eileen said, without my enthusiasm.

Dad started singing the Officer Krupke song and nearly drove off with the speakers still hanging on the car. Mom stopped him just in time. Then he bullied his way into the line of cars aimed for the exit.

"Hey . . ." Mom craned her head around to stare out the back window. "Isn't that Jack's car?"

Eileen and I rolled down our windows to see better. "That's Jack, all right," Eileen said. "Who's he with this time?"

Mom continued to stare. "Donna says it's never the same girl twice."

"That's healthy, if you ask me," Dad commented. "No sense getting tied down to one person at his age. Good for him."

"But who is it?" Mom insisted. "Donna will want to know."

"You mean there's gossip concerning her own family that Donna doesn't know about?" Dad pretended to be shocked.

"She says Jack has gotten so secretive. She can't get a straight answer out of him."

Mom and Eileen were crazy. I couldn't see anybody except Jack. If I'd known he was here, he could have watched up on Buddy's roof with Eileen and me.

"I see her now," Mom said. "It's Maggie Potts's girl."

I looked again. The girl slid a few inches away from Jack. She'd been sitting so close to him that I hadn't seen her. "Suzi." Suzi from the reservoir dance.

"That's who I thought it was." Eileen leaned back in the seat. "Suzi Potts was homecoming queen last year."

I couldn't have said why, but seeing Jack, or seeing Jack with Suzi, or whatever, poured cold water on the musical high I'd been feeling.

I could tell Eileen was searching for Butch's car as we left. Thankfully, we didn't see it.

On the drive home, Mom and Dad babbled on about the movie and the previews. Mom claimed the only way she'd see any Alfred Hitchcock movie was with earplugs and a blindfold.

When we turned off the highway to drive into Hamilton, everybody stopped talking. Hamilton was asleep. We crept up Main Street and crossed the railroad tracks with a *thump, thump.*

"Not again," Mom said. "That poor man." Then she laughed.

Dad laughed too. "You'd think the guy would learn."

"What?" Eileen asked before I could. Then she cracked up too.

Finally, I saw why. In the center of Main Street, on a Mickey Mouse beach towel, sat Officer Duper's official parking sign.

"Now that's funny," I said.

Then just like that, we stopped laughing. A dry silence filled our car. I wondered if Mom and Dad and Eileen were thinking what I was thinking. All the problems that had been facing us before we escaped to the drive-in were still waiting for us. And what if those problems were just previews of worse things about to play out in our lives?

The second we walked into the house, the phone rang.

"I'll take that blindfold and earplugs now, please," Mom said, without her original humor.

We might have taken the stupid phone off the hook if we'd been a normal family. But Dad had to be available for certain patients. He gave a secret ring code to pregnant women and really sick patients so they could reach him in the middle of the night—ring once, hang up, call again. Or ring three times, then two. That way, we didn't always have to answer the regular rings at night.

The phone rang and rang as the four of us stood in the dark kitchen and listened to it.

"Let's have some ice cream before bed," Dad suggested, turning on the lights.

I glanced at Mom, expecting her to tell Dad he was crazy. Ice cream at this hour? After what we'd eaten at the drive-in? I waited for Eileen to say she couldn't afford the calories.

Mom turned toward the fridge. "Hot fudge?"

Eileen was right on Mom's heels. "Whipped cream!"

"Cool!" I grabbed the jar of cherries and followed Dad into the backyard. Branches of our tamarack tree caught my arm when I tried to slip out. Dad wouldn't trim that tree for anything. As far as I knew, Mom had never asked him to. As for me, I would have cried at the loss of a single branch, though I couldn't have said why.

Mom and Eileen bumped the door for help. Dad opened it, and I reached for sundaes, while Eileen and Mom shimmied outside.

We plopped down on the grass, ignoring chiggers and

bugs and whatever mysteries lurked in our backyard. Midge took turns begging for handouts before settling onto my lap.

"There's the Big Dipper," Eileen said.

"And the Little Dipper." Mom pointed, but she didn't need to. Both dippers shone like they were sending us secret, urgent messages from the heavens.

"You can see Boötes the Herdsman and his faithful hounds. Look! There's his shepherd's crook!" Dad sounded as proud as if he'd shot that constellation into the sky himself.

For a second, I wondered if people in Vietnam could see the same sky we were seeing. The same Big and Little Dipper. The same Herdsman. And what if a Vietnamese girl happened to be looking up at the sky at that very moment, wondering if an American girl was gazing up and seeing the same sky as hers?

I breathed in the night and wished the ice cream would stop melting.

And the phone would stop ringing.

But then I thought: Let it ring.

We are the kind of family that sees shapes in stars. We write when we have to, when we want to and need to. We go to drive-ins together and eat hot fudge sundaes after midnight. And we are a family that won't trim a tamarack tree, even though it means we have to duck to get out to the backyard.

37
Creeps

For the second Sunday in a row, the Taylors and the Adamses did not make music together. I didn't know how much more I could take.

The anonymous notes kept coming. I even found one in Midge's doghouse.

```
Most of the basic material a writer
works with is acquired before the age
of fifteen. -Willa Cather
```

Great.

I hadn't forgotten my promise to write about the Kinneys for the *Hamiltonian*. I sure didn't want to disappoint Randy. And I really did want to know what happened—maybe more than ever. I just couldn't figure out how to ask Mrs. Kinney about it without wrecking the little bit of trust she seemed to have in me.

Jack stopped by the pool on Wednesday and we talked. Right away, he picked up on my blue funk. "Tree, you gotta snap out of it. Breaking our Sunday night tradition is a drag. But never fear! I'll get Donna and Bob to your pad next Sunday or my name's not Jack."

In spite of everything, I believed him.

Penny had come by the pool almost every day since Gary's birthday. She and I got to talking more and more. It was Sarah who kept us going. She'd cover for me and give me the nudge to go say hey to Penny. I knew my best friend was already looking out for me, trying to make my future Sarah-free school days less miserable.

Thursday, two weeks before the steam engine show and the Fourth of July, I skipped supper and went out to sit with Penny. I'd been checking in on her progress with *To Kill a Mockingbird*. She'd be reading, her back against the fence, and I'd stroll up, clearing my throat so I wouldn't startle her. But she'd be startled anyways and stare up like she was totally surprised to find me at the pool, and maybe to find herself there too.

Penny looked different than she did in school, prettier, with freckles across a cute little nose. Sarah said Penny looked prettier because I was getting to know her better.

"Still liking the book?" I plopped beside her on her towel.

"I'm loving it, Tree. Can't decide if I like Scout or Atticus more, but I think Atticus. You know, the trial and injustice—this book could have come straight from the newspapers."

She went on for five minutes about what was happening in the nation with black people getting their civil rights. She knew all about Martin Luther King, Jr., and Freedom Rides. "In Birmingham, they arrested Dr. King for nothing, Tree! He didn't do anything wrong."

"I know. Dad wrote a letter. To our senators, I think. Maybe to the president."

"Good for him! I wish I could go on one of those freedom marches. Don't you?" She turned to me, waiting for an answer.

I'd seen reports of the marches on TV. They usually ended with white policemen turning fire hoses or clubs on the marchers. "Yeah. Kind of."

Penny kept going. "Did you know that in Kansas City, black children still aren't allowed to swim in the municipal pools? They have to go to their own pools. And you can bet theirs aren't half as nice as the pools for whites. It's not right. And it's going to change. You'll see. It's already changing."

"I believe you, Penny. You know a heck of a lot more about it than I do."

"Would *you* let a black person swim in this pool?"

"Sure. I mean, if it were my pool. I don't really know what the rules are." I felt like she was accusing me. And maybe I was accusing myself a little because I'd never thought about it before. "I don't think we've ever had a black person ask to swim."

"Sorry," she said. "I get carried away."

"That's a *good* thing, Pen. Jack says we should all get carried away more, especially about things happening to other people and not just us." I was remembering the note I'd found tied to our tamarack the day before. The paper dripped with morning dew, but I could still read the words:

```
Everybody in the world ought to be
sorry for everybody else.
```

It was from something called *The Halo,* by Bettina Von Hutten.

"Jack's right," Penny said, and she went on to talk about segregation in public schools and how claims of equal education were a joke.

I had to wonder who else she got to talk to about this stuff. Karen never seemed to talk to Penny about anything, at least not when I saw them together. And all Chuck did was bark orders at her and call her names. Sarah and I had decided Penny came to the pool to get away from home. We'd only seen her in the water a couple of times, and she wouldn't be taking home any swimming medals.

"Getting back to *Mockingbird,*" Penny said, closing the book but keeping her finger in her spot, "I love it when Atticus tells Scout, 'You never really understand a person until you consider things from his point of view—until you climb into his skin and walk around in it.' You know, Atticus reminds me of your father."

"No lie?" Dad got called out to the Atkinson house for Penny's mother now and then. I thought she got bad headaches. I'd ridden along on some of the house calls, but Dad made me wait in the car.

Penny kept talking, but I couldn't concentrate. Wanda and her flock of admirers, male and female, were lying out on the other side of the pool. I couldn't stop sneaking peeks at them, especially when they exploded into laughter or got into shouting matches.

". . . like that time your dad ran over Rolfe."

That brought me back on full alert. "Rolfe? My dad ran over a Rolfe?"

"Our dog?"

"Not that giant long-haired dog? The one with so much hair in his face, you can't see his eyes?" I'd seen that dog in their yard when I tagged along on calls. Sometimes the mutt pounced on the car door and scratched to get in.

"I think you're talking about Rolfe the Second. This was last year, with Rolfe the First. But his hair was in his eyes too. Maybe that's why he ran in front of your dad's car."

"Penny, I didn't know anything about it! Why didn't you—or Dad—say something?" But I knew why my dad wouldn't have said anything. For the same reason he tried to get birds out of the car grill before Eileen and I could see they'd been smashed there. For the same reason I couldn't talk to him about the Kinneys. For the same stupid reason I already knew I wouldn't be asking him about Rolfe or letting him know I knew.

Secrets.

"I didn't say anything to you at school because I figured you already knew," Penny explained. "And anyway, I felt weird. It wasn't your dad's fault at all, and he felt so bad about it, Tree. Anybody else, except maybe Atticus, would have kept on driving and not looked back. But not your dad. You should have seen him carrying that dog up to the house in his arms.

"He worked on Rolfe for an hour before he died. Your dad cried when he told us Rolfe was gone. He buried him that night—dug the hole himself. Mom and Karen and I kept telling him that Rolfe ran out in front of cars all the time, no matter what we did to get him to stop. The dog was dumb as dirt. It happened late at night—I think your dad had been seeing somebody at Cameron Hospital. He wasn't driving fast. Rolfe just shot out of nowhere."

"I don't know what to say. I'm . . . I'm sorry." I thought about Midge. Lately, I hadn't been paying enough attention to her. I didn't know what I'd do if Midge ever got run over.

"Ed, my stepfather, came home the next day. All he could talk about was trying to get money out of your dad. Mom had to talk him out of suing. It was nuts. Ed hates dogs, especially Rolfe." She shook her head, and her whole face changed.

"Two days later your dad walked up to our house with Rolfe the Second. I don't know where he found a dog that looked so much like Rolfe the First. I do know that he must have gone to Kansas City for him. This Rolfe isn't a mutt like the other one. He's smart and a purebred. That was pretty classy of your dad. He didn't have to do that."

And I'd had zero idea anything was going on.

Chuck strolled up to us. Penny's back was to him.

"There's your brother, Penny."

Penny's body stiffened. "He's not my brother, Tree."

"Hey, gals! What's happening?" Chuck stopped beside our towel. He towered over us, blocking out the sun. He was

242

wearing shades, so I couldn't see his eyes. "So, basketgirl, shouldn't you get back to work in your basket room?" He reached down and took my arm, like he was about to pull me to my feet.

Penny shot up off her towel like a missile from a launchpad. "Get away from her!"

Two seventh graders sunning a few feet from us turned around.

"Penny?" I looked from her to Chuck and back. "It's okay." Chuck had already moved his hand away.

"No!" Penny screamed. "It's *not* okay."

Chuck held up his arms, palms toward us. "Touchy, aren't we, Penelope?" He backed away, chuckling to himself.

Penny snatched up her towel and headed for the locker room.

Sarah walked up behind me. "That Chuck guy is really starting to creep me out."

38

Blows My Mind

On Saturday I pulled out my bike and discovered I had a flat. Great. I'd probably be late for work.

I set out on foot. As I got close to the pool, I heard shouts and laughter. A crowd had gathered along the wire fence. Kids pointed. Adults howled. I pushed through them to see what was so funny.

There, in the deepest part of the pool, was Officer Duper's sign: FOR POLICE DEPARTMENT VEHICLES ONLY, BY ORDER OF OFFICER DUPER.

Ray came up behind me. "Isn't that too cool!" He put his hands on my shoulders, and I felt it all the way down to my toes.

Wayne shuffled up beside Ray. "I guess this was the final straw. Officer Duper is no more. He quit this morning."

"Perfect timing!" Ray cracked up, removing his hands from my shoulders. "Sheriff Robinson got back with a string of bass today. Looks like he'll be staying on another fifty years."

Nobody around us was complaining. In his brief term as sheriff, Officer Duper had given out more tickets than Sheriff Robinson had in fifty years. I felt pretty sure that everybody in town knew they had Jack to thank for the send-off, even though nobody ever said so, including Jack.

Penny showed up at the basket counter in the afternoon, acting as if she hadn't left in such a weird way last time.

I played along. I didn't want to set her off again. I took her basket without looking at her. "So, did you finish the book yet?"

"Stayed up all night. No wonder it's your favorite book, Tree. Mine too now. I'm starting my first Agatha Christie mystery. Got it from the library this morning." She pulled the book from her basket. *The Murder of Roger—*"

"*Ackroyd!*" I finished for her.

"Heard of it?"

"I'm rereading it right now."

"Maybe we can talk about this one too, then."

"And I promise not to give away the ending. I think it's her best."

Someone behind Penny cleared her throat on purpose. Wanda.

"See you later," Penny said, heading for her reading spot.

Wanda, clad in her bikini, set her basket onto the counter but didn't let go. "So, how are you, Tree?"

"Great."

"I saw you at the drive-in the other night. We had a blast! Your parents took you, right? That's so sweet."

"I'm pretty busy right now, Wanda." We both had our hands on her basket.

"One more thing. Aunt Edna and I have been talking about our plans for the *Blue and Gold* next year. I'm thinking about reporting on the steam engine show."

"Really? Me too."

"Why would you write about it?" Wanda scrunched up her nose, trying to look puzzled.

"Because it's a free country, Wanda. And Mrs. Woolsey can't pick her staff until school starts."

"Tree, Tree, Tree," she said, making that *tut-tut* noise with her tongue. "Don't say I didn't warn you." She let go of the basket, then grabbed it again when I tried to take it. "I almost forgot. If Ray shows up, tell him I'll be at our spot by the pool, waiting for him."

A fresh wave of determination rose from "the inner workings" of my "very soul." Wanda was not going to get to me. I would write that report on the Steam and Gas Engine Show. But I'd write the Kinney article too. And not just for the school paper. I was writing it for the *Hamiltonian*. Wanda had never been published in the town newspaper.

We got so busy at the pool that I couldn't even break free to check on Penny until late in the day. Every now and then, I peeked out to make sure she hadn't gone home. I felt like I needed to keep an eye on her, the way I did on the Cozad kids, even though their mother hated me.

Finally, the crowd thinned. Penny and I plopped onto her towel and talked about Agatha Christie mysteries until almost nine. With five minutes left to closing, I got ready for my official countdown. I glanced out to the road, and I thought I saw Chuck driving by. Penny either didn't see him or pretended not to. I just hoped he'd keep on driving.

But no such luck. A minute later, he strutted out from the locker room.

"I can't believe he's here," Penny said through clenched teeth.

I was getting bad vibes again. "Why would he come swimming for only a few minutes? He doesn't have a season ticket. D.J. will make him pay full price." D.J. bent the rules for his buddies, but he didn't like Chuck any better than Jack did.

"He thinks he can make me ride home with him," Penny muttered.

It was a weird thing to say. Penny walked to and from the pool, although she lived farther out than I did. I'd sure take a ride home if somebody offered one.

I watched as Chuck climbed the high dive and jumped. He surfaced, then dog-paddled the length of the pool. When he pulled himself out of the water, he stood up straight and beat on his chest, like King Kong. Then he let out a victory yell before strutting over to us.

"Woo-hoo!" He stood above us, dripping water onto Penny's towel. "That felt good, ladies! Mouse, how'd you like to go off the high dive?"

Penny's eyes grew wide. She scooted away from him a couple of inches, like this was a threat.

"No? That's right—I forgot. The mouse always chooses to go back into its hole." He turned to me. "You look like you could use a nice cool dip." He reached down and grabbed me like he meant to toss me into the pool.

Penny jumped up and attacked. "Get your dirty hands off of her! You're nothing but a big bully!" She hit him, her tiny hands slamming his wrists and clawing his arms.

Chuck let me down. He glared at Penny. "You don't tell *me* what to do. I tell *you* what to do. Got it?"

His icy voice gave me chills.

Then, as if he only now remembered I was there, he backed off, like he'd been kidding, like it was some big joke. "Take it easy! I didn't mean anything by it."

Only he did. My skin still felt the press of his fingers through to my bones. Hard. I couldn't have gotten away from him if it hadn't been for Penny. I had a flashback—Chuck shoving Penny in our Capture the Flag game. Chuck calling her the kind of names that would tear a person down if she heard them every day.

And in that instant, I knew. No wonder she seemed scared all the time. This wasn't an ordinary brother-and-sister feud. Penny and her brother—her stepbrother—had a secret. I'd seen it—the hopelessness, the fear—packed into every inch of Penny's body.

And now, in some way, into mine.

Chuck laughed and headed for the exit.

Penny stayed where she was. She watched him. Even after he was out of sight, her chest heaved in and out. Her rasping breath silenced every other sound.

After what felt like minutes, I broke the silence. "Penny? Has he been hurting you?"

Tears streamed down her face, but her expression didn't change. She could have been a soldier in battle, eyes fixed, mouth a thin line of determination.

"Tell me!" I begged.

Finally, she said, "You wouldn't believe me if I told you." She ran for the nearest exit, through the girls' locker room.

This time, I raced after her. She didn't get her basket. Her clothes. Her shoes. I followed her out to the front. She was walking on gravel. Stomping. Barefoot.

"Penny, stop!"

She didn't.

And then Chuck. He drove up beside us in his old Chevy. He stopped so short that gravel flew. Then he leaned over and opened the passenger door. "Get in!" he commanded.

Penny kept walking. She didn't even glance up.

He rolled along beside us. "Don't be an idiot. Get in the car, Mouse! I'm driving you home."

I turned to him. "She's not going home with you! Penny's going home with me."

He glared at me. Then he looked once more at Penny and slammed the door. When he took off, his tires squealed like they'd been stabbed.

"Penny, tell me. You have to tell me."

She shook her head furiously and kept walking. "Nobody would believe me."

"You're wrong. *I* believe you." I wasn't sure what it was that I believed. Chuck was a bully. He was scaring her. Terrifying her. Hurting her? And Penny was on the edge because of it. She was about to jump over.

"Penny, come home with me. Please? I believe you. So will my dad."

"Your *dad*?" she shouted. "Keep him out of this!"

"Why? You have to tell some—"

"No! I can't!"

"Yes, you can. I'll go with you. We'll go together. Dad can help. He can talk to your mom. He can make Chuck stop."

While I talked, sputtered, tossing out words to her, her head shook back and forth, hard enough to rattle her brain.

"You can't just let him keep on bullying you, Penny. You have to tell. Don't keep this a secret any longer!" I cringed at the word.

She glared at me. "It's *my* secret! Not yours! Just leave me alone!"

Tires screeched behind us. I whirled around in time to see Chuck's car bounce over the grassy path. I thought for sure he was going to run over us.

Brakes squealed. The car stopped right next to Penny. Before I could open my mouth to scream, Chuck slid across the seat, threw open the passenger door, and reached out to grab Penny's arm. He pulled her off her feet and into the car. The door slammed, and they took off, weaving through the grass and back onto gravel.

The last sound I heard, above spitting gravel and squealing tires, was the sound of Chuck's King Kong victory yell.

39
Out of My Tree

I collapsed onto the grass and held my head in my hands. What was I doing? What had I done?

I hadn't asked to see into Penny's life. I'd just stumbled into her web of fear and pain. And now I'd caused her even more pain.

Maybe I'd gotten it all wrong. What did I know about how she felt? I didn't have my imaginary compassion machine. Maybe the whole thing really was brother-and-sister fighting, and I'd just fanned the flames. I would end up making Penny's life even harder if I made a big deal out of nothing. Penny had a point. It was *her* secret.

Only what if I wasn't wrong?

I went back to the pool for my shoes, then walked home, still not sure what I was going to do about anything.

A tiny circle of light in the garden told me Dad was weeding by flashlight. I headed for the light. When he spotted me, he waved. In his dirty overalls and muddy garden gloves, my dad may never have looked less like a doctor than he did right then.

Still a few feet away from him, I said, "Dad, I need to tell you something."

Fifteen minutes later we were driving to Penny's house. Dad didn't want me along, but he finally agreed to let me ride with him as long as I didn't try to go inside.

We didn't talk. We'd done our talking in the garden. I'd spilled every single thing I knew about Penny, about Chuck, about Penny's mother and stepfather. I'd tried hard to keep what I knew separate from what I thought, what I suspected.

Dad hadn't interrupted me or asked a single question until I had everything out. Then he nodded, like maybe he'd already suspected something without me telling on Penny—or maybe I just wanted to believe that.

We were almost there when he turned to me and asked, "Do you think Penny knows you're talking to me?"

"I don't know. She told me not to. She said it was her secret, not mine."

Dad looked right straight at me then, like I was the one being hurt. "Some secrets belong to everybody, Tree. Sometimes the truth matters more than anything else. You did the right thing."

Tears clogged the corners of my eyes. It was what I needed to hear, what I wanted to be true. Only I didn't know if it was true or not.

Dad parked at the far end of the Atkinsons' narrow gravel drive. I watched him take his long strides up the lane toward their house. No hat, no doctor's bag. He hadn't even bothered to change out of his garden clothes.

I lost sight of him when he was still a few yards from the house. Darkness closed around the car like a giant gloved hand. It got so dark that when I tried staring out my side window, all I could see was my own reflection. I turned away. I couldn't stand to look at myself.

What if I'd done the wrong thing? What if I'd messed up everything for Penny . . . *and* for Dad?

He was in that house so long that I started getting scared. I didn't see Chuck's car, but what if he was in the house? I wanted to go in and make sure Dad was okay. But I knew he'd kill me if I showed up at the door. So would Penny.

I tried to think who lived out this way. In ten more minutes, I told myself, I would run to the nearest house and phone the sheriff.

Then I remembered. Did Hamilton even have a sheriff?

The door opened, and my dad came out alone. His face didn't give me the slightest hint about what had happened inside that house. He climbed into Buddy, but he didn't start the engine right away. He just grabbed the steering wheel and squeezed it so hard that even in the dim light I could see the whites of his knuckles. Then he hit the steering wheel. I cringed. He hit it again. And again. And again, the sound echoing inside the car like thunder.

My whole body shook with every slap.

Silently, I watched my dad and wondered how many secrets he'd had to carry in his life—how many he was carrying right at that moment, as he slammed the steering wheel in the dark of night. A picture of Dad and Mrs. Kinney flashed through my head—both of them sitting on the porch, sharing the gun, sharing the secret of what really happened inside that house.

Dad stopped beating the steering wheel. But I could still hear the slapping sound in my head. He stared out the windshield like he couldn't remember where he was or where he was supposed to go.

Finally, he turned the key in the ignition and backed out of the driveway before he thought to turn on his lights.

We were halfway home before either of us spoke. I couldn't stand the silence another second. "Dad, I'm sorry. Did I do the wrong thing? Should I have stayed out of it and let Penny keep her—"

"No, Tree." He didn't take his gaze off the road. "You did the right thing. It may not feel right for a while. I don't think Penny's going to be thanking you any time soon. But her mother might . . . or might not. I think she knew more than she wanted to believe. She needed to hear what you had to say. She's a good woman. And I guarantee that Penny's stepbrother won't be hurting her anymore. He's leaving tonight . . . for good. You did the right thing."

"Did I?" Swallowed tears made my voice come out rough, salty. "It was *her* secret. Maybe I didn't have any right to tell."

"This was her secret. But once you saw into it, this was one secret you couldn't leave alone. You had to push to the truth."

"But how do you know? How can I tell which secrets to leave alone and which secrets not to? I didn't know for sure he was hurting her."

Dad looked at me like he was seeing me for the first time. "That's the problem, Tree. We don't always know. Only God sees everything. There aren't any secrets with him. The rest of us have to do the best we can."

A firefly smashed into the windshield, leaving a glowing smudge.

Again, I thought of the promise I had made to Randy to write about Mr. and Mrs. Kinney. It had sounded so easy . . . until I got to know her, Mrs. Kinney, a real live person. "What if I become a writer and dig for the truth and uncover all these secrets? How am I supposed to know which ones to write about and which ones to leave alone? I don't get it, Dad."

"I think you do get it, Tree. Or you're starting to."

Was I? Was he right?

Dad glanced over at me with the saddest smile I'd ever seen. "Nothing weighs on us so heavily as a secret."

I knew that quote. My dad recited it like he didn't have to think about it. Like he'd already thought about it more years than I'd been alive.

Like he'd already written it.

Because he had.

Nothing weighs on us so heavily as a secret.

That was one of my anonymous notes. All the notes, the *anonymous* notes, fanned through my mind, swirling words across my brain like a Missouri tornado. Notes about truth and life, about gossip . . . about secrets. "Dad? The notes . . . that was you?"

He took a minute before answering. "There were things I

wanted to say to you, Tree. Only I knew you needed to find out for yourself." He let out a one-note laugh, if you could call it that. "I got the feeling you wouldn't have appreciated the thoughts if they'd come right from me. I couldn't blame you. I haven't exactly had my head on straight lately."

"Me neither."

Dad took in a big breath and let it out so long, it filled the car. "I guess all we can do is make sure that when we do reach into other people's lives—or when we don't—we act with the best motives we can."

I tried to look inside myself and make sure I'd told Penny's secret—or what I knew about it—for the right motive. Not from gossip or curiosity but because I was afraid Penny was being hurt.

From the frown of concentration on my dad's face, he might have been looking inside himself too. "I don't always get it right, Tree," he admitted. "I try. I really do. And if I get it wrong, that's something I have to live with."

"Then maybe stepping into other people's truths isn't worth it."

"I hear that," Dad said. "Maybe that's why most Americans don't really want to know the truth about Vietnam. They're content to call a war a 'conflict.' They want to hear 'The casualties were light.' I suppose that's why every day so many folks skim over the secrets they just might uncover if they went deeper."

I thought about Eileen and the way she managed to stay out of things like the Kinneys or Vietnam or even Butch and Laura.

"Sometimes I envy those people who can ignore all the uncomfortable secrets," Dad said. After a second, he smiled over at me. "But you and I aren't like those guys, Tree. We can't look away. Some can. *You* can't. You need to know things. You have to get to the truth . . . even if it means proving other people wrong. And that's okay. That's just the way it is. Only once you unwrap a secret, whatever you choose to do with what you uncover—that becomes your responsibility, Tree."

Dad and I hadn't once mentioned the Kinneys, but they were right there in that car with us. I wished it weren't so, but I had to know what Mrs. Kinney did and why she did it. Even if I never wrote about that shooting, never told another living soul, I had to know the truth. I hadn't just stepped into her secret—I'd stepped into her life.

"Dad, I need to ask Mrs. Kinney what really happened."

In the dark, I felt Dad's arm slip around my shoulder. "I know, Tree. I know."

40
Checkmate

Jack proved true to his word about reuniting the Adams-Taylor quartet, although it took him a week longer than he planned. When the Adams family finally showed up at our house Sunday night, I could have blown the trumpet myself. I yearned for *normal,* if only for a night.

I'd been feeling like the Lone Ranger minus Tonto. I missed Sarah already. Her parents made her go with them to look at houses in Kansas. I schlepped baskets alone all week, or with the help of D.J., who made a better manager than a basketgirl.

Eileen had gone back to Butch—not that she'd ever admitted a separation. When she wasn't out with him, or waiting by the phone, she was holed up with her textbooks.

And Penny. Penny wouldn't talk to me. She wouldn't come to the phone. The last time I called her house, Karen relayed the message that her sister would not be coming to the phone—or to the pool—ever again.

Dad told me to give her time.

It was hard not to keep thinking about her and wondering if I should have done something different, or *not* done something, or done it sooner, or . . .

And I missed Mrs. Kinney and our talks over hot chocolate with nutmeg. I hadn't been to see her because I knew that when I did, I'd have to ask her about the shooting. I'd finally know the truth, and I didn't know what would come after that.

I needed Sunday night with the Adams family. When the grown-ups settled into making music together, Jack and I exchanged victory arm punches.

"You did it!" I shouted.

"I did." Jack took my hands, and we did a rock-'n'-roll bridge, both swinging under.

Eileen folded her arms and tilted her head at us. But even she couldn't hide a grin. "Can't you wait until they start playing music before you dance?"

"Guess not." I back-stepped into the mashed potato, with a little monkey thrown in.

Jack gave the signal, and we broke into the madison, the coolest line dance ever.

"Well, I'll leave you kiddies to it," Eileen announced. "Lots of planning to do. The steam engine show is this Thursday, in case you've forgotten. I need to call Butch."

As if we'd rehearsed it, Jack and I jumped into the jitterbug and burst into a terrible Elvis Presley imitation of the Hound Dog song: "You ain't nothin' but a hound dog! Cryin' all the time!"

Eileen caught the slam, that her Butch was nothing but a hound dog. Jack and I did sometimes call him that behind his back—and also behind Eileen's back. She tried to ignore us, but it wasn't easy. Jack and I jived all over the living room.

"I know you think you know him," Eileen began. "But I'm telling you that Butch—"

The second we heard "Butch," Jack and I launched into the few lyrics either of us remembered from that song: "You ain't nothing but a hound dog! Cryin' all the time! You ain't never caught a rabbit, and you ain't no friend of mine!"

When poor Eileen couldn't make herself heard above our howling, she shouted, "You guys think you're pretty funny, don't you!"

Jack and I looked at each other, then nodded in unison.

Eileen shot us death glares. "You two should be locked up."

Which, of course, set us off with a new Elvis song and dance: "Jailhouse Rock"!

Once Eileen left, Jack asked if I wanted to round up anybody for Capture the Flag. I didn't. I no longer had anybody to round up.

Instead, we stayed inside and tried chess again. Jack had attempted to teach me that boring game on and off for a couple of years. I'd never come close to winning, which made it the right choice for me. Maybe I could feel even more like a loser than I already did.

Jack studied the board, and I knew his brain was seeing ten plays ahead. I was still trying to figure out which way knights moved and why pawns had to go crossways to capture anybody.

At least stupid chess gave us lots of time to talk. I had so many things on my mind that I would have loved to talk to Jack about.

I moved the bishop. Why? Because I could.

"Tree." Jack slid diagonally with his bishop and lifted mine off its square. "Want a do-over?"

I shook my head. "Why delay the inevitable?"

He took the piece and studied the board again. "What's on your mind?"

I shoved a pawn forward. "Lots of things."

"Like?"

Can't tell him about Penny. . . . I've avoided Mrs. Kinney all week. . . . Wouldn't do any good to whine to him again about Sarah leaving me. . . . Jack will be leaving me too. . . . Ray with the sky-blue eyes?

For some reason, I couldn't quite bring myself to come right out and talk to Jack about Ray. So I took the back door to the discussion. "I saw you in Cameron."

"Yeah?"

"At the drive-in movie. With Suzi."

"Right." He didn't glance up from his dippy chessboard. "*West Side Story*. Did you like it?"

"It was okay. You?"

"Not much of a plot. But I'd watch that fight scene again. Great dancing." Jack looked up at me then. He set down the queen, who had no doubt been on the verge of making a killing of some kind. "Spill, Tree. What's wrong?"

I sighed, not really sure I knew the answer to that question. "I don't know. It's just that a bunch of guys . . . and girls . . . from my class were at the drive-in too. I think they were pretty paired up. But I wouldn't know, would I? Because nobody asked me to go with them."

"Then they're nuts," he said simply.

261

"Well, it isn't fair. You get to ask any girl you want. And she has to sit at home by the phone and wait to be asked."

Jack grinned. "It's not *quite* as easy as that. I don't think *every* girl is sitting by the phone waiting for my call. Some probably stand."

"I'm not kidding here, Jack." And I wasn't. I could feel tears burning behind my eyes, pushing at my eyeballs.

The grin disappeared from Jack's face. "Go on."

"Why is it like that? Butch can ask Laura *and* Eileen out, and they both go. Ray . . . other guys I know . . . they can ask anybody they feel like. But girls? We can't ask guys out. Guys have all the clout. Why don't girls have any power?"

Jack didn't answer me right away. I was glad he didn't. If he had given me an easy answer, or if he'd tried to laugh it off or joke me out of my funk, I would have kicked the chessboard over.

Finally, he stopped staring at me and looked at the board again. "Tree, you have all the power. You just don't know it yet."

"That doesn't make any sense," I snapped.

He picked up a game piece, the king. "Some people think this is the most important piece in chess. The mighty king. The whole point of the game is to capture him, right?"

I was still sulking. "If you say so."

"But he's nothing. Oh, he thinks he's king. King Butch."

I almost grinned, but I swallowed it.

"Tell me how the king can move, Tree."

I leaned back in my chair and folded my arms across my chest. Very Eileen of me. "I'm not stupid. One square, any direction."

"Unless he'd be moving into a trap," Jack added.

"I knew that."

"Now, how can *this* piece move?" He held up the queen.

I grinned a little. "Any direction, any number of spaces."

Jack smiled. "Yep." His gaze locked onto mine then. "You are the queen, Tree. Never forget that. You have the power to move in every direction, as many squares as you want. You have the ability to plan ahead. To lure, to attract, to charm. Guys may like to think they're kings, and you may allow them to believe it. But that's just part of your overall game, your strategy. No matter what they think, guys can only move one square at a time. They're on defense."

"I'm the queen?" I tried to act like I wasn't buying any of it. But the truth was, I wanted to buy it.

"You are absolutely the queen," he answered, totally serious now. "You have no idea the power you're going to wield over those poor, hapless kings. You are going to be beating guys away with your crown and staff in high school. And you have my guarantee on that."

"Right," I said sarcastically.

"I *am* right. Things are going to change for you, Tree. Just don't *you* change too much. Promise me that."

Neither of us said anything for a minute. I was trying to use Dad's memory system to hang Jack's words on hooks so that I'd never forget them.

"One more thing," Jack said.

"Yeah?"

He moved his queen to my king and flipped my king over onto the board. "Checkmate."

41
Get a Grip

The day before the Steam and Gas Engine Show, old ma-
chinery and cars and tractors started rolling into town, pulling up on Main Street and out at the fairgrounds.
Firecrackers popped every so often. Some kids couldn't wait
for the Fourth.

I'd promised Randy Ridings an article about the Kinneys,
and tomorrow was the deadline.

When Jack stopped by the pool and asked if I needed a
ride after work, I told him I had plans. I needed to see Mrs.
Kinney. I knew Jack would come with me if I asked him to.
And I would have loved having him beside me when I finally
asked Mrs. Kinney if she had shot her husband.

But I remembered what the deal was with secrets, the
responsibility that came with finding out the truth. If I
brought Jack with me, I'd make him part of whatever truth I
might unwrap. I couldn't do that to him.

★ ★ ★

After work, I changed into an outfit Mom got for me in Kansas City—a kick-pleat gray skirt, sleeveless blue-green blouse, wide belt, and sandals. Then I walked straight to Mrs. Kinney's house and knocked at the door. I had to know what really happened. I still didn't understand why, exactly, except that Dad was right: for better or worse, I was not one of the lucky people who could choose not to see beneath the surface, down into truth, even with a friend. Maybe especially with a friend.

When Mrs. Kinney didn't answer the door, I walked around the side of the house and found her in the backyard, planting something.

She looked up when she saw me. "Strawberries. Everbearings." She pointed to the end of the row, where aluminum foil pie pans dangled from strings tied to poles. "That there contraption is how South Africans keep birds off their berries. I'm trying it on crows. Birds don't like seeing their reflections. And they hate the noise."

"Is it working?"

She brushed her hands together and walked toward me. "Not a bit."

I followed her inside and went straight to my chair—no more small talk.

She must have gotten the message because she sat right down too. No hot chocolate. Not today. "I take it you didn't stop by to hear about Mandalay Bay and them starfish that ain't got no brains?"

I shook my head. "Please don't get mad at me for asking you what I'm going to ask you, Mrs. Kinney. Or for what I'm about to tell you, either. I couldn't stand it if you stopped wanting to be friends."

She didn't move. Didn't rock. "I figured something was up when you stopped dropping by."

"I . . . I was here that morning. I heard the shot and followed my dad. I hid behind your cottonwood. And I saw things. I saw you come out with the rifle, and I saw my dad take it away from you. I heard Dad tell Sheriff Robinson that it was an accident. Only . . . only I don't think it was an accident."

We were both silent for a minute. I studied her face, the lines at her mouth familiar to me now. Most of the wrinkles in her forehead had smoothed themselves out. She still didn't look as young as my mother or Donna. But she didn't look old enough to be their mother anymore.

I took in a deep breath and smelled lilacs. She'd filled a chipped vase with branches and set it on her rickety coffee table. A bully had lived here—a bully worse than Chuck Atkinson. I kept going. "I know you had your reasons, Mrs. Kinney. I know you're a good person. You're smart. And you're kind."

I tried to bring up the image of her standing in the doorway, clutching that rifle. Only the picture wasn't as sharp as it used to be, back when that was the only picture of her I had.

"Mrs. Kinney, I know *you* were the one with the gun."

"I was," she agreed.

"Everything else is guesswork," I admitted. "I'm guessing your husband used to hurt you. I guess you might have been scared of him. I guess he might have come at you to hurt you again. And I guess . . . I guess you shot him." I stopped talking because words were spilling out of my mouth without passing through my brain first.

But it was out now.

Mrs. Kinney stared at me, her eyes never blinking.

"My dad—does he know the truth?"

"He knows what he knows, I 'spect. We ain't said nothin' about it, him and me."

"But he's keeping your secret, isn't he?" I couldn't help raising my voice. I'd seen the weight of her secret on him.

I think she shook her head, but it might have been a twitch.

"I'm sorry, Mrs. Kinney. I tried to let it go, but I couldn't. I have to know what happened."

She sighed. "You want to know the facts? Or the truth?"

I frowned at her.

"Fact is, I shot Alfred."

There it was. I didn't move. My head buzzed. I'd known all along that she shot him, hadn't I? From the moment I saw her holding that rifle, from the moment Dad refused to talk to me about it. So why did I feel like somebody had just punched me in the stomach?

"Fact is," she went on, "I was mighty scared of that man. He done me harm in the worst way, and that's a fact." She shivered, as if remembering. Her gaze flitted from the broken leg of the coffee table to the empty knickknack shelves to dark corners of the room, where terrible scenes must have replayed in her head.

She looked at me again. "Also a fact, I know my way around a rifle. My daddy used to take me hunting. He liked to tell his drinking buddies there wasn't but one thing his daughter was good at. Said I could shoot the eyes off a fox. And that gives you another fact. I coulda hit something a heap worse than Alfred's shoulder, if I'd a mind to."

I gazed around at the broken furniture, the bare walls, the emptiness. Then I looked back at the woman sitting across from me. She was right. Now I had the facts. But the truth? The truth went right past facts and into people—people with as much going on inside of them as I had going on inside of me. "How did you know my dad would keep your secret?"

Her lips parted, revealing a missing tooth I hadn't noticed before. "He's a good man, your daddy. Fine as I've come across."

So now what? I had the facts. But this truth, this secret, didn't belong to me.

I made my way to the door, but my fingers wouldn't turn the knob. Mrs. Kinney had confessed. She'd really and truly shot her husband. I'd thought that once it was all out, I could move on. But it wasn't as easy as that. I couldn't tell how I felt now that her secret was open between us. I suspected it would take me a long time to figure that one out.

I turned back. "Mrs. Kinney?"

Her head was bowed. A shaft of light squeezed through the window and landed on the toe of her worn shoe, the same shoe my mom would have called sensible.

"Jack's coming by for me at nine tomorrow," I said. "If you'd like to go to Hamilton's first-ever Steam and Gas Engine Show, we could take you."

42
Steam Engine Secrets

Jack arrived a few minutes before nine. He looked great in the role of Jesse James, with chaps, cowboy shirt, boots, and hat. Donna had even managed to get him a gun belt with fake pistols and an old bank bag from the Gallatin bank. Jesse and his brother Frank had robbed that bank without much success—no money, just worthless banknotes.

"Not bad, Tree." Gentleman Jesse eyed my costume as I slid into the front seat.

"At least I didn't rob anybody." I had to admit that I liked my yellow prairie dress, though I suspected I'd resent the long sleeves and full skirt before the day ended. "Eileen's waiting for Butch. But we need to make another stop."

I didn't tell Jack about Mrs. Kinney's confession. He didn't ask. He just carried her baskets and helped her into Fred. She'd dressed like usual, but her long black dress fit right in.

"Have you ever seen Hamilton so packed?" I asked when we hit Main Street. Most of the people were wearing prairie costumes. Some rode horses. Others drove ancient cars. Merchants had items set out for show or sale all up and down the sidewalk. A steady waft of gas fumes blew in from the fairgrounds.

Jack and I escorted Mrs. Kinney to the church bazaar, where Mom and Mrs. Overstreet fussed over her baskets.

"I'd like to buy this yellow basket," Mom said. "These are all wonderful, Lois. Think you could give us a hand here at our table?"

"Marvelous idea!" declared Mrs. Overstreet. "My arthritis is acting up. You can handle the money and whatnot."

Mrs. Kinney glanced at me before answering. "I reckon I'd be pleased to help."

Jack and I left Mrs. Kinney and wandered back up Main Street. We checked out the weird tools and kitchenware in front of the hardware store.

Jack picked up a silver doodad with a hook on the end. "Brother Frank James and I used to pick our teeth with this."

I grabbed it from him. "Nonsense. This is my back scratcher."

And on and on we went, making ourselves sick laughing so hard.

"There's Eileen." Jack motioned toward the table in front of the J. C. Penney store.

Butch stood back, hands on hips like he wanted to move on. Eileen, though, was fingering the knickknacks on the table. She looked gorgeous as a prairie woman, with bouncy spiral curls.

"Hey, Eileen!"

Eileen wheeled around so fast, she dropped the bag she was carrying. Four plastic dragons spilled out.

I picked up the bag and replaced the dragons. She had a stuffed dragon under one arm. My sister didn't buy things like that. Not dragons.

Not for herself.

Butch laughed. "She picks those dumb dragons up everywhere."

I took her elbow and moved her away. Jack caught my cue and started talking up Butch so he wouldn't follow. "*You're* Gary Lynch's Secret Dragon?" Never had I suspected my sister. Dad, maybe. Jack, maybe. But Eileen?

"You can't tell anybody, Tree."

"I don't get it. Why does it have to be a secret?"

She bit her lip, then grinned at me. "Because it wouldn't be as much fun for either of us if Gary knew."

I nodded, thinking that people can surprise you. Even sisters.

In the afternoon, we dragged Mrs. Kinney away from the church bazaar and off to the newspaper office. It was time to face the music . . . and Randy Ridings.

I'd stayed up half the night typing all the weird facts Mrs. Kinney had told me. Now I pulled my folded fact sheets from my pocket. One good thing about prairie dresses—great pockets. "Randy, I know I promised you a feature story today."

Randy took off his top hat, frowned at Mrs. Kinney, then raised his eyebrows at me. He must have been sweating like crazy in his getup—a silky white vest, white gloves, shiny slacks, and a black coat with long tails. He might have been dressed like an old-time politician. "You want to talk about this inside my office, Tree?"

"No need," I answered. "I don't have what I promised you. But I think I have something better." I smiled at Mrs. Kinney, who looked more perplexed than Randy did. "See, Mrs. Kinney knows a ton of weird-but-cool facts from all over the world." I held out my typed sheets. "These are just a few of them. I was thinking people in Hamilton might like a good laugh, plus learning about the world."

Randy frowned as he took the pages from me. But his grin peeked out as he read. "Fancy that," he muttered. "Hmm." He squinted over the paper at Mrs. Kinney. "Let me think about this. Could you come by the office on Monday, Mrs. Kinney? Maybe we can work something out."

Only then did I dare look over at Mrs. Kinney. Her eyes were watery, but she was smiling. "I reckon I can do that."

43
S.W.A.K.

The sun was setting by the time Jack and I took Mrs. Kinney home. Fireworks sounded from all over town. I held it together until Jack and I were on our way back down the porch steps, where the shadow of my dad and Mrs. Kinney would always be, the rifle between them.

For no reason I could put my finger on, tears exploded from me like sparks from a Roman candle. I could hardly see where to walk. Jack held on to me until we made it back to the car. *Jack.* I had never been so glad to have anybody beside me. He put his arm around me, and I rewarded him with a full-fledged, shoulder-shaking, snot-dripping cry.

When I stopped bawling, more or less, he started driving. I didn't know where he was headed, and I didn't care. I stared out the window as my mind dredged up every secret I'd stepped into so far that summer.

Jack turned into the reservoir and parked Fred at the water's edge, just beyond the spillway, where couples went to watch submarine races. The whole reservoir wrinkled under a half moon, leaving a silvery carpet on the surface of the water. The sky filled with colors and light from fireworks all over Hamilton.

He shut off the engine and waited.

I gulped down saltwater tears that flooded my throat faster than water over the spillway. "I know Mrs. Kinney's secrets, Jack. And Dad's. And Penny's. And Eileen's. And maybe, one day, the whole stupid world's!" I looked up at him. "Only what do I do with all of them?"

He sighed. "I don't know, Tree."

"This whole summer has been nothing but secrets, and I'm afraid my whole life will be like this. It's like life is a spiderweb of secrets, holding everything together by these tiny threads that hide the truth. And I keep stumbling into webs I can't get out of."

When I looked over at Jack, he was staring at me. I had never seen him look at me like he was now, as if he felt everything inside of me, times ten.

"Tree, this may be the worst timing in the history of spiderwebs. But I have to add another secret to your web." He gazed out at the ripples of water, and the moonlight caught his profile, his strong nose and chin, long eyelashes I'd never noticed before. "I shouldn't be telling you this. You shouldn't have to hear it, not with all you've been going through. But I can't tell anyone else. You're it."

I swallowed hard, and when he turned back to me, I didn't look away.

"I'm going to Vietnam."

"You're what?" I stared into his eyes, hoping they'd get that twinkle, the mischievous squint that would let me know he was kidding.

But there was no twinkle. Only an agony so deep I fell into it with him.

"I'm not going to college, Tree. Not now, anyway. I need to do this. I believe in what we're fighting for over there. We have to stop Communism now. If Vietnam goes, so will Cambodia. And Laos. And then the world. Communism could take over the whole world. I want to keep us safe."

"You can't go, Jack!" I pleaded.

"I can't go until I'm eighteen. So I'll head for Maryville, like I'm planning on getting that business major. But I'm not. And I'm not telling my parents until I've signed up. Especially not Donna. Only you. I couldn't lie to you, Tree."

"Jack . . ."

It was all I could say. I didn't want him to leave. I didn't want him to go where people were killing each other. I did not want to lose him.

"Will you write me when I'm over there?" He asked this like his life depended on it. "Even when you're officially reporting for the *Blue and Gold,* will you still write me?"

I nodded. Tears were flowing again, silent but harder than ever. Deeper.

In the background, from somewhere above us, music drifted down. Cars must have been circling.

Jack touched my chin. Lifted it. Then he kissed me on the forehead. A soft kiss. Long and sweet and real.

I didn't care if it was the music or the moonlight, the

mystery of submarines, the threat of Vietnam, or the secrets of summer—I knew that kiss was the fulfillment of Goal Number Two. Not what I'd expected. But true.

Jack and I joined five cars in a jagged circle of headlights. With no more talking, we raced to that circle of light, and we danced. I danced so hard I couldn't breathe or see or think. With everything in me, I rock-'n'-rolled, prairie girl with Jesse James, through the thin lines of the spiderweb, trusting Jack and I would hold each other up, at least for tonight.

A slow song came on, "Soldier Boy" by the Shirelles. Jack and I usually skipped the slow dances, but we didn't skip this one. I was figuring out that when I turned twenty-four, Jack would only be twenty-eight. No difference at all.

Halfway through the song, Jack whispered, "What are you thinking, Tree?"

"I'm thinking that people are like music. The better you know them, the more there is to know. Like you think a person is one way—smart or funny or mean. But nobody is just one note. God created people like music. We're all symphonies and rock-'n'-roll."

He nodded, laughed a little. "Who said that?"

"Me."

Then he pulled me in a little tighter and rested his chin on top of my head. "You know, Tree. You should be a writer."

"Right on."

Not the End

So many things have happened to America and me this past year that to do it right, I'd have to write a whole entire book about it. And I don't want to spend that kind of time reliving that year. The last quote in my writer's notebook was anonymous:

All good writing is swimming underwater and holding your breath.

That's what I'll have to do to sum up the year.

On August 2, 1963, Sarah moved to Iola, Kansas, and it's rumored she only wore black and gold, Mizzou colors, the entire year. We've kept in touch through letters, and Mom lets me phone her long-distance on holidays, including her birthday. But I never got used to her not being in classes with me. In some ways, I missed her more and more as the school year progressed without her.

On August 9, 1963, Mrs. Kinney's first piece came out in the *Hamiltonian,* kicking off her weekly column, *Mind Travel.*

In her third column, she urged everyone in town to send travel postcards to Gary Lynch wherever they went.

On August 23, 1963, I was awarded the freshman position on the *Blue and Gold* staff. I won it fair and square. I never gave Mrs. Woolsey anything I'd written about the Kinneys. Only Jack got to read that. But I turned in a feature on Officer Duper and an op-ed piece on the power of rock-'n'-roll. Plus "Ode to a Lifeguard."

On August 26, 1963, Wanda Hopkins dropped out of school and married a Cameron basketball player. Seven months later they had a baby girl. Ray told me Wanda's secret right after she dropped out, but it wasn't a truth I wanted to write about. I gave her three Dr. Seuss books at her baby shower.

On August 28, 1963, Dr. Martin Luther King, Jr., gave his "I Have a Dream" speech. The following week, Penny gave a report on it. She got an A+. And when I told her I thought it was the best report we'd ever had in school, she said, "Thanks, Tree." After that, we started eating school lunch together.

On September 28, 1963, Jack Adams took a bus to a recruiting station in downtown Maryville and joined the United States Army. I knew what he was planning to do. I couldn't eat the whole day, and I snapped Eileen's head off for no good reason. I couldn't tell anybody why I was acting like I was.

Jack called me from a pay phone outside the recruiting office. He sounded so excited that I felt guilty for crying through the whole conversation. After we hung up, Jack called his parents. Donna was crying when she called Mom with the news. After that, Donna phoned every person in Hamilton.

On November 1, 1963, the South Vietnamese military, backed by the United States, overthrew the South Vietnamese government. President Diem and his brother Nhu were killed the next day. That night Dad sat next to me on the couch and read the whole newspaper article out loud. I stopped him every time I had a question, and he answered it. We talked about what might happen next in Vietnam. Neither of us mentioned Jack, but he was in every word of that article and in the middle of every question I asked.

That week Dad wrote another letter to our senators, urging them to get out of Vietnam and bring our soldiers back home.

On November 22, 1963, I was in English class taking a quiz, when the loudspeaker crackled and squawked in our classroom. Penny and I giggled. The whole class stopped writing and stared at the speaker high on the wall above the blackboard as our principal gave us the news that President John F. Kennedy had been shot, assassinated, in Dallas, Texas.

Later, Mom, Dad, Eileen, and I sat on the couch, closer together than we had to, and watched Walter Cronkite on the *CBS Evening News*.

By Christmas, I had written three letters to President Lyndon B. Johnson, urging him to bring home our soldiers. On December 29, I got my first letter in return. It stated simply that my letter was now on file with the F.B.I., along with other suspicious and threatening letters. Mom and Dad both agreed there was nothing suspicious or threatening in any of my letters.

On January 7, 1964, Private John "Jack" Adams joined a

ground force of thousands sent to Vietnam. Jack wrote me about every soldier in his platoon—guys with names like Mojo, and Loon, and Shooter Bill.

I began writing Jack every day, instead of once a week.

April 30, 1964, was the worst day of my life, although I didn't know it until May 5. According to official army records, "On April 30, 1964, Private John K. Adams, in an act of bravery to protect three wounded men under Viet Cong fire, ran headlong into an ambush. He was wounded and is officially missing in action."

I don't remember what I did on that Thursday. Went to school, of course. Laughed? Worried about tests? Flirted with Ray? I didn't know that my whole world had changed.

I have pictured that ambush so often that it feels like I was there to see it. The heat and mosquitoes cling to Jack's skin while he waits with his platoon for help to arrive. The men are pinned down. No reinforcements in sight. No helicopters. Nothing, except the enemy. The Viet Cong keep firing as if they have so much ammunition they need to get rid of it. Bullets hit their targets. Three men fall wounded as the platoon dashes for cover. The fallen men lie in an open field, while Jack and the rest watch from behind thick vegetation. Surely a helicopter will come and rescue the men. Surely the army has reinforcements on the way.

But no help comes. Jack knows somebody has to do something. Their lieutenant is one of the men down. Everyone now looks to Jack for leadership. The others beg him not to go himself. Someone else should go instead. Not their best shooter. Not their leader. Not Jack.

But they don't know Jack like I do.

He runs out of the bushes, crying out to the wounded that help is on the way. I see him running and screaming, much like I've seen him a thousand times in our games of Capture the Flag. Dodging bullets, he races toward the injured soldier, his buddy. "It's okay. I've got you," he says, tugging the soldier to safety. A bullet grazes his leg—a shallow wound, like Mr. Kinney's. Somehow, Jack reaches the second soldier and drags him to the nearest cover. He is headed toward the third soldier when scores of Viet Cong appear out of nowhere and grab him.

Did he have time to salute his fellow soldiers? Did he have time to hear music? To think of me?

On May 5, 1964, Donna called Mom. She had just received a telegram telling her that her only child was MIA, missing in action. A telegram. Black words on a piece of flimsy tan paper. Words that changed everything.

Mom called Dad at the office. He drove directly to school and pulled me out of class. I didn't return for a week. Only Penny called. And Sarah. Penny had called her.

On May 14, 1964, I received a letter from Jack, posted three weeks earlier. It read:

Dear Tree—Miss you. I have a secret. But no sweat—it's the good kind of secret. I'm coming home the first of the month! Let's dance our kicks off! Love, Jack

It's the last Jack letter any of us has received.

I imagine Jack hiding in the jungle. I picture him in a jungle prison. He's still Jack. I see him dancing, working out new steps to the songs in his head. He's swinging and jiving so hard, his Viet Cong guards step back and watch, in awe.

He'll be back.

Last night I attended the Hamilton High spring dance with Ray Miller. Afterward, I taught a new generation of Hamiltonians to dance in a headlight circle at the reservoir— but only and always beginning each dance session by shouting "To Jack!"

Acknowledgments

I feel as if I should thank the entire town of Hamilton, Missouri, where I grew up dreaming of becoming a writer. This book is a work of fiction, but I hope it reflects my gratitude for the spirit of the people there. It was an amazing time and place to come of age.

Thanks, especially, to my sister, who embodies all of Eileen's good traits and none of her bad.

I will always be thankful for the memory of Jack House. *To Jack!*

I'm grateful to my agent, Elizabeth Harding, at Curtis Brown, Ltd., for doing all the things I don't like to do so that I can do what I love—write.

It just doesn't get any better than being part of the Knopf family, where each comma is carefully discussed with heartfelt emotion. I am the luckiest writer in the world to have Allison Wortche as my editor. Thank you so much for your perceptive eye all the way through this project. I've watched my simple story transform into something much deeper because of you.

And I can't miss another opportunity to thank my wonderful family for pitching in when I'm too locked into writing to do anything else. Thanks to my hubby, whose writing challenges me, and whose love keeps me going.

About the Author

Dandi Daley Mackall is the award-winning author of many books for children and adults. She visits countless schools, conducts writing assemblies and workshops across the United States, and presents keynote addresses at conferences and young author events. She is also a frequent guest on radio talk shows and has made dozens of appearances on TV. Her young adult mystery published by Alfred A. Knopf Books for Young Readers, *The Silence of Murder,* won the Edgar Award.

Dandi writes from rural Ohio, where she lives with her husband and family, including their horses, dogs, and cats. Visit her at DandiBooks.com and SilenceofMurder.com.